Critical Acclaim for Dig.

Winner of the **Michael L. Printz Award**
A **Los Angeles Times Book Prize** Finalist
A *BCCB* **Blue Ribbon** selection
A *Horn Book* "Fanfare" selection
A *School Library Journal* Best Book of the Year
A Chicago Public Library Best Book of the Year
A YALSA Best Fiction for Young Adults selection

★ "This visceral examination of humanity's flaws and complexity cultivates hope in a younger generation that's wiser and stronger than its predecessors." —**BOOKLIST**, starred review

★ "This combination of masterly storytelling, memorable characters, and unexpected twists and turns make this book into an unforgettable, lingering read."
—**SCHOOL LIBRARY JOURNAL**, starred review

★ "A.S. King's novels ... are in another solar system entirely."
—**BOOKPAGE**, starred review

★ "Engaging ... a story of racism, family, secrets and how many things are hidden beneath the surface." —**SLJ**, starred review

★ "[A] haunting exploration ... of the advantage and poison that is white privilege, and the resentment of young people at the toxicity of what they inherit. King fans know to expect the unexpected, and they'll be richly rewarded with this intricate, heartfelt, readable concoction."

"[A] haunting exploration of the advantage and poison that is white privilege..."

"A.S. King challenges readers from the first page to the last. *Dig* will make you question the confines of your comfort zone—if you have one. An incredible addition to an already impressive body of work."

—**Erin Entrada Kelly**, *New York Times*
bestselling author and Newbery medalist

"I've had a long love affair with the work of A.S. King. I have read every book of hers. I've wept. Laughed. Marveled. Raged. There is no other writer like her. She has the power to astonish like a natural wonder. And her books—the raw honesty, beauty, and singular strangeness of them—make me feel less alone in the world."

—**Martha Brockenbrough**, author of *The Game of Love and Death*

"No apologies necessary. *Dig* is writing at its finest."

—**Book and Film Globe**

"[This] strange and heart-wrenching tale is stunningly original."

—**Kirkus**

"Profound. Offers hope that at least some of these characters will dig themselves out from under the legacy of hate they have unwillingly inherited." —**Publishers Weekly**

"Taut, mesmerizing . . . The story fearlessly navigates intellectually and emotionally challenging terrain—racism and whiteness, abuse and assault, misogyny, and other violence—as the teens consider and confront painful truths." —**CCBC**

"*Dig* leads the way toward a critique of racism and white privilege that must be undertaken by all of us." —**Public Books**

Dig.

BY A.S. KING

PENGUIN BOOKS

For Pam, who said, "Those are your people."

PENGUIN BOOKS
An imprint of Penguin Random House LLC, New York

First published in the United States of America by Dutton Books,
an imprint of Penguin Random House LLC, 2019
Published by Penguin Books, an imprint of Penguin Random House LLC, 2020

Visit us online at penguinrandomhouse.com

THE LIBRARY OF CONGRESS HAS CATALOGED THE DUTTON EDITION AS FOLLOWS:
Names: King, A. S. (Amy Sarig), 1970– author
Title: Dig / by A.S. King.
Description: New York, NY : Dutton Books for Young Readers, [2019] |
Summary: Five white teenage cousins who are struggling with the failures
and racial ignorance of their dysfunctional parents and their wealthy
grandparents, reunite for Easter.
Identifiers: LCCN 2018017878| ISBN 9781101994917 (hardcover) |
ISBN 9781101994924 (ebook)
Subjects: | CYAC: Cousins—Fiction. | Family problems—Fiction. |
Family reunions—Fiction. | Prejudices—Fiction. | Easter—Fiction.
Classification: LCC PZ7.K5693 Dig 2019 | DDC [Fic]—dc23
LC record available at https://lccn.loc.gov/2018017878

Penguin Books ISBN 9781101994931

Design by Samira Iravani
Text set in Joanne & IM Fell Great Primer

Printed in the United States of America

10 9 8 7 6 5

A man who prides himself on his ancestry is like the potato plant, the best part of which is underground.

—*Spanish proverb*

Without the potato, the balance of European power might never have tilted north.

—*Michael Pollan*

I'm pleading with my loved ones to wake up and love more.

—*Kate Tempest*

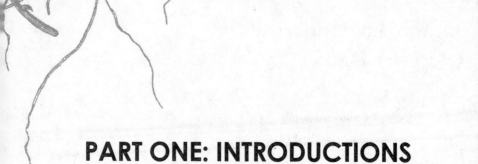

PART ONE: INTRODUCTIONS

CAST IN ORDER OF APPEARANCE:

Marla & Gottfried
Two Dead Robins
Jake & Bill: The Marks Brothers
The Snake

Marla & Gottfried's Easter Dinner

April 1, 2018

Marla Hemmings is hiding neon-colored plastic Easter eggs in the front flower bed. Four feet behind her, Gottfried is hacking at a patch of onion grass with a trowel. He stops to watch two spring robins chirp from a limb.

"Do you think these are too hidden?" Marla asks.

Gottfried goes back to his onion grass. "They'll find 'em."

"That's not what I asked."

"They always find 'em."

Gottfried looks back at the robins. He thinks of a day back when he'd just learned to drive. *Seventeen at the most.* Did he say that out loud? Marla looks at him as if he did. He thinks it again. Seventeen years old. Driving that finned 1960 Dodge Matador wagon his whole family used to fit into for trips to the beach or his faraway track meets. Warm day, just like this one. Easter coming. The two robins dancing in the middle of the road. He thought they were dancing. Then he thought they were fighting. Then he knew what they were doing. Seventeen is old enough to know what robins do in springtime.

"I'm going to the side now," Marla says. She adjusts her gardening apron, picks up her basket of gleaming plastic eggs, and watches Gottfried looking at the robins. "You'll have to get the ham on soon."

"Ham," Gottfried says. "Gotcha."

Marla shakes her head. She wonders sometimes if her husband is losing his mind. He only ever needed to go to work and mow the lawn. She raised five children and did all the work that came with it and she isn't losing *her* mind.

The car was going too fast to stop. The robins were jumping up and then landing for another session, then rising again. By the time Gottfried got near enough to them to know he was going to hit them, he couldn't slow down more than he had already. Thirty miles per hour to a robin is fast enough. Before he took the car home, he drove all the way across town to the automatic car wash. During the spray cycle he'd cried.

Gottfried never believed in the resurrection. Marla's insistence on perfect Easter egg hunts since the kids were little annoyed him. Her obsession with them now that there were grandchildren was infuriating, especially considering their grandchildren were mostly grown—teenagers. When she asks questions like that—did he think the eggs were *too hidden*?—he wonders if Marla is losing her mind.

She says, "And don't forget to peel the potatoes!"

He throws the lumps of onion grass into the woods that surround the house.

He goes inside and washes his hands.

He puts the ham in the roaster.

He empties a five-pound bag of potatoes in the sink and retrieves the peeler from the drawer. As he slices the skin off inch by inch, he thinks of the robins again and cries.

Jake & Bill can bring the snake out now

April 1, 2018

Jake Marks and his older brother, Bill, walk through the high school parking lot. Bill has his snake with him—wrapped around his neck and tucked into his coat. Jake has the look of skipping school on his face even though it's a Sunday and a holiday. Could be a school day for all he knows. He gives no fucks. Jake never gives any fucks. It was once suggested that the school should rename the in-school suspension room the Jake-Marks-Gives-Zero-Fucks Room.

Jake's just flowing in Bill's wake. Six years between them, and the two act like twins, which is sad if you think about it. Either Bill is seriously immature or Jake is growing up too fast. Smoked since he was ten. Crashed his first car at twelve.

PART 1.1: INTRODUCING THE SHOVELER AND THE FREAK

CAST IN ORDER OF APPEARANCE:

The Shoveler

Mr. _____son

The Shoveler's Mom

Mike the Neighbor

Mrs. Second Grade

Penny & Doug or Dirk or Don

The Freak, Flickering

Half-Wit High School Bitches Kelly & Mika

The Freak's Mom and Dad

The Shoveler's Shovel

Bill with the Neck Tattoo

The Talking Dirt

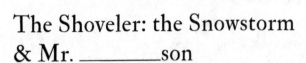

The Shoveler: the Snowstorm & Mr. _____son

84 Days before Marla & Gottfried's Easter Dinner

5:33 A.M.

My phone rings and it makes no sense that my phone is ringing because I'm in the ocean. It's dark—storm coming in, threatening sky, and I'm trying to make it to shore ahead of the storm. It's not a scary place, even though the waves are twenty feet high and getting higher. But I am at one with the ocean. Every time a wave rises behind me, I turn to look and then dip my head calmly under water until the wave passes. Then I walk toward shore until the next wave comes and I do the same.

There are people on shore, but I don't know who they are. They seem worried about me, but I'm fine.

I picked up the phone. There was a man on the other end and it wasn't my father.

It's never my father.

"Hello?" he said.

"Yeah."

"Is _____ there?" I don't remember the name—I didn't even hear it when he said it. It was Sunday morning at 5:33 a.m.—I was still chest deep, walking to shore. He'd heard my answer—scratchy, tired, and dreaming. He knew he had the wrong number.

"I think you have the wrong number."

"This is Mr. _____ son."

"Wrong number," I said again.

"Sorry to bother you," he said. He sounded like he was heading to church. His voice was the choir. Soft, understanding, sorry. He hung up.

Before I fell back to sleep, I knew what his name was. I repeated it to myself a hundred times so I'd remember. But I didn't remember it when I woke up. I ran through all the names. Stephenson, Richardson, Davidson, Hutchinson, Robinson, Johnson, Morrison, Nicholson, Jefferson. None of them were his name.

But he was somebody's son.

I check to make sure the call wasn't in my head. But it's there on my recent calls list. 5:33. A call from 407-555-1790. Maybe it was the coast guard calling to make sure I got out of the ocean okay. Maybe it was just a guy trying to wake up his church buddy. Maybe they were going fishing after the sermon. Maybe they were going to rob a convenience store. Maybe they were going to visit a friend in the hospital. Maybe they were going to drive to New York City to see a show.

I don't know how to stop the variables.

I know Mr. _____ son wasn't calling for my mother. No one calls for my mother. It's not that she's unlikeable; she's just hard to locate. Today, Sunday, she's trying to organize the kitchen. We moved in three days ago and she can't find her big potato pot. This is a problem.

"Are you sure you didn't use it for something?" she asks me.

"I'm sure."

"I don't understand where it could've gone," she says.

"Still three boxes in the shed out back that we never opened."

She sighs and frowns. "Those are all clothes. Not pots. I put all the kitchen stuff in kitchen boxes. I know how to pack."

We've moved seventeen times as far as I can remember and I'm sixteen. She knows how to pack.

"It's not like I have a lot of stuff," she says.

"I'll go check the boxes anyway. Maybe things got mixed up. Can't hurt."

She smiles and the teakettle on the stove whistles and she turns off the blue gas flame and pours the steaming water into a bowl of instant oatmeal and makes a cup of tea with the rest. The way she stirs the oatmeal. The way she wrings out the teabag with the string—it's confident. My mother is confident about oatmeal and tea and she knows how to pack.

She has trouble with money. Paying rent. Communicating effectively with bosses, landlords, and the electric company. She has trouble telling the truth.

She won't tell me who my father is, but I know she knows.

I go to the shed—there's light snow falling—and I find the boxes already opened. It's a shared shed, for all the tenants of the building. I don't know if she opened the boxes or if someone else did. They weren't open yesterday when I came out here to sneak a cigarette.

Now the boxes' flaps lie open, and the items inside seem vulnerable and frightened. My summer clothes that probably

7

won't fit me by summer. My swimming trunks. My flip-flops. All shivering.

I reach my hand down the sides, inspecting every layer. I find the potato pot in the second box and pull it out and put it on the floor of the shed. Then I find a shopping bag full of kitchen utensils. I put it inside the pot. Then I fold the boxes back the way they should be—flap over, flap under—and stack them in the back corner as far away from the lawn mower as I can so our stuff won't smell like cut grass and gasoline.

I light a cigarette. I think about my summer clothes. I think about Texas and Arizona and Nebraska, my last three summers. Sometimes I try to remember the names of my friends in the places I remember living, but their names are as inaccessible as Mr. _____son's. I remember such little things. I remember the name of a lizard in a third-grade classroom. Pollo—pronounced the Spanish way with the two *l*s as a *y*. Dumb name for a lizard. *Pollo* is Spanish for "chicken"—the kind you eat, not the animal. Maybe it was a joke. Maybe lizard tastes like chicken. I can't remember the teacher's name or else I'd write to him and ask about why he named his lizard *chicken*. He had a reptile tie for every day of the week.

I remember one best friend per location, if I had one. My other friends all blend into one another. JoshSethJaiquanRayRay-BillSumo. Before this apartment, we lived in a smaller one with brick walls; and next door lived Barry, the Texan boy who taught me how to smoke. I would always remember Barry. A kid doesn't forget the boy who taught him to smoke.

Barry thought it was weird for me and Mom to share a bed, but we only had one bed and one room and I got sick of sleeping on the floor and she didn't mind and it wasn't like we did anything inappropriate because that's not how we do things. We just survive. Potatoes and corn bread. Potatoes and pork chops. Potatoes and sweet corn. Potatoes and roast chicken. Who cares where we dream?

The weather forecast says we're about to get a real blizzard—maybe three feet. I walk back up the stairs to the apartment—a two-story, two-bedroom with thin windows—and I hand the potato pot to Mom and she looks like I just gave her a Cadillac with a million dollars inside. Then her face changes direction.

"Don't think I don't smell that on you," she says. "How are you even affording those things?"

"I had a pack I brought with me," I say.

She starts the hot water so she can wash the potato pot. "We need jobs," she says. She points to the newspaper, open on the breakfast bar.

"We do."

"Tomorrow morning I'm going to the temp agency and see what they can find for me."

"You probably won't get there until Tuesday or even Wednesday. Blizzard."

She doesn't say anything because we both know the last thing Mom wants is a job.

I open the newspaper to the help-wanted section. Truck drivers, a battery plant, and third shift at the factory a block down the road. The neighbor guy, Mike, who loaned me his snow shovel yesterday, told me the factory makes mousetraps. I made a joke about how there's probably no mice on 3rd Street, which is good because our last two apartments had mice who ate the junk food I used to hide. When he laughed, I felt like life could be okay here.

At my age I'm supposed to be chasing girls, doing homework, hanging out at McDonald's on Friday and Saturday night goofing around with other high school sophomores. But Mike is more my style, even though he's in his thirties. He has a good job and a Harley-Davidson motorcycle, and in winter he drives a small pickup truck. I think he's a happy guy even though he lives with his mother. I'm a happy guy and I live with my mother.

"If you see anything part-time, let me know," I say. "Only jobs in here are full-time."

"Will do," Mom says. She's done peeling potatoes now. "I have to walk over to the grocery in a minute. Will you keep an eye on these? I don't want 'em to boil over."

"No problem."

She thinks I don't know that she's going to be gone for more than an hour. She thinks I don't know that she shoplifts pork loins and chicken breasts. She thinks I don't know that she's choosing to walk to the grocery before a snowstorm because it'll be packed with people buying milk and toilet paper so her bulging pockets will go unnoticed. She thinks I don't know she flirts with Mike next door, even though we've only been here three days. She thinks I don't know about the calls from the last landlord who took her to court. She thinks I don't know about how she has bad credit. She thinks I don't know about her using other people's details to get the electric hooked up—stealing people's trash bags and digging through them for anything she can find. She thinks I don't know that she steals a single cigarette

10

from me every Saturday night and smokes it on the front porch.

I can't stop the variables.

She can't stop the variables.

Every night, we eat potatoes.

The Shoveler: Old Business

When it snows, it snows fast. Under the streetlight, it moves sideways and sometimes defies gravity and moves straight up. I watch it from the living room window. This is the most space we've had since Arizona. Mom told me it was because she had more money to put down, but Mike next door told me that it's because the roof leaks.

Mom checks her phone. "You don't have school tomorrow."

I nod. "How much do they say we're getting?"

"Another foot or foot and a half."

"Maybe we should've gone to California."

"I have business here," Mom says. She's looking out the window and it's not her usual business face.

"What do you mean?"

"Just some old business."

As always, variables. As always, the first variable is my father. As always, I can't say a word about it. As always, Mom doesn't extrapolate. So I just sit and watch the snow. I get bored after an hour.

"I'm going out to start on the car," I say. "Less for me to do tomorrow."

"Stay in," Mom says. "Mike will help you in the morning."

Mike. Okay. Sure.

I go out anyway. When I stand on our porch, there isn't a footprint anywhere around me. It's like landing on the moon. Quiet. Muffled. Cold. I start with Mike's borrowed shovel in the most logical place—where I'm standing. I cut a path down our

12

walkway to the sidewalk. The snow comes down so hard, I have to brush off my shoulders every five minutes.

Once I start on the sidewalk, I can't stop. I do the run in front of our building and then I do Mike's building, then I do the old lady's building next to Mike. He told me he usually does her shoveling for her, so this feels helpful.

A snowplow turns down the street. It pushes the snow from the middle of the road to the edge of the parked cars. The drifts are so high already the cars look like space pods on the moon. I look up at the streetlight, and the snow's still coming down fast.

"Hey!"

It's Mike. I wave. By the time he gets to me, his goatee is caked with snow.

"Your mom said you were out here. You should wait for me, man. We can do it in the morning. I got my brother's old snowblower in the garage."

"You told me it was a piece of shit," I say.

"It is. But it's better than doing it by hand," he says. "Come in for a beer or something."

"I'm sixteen."

"Whatever. Come in. I have the stove going."

Mike has a wood-pellet stove. And his brother's old snowblower and an impressive collection of snow shovels and the biggest flat-screen TV I ever saw. He records baseball games all season and then watches them in winter. He says it makes him feel warmer.

I think this is why I like Mike.

He doesn't seem to be the type of guy who shoplifts or digs through anyone's trash for their Social Security numbers. Just baseball and beer. And his mother upstairs, who I've never seen.

I stop on his back stoop—where a flight of snow-covered steps leads up to his back door—and pull out my pack of Camel Lights. I offer him one and he takes it.

"Come around this side," he says. "Your mom can't see us here."

We smoke and blow out huge clouds. Smoking in a snow-storm is something special. It's not like smoking in Texas. It's hard to explain.

"How are you settling in?" he asks.

"Good." I shrug. I'm not sure if I've ever settled into any-thing, anywhere.

"Your mom says you're a good kid."

"Sure," I say.

"Sorry. You're not really a kid," he says.

"I don't know. Can't tell." I think for a second and add, "It's a gray area, really, isn't it?"

"True," Mike says.

When we go inside, Mike presses a button on his remote to make the frozen baseball batter on the screen come to life again. He says, "Watch this!" and the guy hits a home run. I don't really watch baseball, but the home run is impressive. Right over the stadium. Out of the park.

I sit next to the wood stove and warm my hands. Mike goes into the fridge and gets a can of beer for each of us, but I say, "No thanks, man."

He nods and sits down and I get up and put the beer back in the fridge. In the kitchen, I take inventory of kitchen appliances. Mike has a blender, a toaster, a coffeemaker, a bread maker, a dehydrator, a food processor, a juicer, and something called a seed starter that looks like the cage Pollo the lizard lived in.

Mike has a lot of kitchen appliances for a guy who lives with a mother who never comes downstairs.

And yet, in the fridge it's just beer and the usual condiments.

I want to ask him what he eats, but it seems stupid. I go in and sit on his couch and watch baseball by the wood stove. I say, "You're right. Baseball makes me feel warmer."

He points to his brain with his index finger. "It's all in the head, man. Control the brain, and the rest is easy."

The Shoveler: Tunnels on the Surface of the Moon

Control the brain and the rest is easy. I think about this as I walk home from Mike's.

He probably wasn't talking to me, directly. He probably doesn't know about my brain. Mom doesn't even know about my brain. How would I tell her? When would I tell her? Is there a certain time of day that she can actually stop thinking about herself?

My brain is none of her business.

Even if it's trying to drive me crazy.

Every hour since that 5:33 a.m. phone call, my brain has a new distraction. *Stephenson, Richardson, Davidson, Hutchinson, Robinson, Johnson, Jefferson.* Every day since I could wonder, it wonders where half of me is. Ever since I could tally myself, I am half here.

> Family tree project. Second grade. I'd have preferred to dissect my own foot. While it was still attached to my ankle. Florida. The teacher drew a tree on the whiteboard. Drew lines around it. Filled in the lines. Her mother. Her father. Her sister. Her two brothers. Her husband. Her children. Her nieces and nephews. Her pets. *Just for fun,* she said. I drew my tree. I drew my tree big on the paper, and she said, *Sweetheart, you haven't left space for your family!* I had one of those fat crayons in my hand. I wrote *MOM* across the top of the tree. I wrote *ME* in the middle of the trunk of the tree. Mrs. Second Grade stood for a minute and I heard it. I heard it click in her head and I heard her heart break for poor little me. Never had a chance. No limbs. No leaves. No twigs. No pets just for fun.

I got an A. This kid in my class did his tree on a piece of paper so big he had to unroll it. Went back four generations. Four generations. The handwriting wasn't even his. He called me out for getting an A. He said he should be the only one with an A. Mrs. Second Grade said, *Your grades are not based on your family size.*

Recess. Same day. Kid calls me a bastard and says my mom is a slut. I tell him he should eat a giant dick. He tries to punch me, but Florida kids are slower than me. I punch him instead. He bleeds.

Find myself in the office. Tell the principal the kid called my mom a slut. Get sent home anyway. Walk in on Mom and her boyfriend doing things I don't want to hear.

I never brought my family tree home. Shoved it into the classroom trash can. Spat on it for good measure.

My brain makes tunnels. The tunnels get smaller. They eventually close. Usually. The family tree tunnel never closes all the way.

Stephenson, Richardson, Davidson, Hutchinson, Robinson, Johnson, Jefferson. I am somebody's son.

I'm still warm from Mike's baseball game and decide to clear a path to the car so I can start clearing it off. When I shovel, I feel like I was born to shovel things. I consider shoveling things for the rest of my life. Shovel snow, shovel dirt, shovel Mom, shovel myself. Eventually I might get to the answer. Sounds stupid, right? A sixteen-year-old kid looking for the answer when he doesn't even know the question.

But we all know the question.

The question is: What am I even *doing* here?

I watch the plows and the salt trucks go up the main road and pass through the intersection with the traffic lights. Then the plow goes past and pushes the road snow back to where I shoveled, and I think maybe the answer is to constantly do things and never get anywhere.

There's something about being out in a snowstorm, though. The answer is a snowflake. It's a blizzard. It's the way I feel hot on the inside and my nose is numb at the same time. Sweat is running down my back. My fingers are frozen because my gloves are wet. Maybe these are the answers.

Another foot of snow has fallen. I don't know how long I've been out here. Mike's lights are still on, so I'm guessing it's still early enough for watching baseball and *controlling the mind* to think it's summer. The roads are frozen. There is no way anyone is getting anywhere tomorrow. I look at the church across the street and the snow has weighed down the branches of the fir trees around it so much they look like they could snap.

I turn around and look at our house. It's pretty in the snow. Downstairs lives a woman named Penny who's a music teacher. We have the next two floors in the front. A guy named Doug or Dirk or Don or something lives in the back apartment. Mike says he works third shift, so we never see him. Penny keeps the front porch nice and it looks like she has flower beds and stuff. I mean, before the snow. Now it just looks like she grows the surface of the moon.

Only a week ago I was sweating my ass off in jeans in the South Texas sun. I just moved into a blizzard. I'm sixteen years old and the only constant in my life other than my mother is our potato pot.

The answer has something to do with potatoes. It has to.

MAKE THE FREAK VANISH!

It was a Saturday night about two years ago, and The Freak decided to drive to the mall cinema and see a movie. Something animated. Childish.

Kelly Pointer and her best friend, Mika, walked toward The Freak when she was at the concession stand, buying popcorn. They stopped a few feet from her and talked low, then Mika walked away and toward the arcade. Kelly stepped in with a panicked look on her face. The Freak could tell it didn't seem right. The Freak moved here only a few weeks before, and Kelly Pointer had been nothing but territorial.

Kelly said, "I have to talk to you about something."

The Freak said, "Okay."

"You can't tell *anybody*, okay?"

The Freak said, "Okay."

"I'm pregnant."

The Freak asked a few questions. The *Are you okay*s and the *Are you going to keep it*s. Kelly Pointer went on her way and The Freak knew she just got set up. And if it had anything to do with the best friend, Mika, good freakin' luck because the girl couldn't think her way out of an open shoebox.

An hour later, mid-movie.

Mika leaned over to The Freak and said, ". . ."

The Freak had a freeze frame right there.

The Freak couldn't figure the game, but she knew she was in one. The Freak thought Mika was going to say *What's up with*

Kelly tonight? She won't tell me anything! The Freak knows the bitches. All the bitches. The Freak is in tune with the bitch playbook.

So Mika leaned over to The Freak and said, "Did you hear Kelly's pregnant?"

The Freak had no idea what to say. This was not in the playbook. So she said, "Is she okay?"

Mika nodded and turned her attention back to the movie.

An hour later, the movie was over, Kelly Pointer marched up to The Freak at the soda machine and said, "You told Mika I was pregnant!" Now, thanks to Kelly's own lack of volume control, everyone in the cinema lobby knew Kelly Pointer was pregnant, so The Freak guessed it wasn't a problem.

The Freak said, "Mika told *me* you were pregnant."

Kelly said, "No, she didn't."

The Freak said, "Yes, she did."

Kelly said, "You told her and you know it."

The Freak looked over at Mika, who was completely clueless about what was going on and was staring at a boy across the lobby.

The Freak said, "She told me during the movie. I just asked if you were okay."

Kelly launched her allegedly pregnant body at The Freak with her right hand cocked and ready to punch. The Freak ran.

The Freak has been running ever since. Nearly two years.

Running on every continent, through every climate. She just closes her eyes and flickers from one place to the next. She is permanently out of danger. Whether she's in some war-torn country at gunpoint or in a random town about to get beat up

21

by a girl like Kelly Pointer, all she has to do is close her eyes and she flickers to the next place.

She spent most of yesterday learning how to belly dance in Berlin.

She spent most of today in the desert poking a poisonous snake.

She's testing her reflexes. The snake rears up, ready to strike, and she flickers herself out of there before she gets hurt. She lands on the planet snow moon in the middle of a freshly plowed street.

THE FREAK HATES HALF-WIT HIGH SCHOOL BITCHES!

The Freak is angry. She knew better than to be set up by two half-wit high school bitches. Nearly two years have gone by, and she's still angry about it.

The snow calms her. It's falling so fast she can't see thirty feet in front of her. She doesn't try to catch any snowflakes on her tongue. The Freak doesn't catch snowflakes on her tongue. She reaches into her pocket and pulls out a lighter and tries to light the snowflakes on fire before they hit the ground. Before they cover everything up. This is a pointless task.

Last Friday, The Freak's father moved out of the house. Again. Good riddance. He was a series of dials and switches that controlled everything from when she took a bath to how she brushed her hair. He said bras were too expensive when her boobs came in so she wears layers to hide her nipples. He said tampons and pads were too expensive when she got her period, so she's used everything from a menstrual cup to random washcloths since day one. This could be the reason people call her The Freak, but there are others.

The Freak is angry at Kelly Pointer and her dumb friend, Mika. She's angry at her mother already for the day she'll let her father move back in. Happens every time, like a yo-yo. The longest they ever managed to stay separated was three months. That was two years ago, when her mom moved the two of them to Pennsylvania.

She tries to burn snow that's sitting on top of a car. It melts and that's satisfying. She doesn't know where she is, but she never does when she flickers. Flickering can be dangerous. She could have landed anywhere. It's nice to see snow again.

"Hey! What're you doing to my car?"

The Freak forgets that people can see her.

The guy yelling at her is standing in his doorway in a thick flannel shirt and a pair of unlaced snow boots. She moves along. Whispers, "Sorry." It's so quiet in the snow, she doubts the guy hears her but then he says, "Aren't you cold? Want to come inside?"

The Freak is sick of pervy older guys already. She's been sick of them since she was twelve. She isn't cold. She just spent eight hours in a desert. She keeps walking and waves him off. He closes the front door and she's alone again. No traffic. No people. No noise. Snow makes everything that's wrong with the world disappear.

The thing about flickering is she can't stay in one place forever even if she wants to. The Freak is at the beach. The Freak is in the boardroom. The Freak is hiking in the Alps. The Freak is on a boat. The Freak is harvesting Russian wheat. The Freak is on the snow moon.

When The Freak was sixteen, her boyfriend cut her arm with a steak knife. The Freak told him to fuck off. But the next day he said he was sorry. A week later, The Freak was douching with turpentine. It hurt a little, but not as much as other things.

Flickering doesn't hurt. Flickering is easy.

Now The Freak will never have to douche with turpentine again.

She can just go to the beach.

The Freak's feet are in sand.

The Freak's feet are in surf.

The Freak's feet are in woolly boots and she's melting snow with her lighter.

The Freak's bumming a cigarette from a stranger in New York City.

The Freak's snowboarding in Tahoe.

The Freak is sober. The Freak is drunk. The Freak is angry. Adults tell her to smile. Adults tell her not to be so angsty. She says, "You douche with turpentine and get back to me."

The Freak has emotions. She doesn't plan on stopping those up with stupid wine conversations or political debates. Red, white, red, blue. The Freak's mother is a fan of red. Big, round glasses—she'd swirl the wine around and sniff it. By the end of the night, who cares what it smelled like? By the end of the night, The Freak's mother was stumbling around the house, talking to the cat like the cat could really understand her. The cat and The Freak would both recoil from the curse of red wine: black gums and teeth and the unmistakable sour of sulfur.

Jake & Bill are shoveling

Jake and his brother, Bill, are shoveling their driveway in the dark. They live in a nice place—part of a development. From the outside of the house, you'd never guess that minds like theirs could call it home. It's so standardized—as if a house machine had just dropped two hundred houses perfectly aligned along the streets, only changing the color from light beige to dark beige to gray each time. Inside is just as normal. Kitschy decorations from their mother's trips to Amish country. Framed childhood pictures. A wall-hanging-sized quilt that says FAMILY. Whole place smells of cinnamon and vanilla. The kitchen is clean, and the den next to it is filled with normal-looking furniture and lamps and a nice carpet with no stains.

The only thing weird about the house is the heated tank in Bill's room for his snake. But boys will be boys, and boys like weird things like snakes. From the outside, they're as normal as anyone on the block.

Jake shovels faster than Bill, like it's a race. The blacktop of the driveway is the same blacktop as everyone else's driveway. The minute Jake sees it under the snow, he wishes the whole driveway was exposed. Shovels faster. As deep as he can. Daydreams of moving south.

"Fuck this," Bill says, and goes inside, leaving Jake to do all the work.

The Shoveler: Brain Man

There's a girl walking up the street, in the middle of the street. I don't know where she came from and it doesn't look like she knows where she's going. She's just meandering. She doesn't see me and I stand here quietly because for some reason I don't want her to see me.

I can't keep my eyes off her, though.

For some reason I think: *She is the answer.*

For some reason I think: *She is the meaning of life.*

We look at each other for a second, and she walks toward me slowly. Still meandering. Stopping to light her lighter, but I'm not sure why. I think she's trying to light the snow on fire.

Eventually, "Hi."

I say, "Hi."

"Was that your dad asking me to come in?" she asks, pointing to Mike's house.

I shake my head. "That's our neighbor. I don't have a dad."

"Immaculate conception?"

"Sure," I say.

"Cosmic." She reaches down deep into her parka pocket and seems disappointed that nothing is in there. "Dads are overrated anyway."

"You probably only say that because you have one."

She says, "My mom told me that my dad was an ass man when I was five years old. I didn't know what it meant. She told me later that some men are ass men, some are breast men, and some are leg men. I'm looking for a brain man. Haven't found one yet."

I don't know what to say to her. I never thought about it this way. Also: hell of a way to start a conversation.

"It's like they have us carved up before we're even in middle school. Fuck men. No offense, but y'all are a bunch of assholes . . . fathers included."

I don't know what to say to that, either. I want to tell her I'm a brain man, but I'm not one. I've looked at breasts. I've looked at legs. I've looked at asses. "Maybe it's because no one can actually see the brain," I say. "Like, you have to get to know someone before you know their brain."

"No shit."

I let too many seconds pass. "We're all assholes," I say. She looks at me and rolls her eyes. "Sorry. I'm trying to think of a guy I know who's a brain man and I can't think of one."

"Doesn't make you all assholes. I mean, are you an asshole? Out here shoveling snow in the dark? Assholes are usually lazy."

I've never been lazy. This makes me feel good.

"Anyway, it's not like you're an orphan," she says.

"True." I think of Mom. Sometimes I feel like an orphan, but I'm not an orphan.

"And you'll get a good job soon. It'll be in your mailbox tomorrow. Watch for it."

I don't know what to say.

"You got a smoke?" she asks.

I hand her one and she lights it with her lighter. I don't feel like smoking another one so I just watch her smoke. I notice her lips. Full and red. No lipstick. Just naturally perfect lips. I've never wanted to kiss anyone in my life. Never. But right now? Right now I want to feel her lips on my lips and taste what she tastes like.

I watch her take another pull off the cigarette and I can't stop thinking about my father. This is my main tunnel. It feeds the other tunnels. I can't get away from him and I don't even know who he is. I'm sixteen years old and I've never wanted to kiss a girl before. What the fuck is that about? Seriously. A man I never met—a man whose name I don't even know—he's crippled everything about me.

THE FREAK IS PART
OF A TEAM NOW!

The Freak loves how the exhale is a mix of smoke and steam. It's proof that she's there, on the snow moon. She's talking to a boy. It's not something she likes doing, but this boy is different. He's shoveling snow while she smokes. He doesn't seem interested in her at all, outside of random conversation. No flirting, no innuendo, no tips on how to be prettier or more fashionable, no telling her how to talk because *swear words put boys off*. Mostly he moves snow and breathes heavily. There's something about him. She likes him too much. Not even halfway to the filter. That's not good. So she places her cigarette on the edge of the curb, as if the street were a giant ashtray, and flickers to her bedroom.

In it, she finds the note from her mother.

> *You can't just disappear without telling me where you went. I know your dad leaving has been hard on you, but we have to be a team now. I want your car keys on the kitchen table before dinner.*

The Freak was fond of disappearing from the minute she could drive. At first, she was staying out all night with the turpentine boyfriend. After that, she swore off boys and drove around by herself so she didn't have to hear the arguments. It's funny, this note. Still here in her old bedroom in California. As if Pennsylvania never happened. As if car keys mean anything now.

30

The Shoveler: Transparent Backpack

She just vanished. Bummed a cigarette, smoked half of it, then I looked up and she was gone. Her cigarette is still burning on the curb where she left it, but it's wet from the snowfall, which seems impossible—a burning, wet cigarette. She isn't walking up or down the street. She isn't sitting on the front porch. She isn't sneaking through side alleys. Her footprints stop where she stopped. It makes no sense. The variables try to take over. I look at the church across the street. It has one of those tiny old grave-yards next to it. Maybe there are ghosts here. I'm not scared of ghosts, but she didn't seem like one.

By the time I stop clearing off the top of the cars—ours and Penny's—the snow has slowed. Maybe five more inches to come, tops. I bring the shovel and the broom to the porch, knock off as much snow as I can from my boots and coat, and take them off inside the foyer.

When I get upstairs and inside the apartment, I see it's 1:30 a.m. Mom is asleep on the couch, curled up facing the wall. I'm wide-awake and I put the teakettle on and make hot chocolate.

I change out of my damp clothes and put on a pair of flan-nel pajama bottoms and a long-sleeved T-shirt. My room is small and empty, aside from my bed, the school handbook, two trash bags of clothing, and a new backpack Mom got me when she went on her first-day-in-a-new-town shopping spree. The back-pack is made of transparent plastic. This is never a good sign.

I open the handbook and close it again. What could it say

that isn't obvious—other than all backpacks must be transparent? *Don't be late; don't leave early. Don't skip school. Don't hit anyone. Don't stab anyone. Don't wear clothes that show your private parts. Don't fail your classes. Don't be a dick in the cafeteria. Don't be a dick on the bus. Don't be a dick in the library. Don't be a dick during class changes. Don't be a dick on school property after school ends.*

First day in a new school. Never goes well. Always too nervous. Always sweat through all my layers. Always hiding from the kids who want to beat me up. There are always kids who want to beat up the new kid. It makes no sense. Texas, it was a kid name Kyle. Arizona, it was a kid named Paco Taco, which was a racist nickname, but he was known for his love of tacos, and he called himself that, so I guess it was okay? Nebraska, it was a girl. Her name was Julie. She beat everyone up at any chance she could. One time in Kentucky, in the fourth grade, it was the principal of the school. Wanted to beat me up on day one. Said free-lunch kids should at least wash their hair.

I washed my hair every day in fourth grade but the principal always told me it was too greasy. Said free-lunch kids shouldn't have dirt on the knees of their jeans, and he was sick and tired of kids like me bringing his test scores down.

One day he produced the cheese paddle. Holes in wood. Made a whooshing noise. I puked my free lunch onto his carpet.

Got expelled.
Moved. Tun-
nel closes.

I don't have any curtains in my bedroom so I wake up early on
Monday with blinding snow sun in my eyes. The storm is over.
I go out to survey the job ahead. I'm glad I did what I did last
night because there's only about six inches on our walkway and
the sidewalk. Our cars are visible while the rest of the cars on the
block still look like curvy icebergs in an ocean of snow.

I turn to go back inside and I see there's a small newspaper
in our mailbox, the *Merchandiser*. No footprints. Penny's mailbox doesn't have one. Just ours.

There's a job in this paper for me. That's what the girl told
me. I still can't tell if she was real. She looked real. When she
breathed, steam came out of her mouth and nose. She lit snow
on fire. She cursed at the snowplow. She talked about asses. If she
was a ghost, she was a beautiful and very strange one.

I turn to the help-wanted section and there's an ad that's
outlined in purple highlighter.

Worker Needed. Am I a worker?

Interior house painting. I've painted a few of our apartments.
Usually I have to paint them back to neutral, too, because Mom
decides she wants a purple bedroom or a lime-green kitchen
and landlords like white.

*Ten minutes from city. Perfect job for student. Nights and week-
end hours only.*

Mom shows up in the kitchen. "You're up early," she says.

"Got this in the mailbox last night." I hold up the *Merchandiser*.

She grunts and makes coffee, then plops down on the couch next to me.

"Did you shovel all night?"

"Just until I was done."

"I saw you talking to that girl."

"Yeah," I say, and I smile because that means she was real.

"Mike said she was melting snow with fire or something. Weird girl. Maybe you want to stay away from her."

When Mom goes for a shower, I decide this is a good time to call the painting-job people. They don't answer so I leave a message on what sounds like the oldest answering machine in the world—a message recorded underwater and the beep that takes me by surprise. I can't remember what I said, but my last sentence echoes. *I look forward to hearing from you!*

I'm annoyed at how perky I sound. But it seems like a cash job, so perky is probably good. Cash job means Mom can't take my check, deposit into her account, and give me forty bucks for a week's work like the last two jobs.

NAKED FREAK CAN'T CRY!

The Freak wants to go back to the shoveling boy. She needs to tell him about what to expect at school. She needs to tell him not to talk to anyone who carries a snake. She needs to tell him you can't always see right away who's carrying a snake.

But she's stuck where she is. In her dusty old bedroom, listening to her parents argue downstairs.

She can't believe her mom let him back in the house again. She can't believe it, but she understands it. Times are rough. Shit like this breaks people into pieces and somehow her parents' pieces fit together even though it was never good for any of them.

The Freak isn't afraid of a little fighting, though. She sits on her bed and listens to them.

"I should have never let you move out there," he says.

"I wanted to go," she says. "And we needed the money."

"I should have just gotten another job. Or begged my dad. Or . . ."

Her father is crying. This is new. Her mother starts, then. The two of them fill the whole house up with sobs. The Freak tries to cry but she can't work up one single tear—not even an angry one. She looks at herself in the mirror. Strips naked. This usually works, but still, no tears. This makes The Freak angrier. She kicks her trash can over. She punches the mirror and it cracks.

"Did you hear that?" her father says.

"I hear things all the time," her mother answers. "All the time."

The Freak tries to open her bedroom door but it's locked from the outside.

Sits on her bed. Still can't cry even though she's sadder than she's ever been.

Flickers.

The Freak is still naked when she appears in a university lecture hall where a professor is talking about *Solanum tuberosum*—the potato plant.

"Who would have thought Northern Europeans would rely so much on a plant so poisonous? Everything about it is toxic except for the tubers themselves. Leaves, stems, roots, seeds, all poison. The secret," he says, slapping his hand on a stack of books, "is keeping the spuds beneath the soil. Because any part of the plant that sees light can hurt you if you eat it. Even kill you—but only after making you puke your guts out and go crazy."

The professor talks about Europe in the sixteenth century—how, before the potato, the people were dying from disease and famine—and then, in closing, says something that makes the room erupt in mumbling. He says, "The world we live in—this dominion of Northern Europeans—is the way it is because of *Solanum tuberosum*. If you ask me, it's ironic that our ancestors were able to avoid poisoning themselves on the plants, and yet rose to poison the whole world with themselves."

While the mumbling students debate this claim among themselves, The Freak writes a poem on her desk.

Earthworms Tell The Freak Secrets!

(Earthworms know the
history of the whole world

36

because they eat the
history of the whole world.)

If you want to learn the history of dirt,
you listen to worms.

    The professor slaps his pile of books again and starts to take questions.

    The Freak always wanted to go to college, but she's naked and the students are staring.

    In many ways, The Freak feels naked all the time.

    In many ways, The Freak is naked all the time.

    It's probably what scares people most about her.

Marla & Gottfried's Drive-In Movie

"You're too old to do that yourself," Marla says. "We don't have anywhere to go. We can just call that guy with the plow who does Helen's place."

Gottfried finishes putting on his last layer of clothing. So far he's put on a thin layer of long underwear, then a thicker layer, then two pairs of socks, then jeans and his belt and two sweatshirts over his turtleneck. As Marla talks to him, he walks to the hall closet and takes out his fleece face shield and scarf and a pair of earmuffs.

"You really shouldn't be doing this anymore. You could fall again!"

Two winters ago, Gottfried fell and hit his head on the ice. He still doesn't know how long he'd been out, but he remembers having a nice dream without the robins.

He puts on his hat, his coat, and stuffs his gloves into his pockets and heads for the garage where his boots are waiting for him with special metal grips stretched over their soles.

"Gottfried! Why aren't you listening to me!?" Marla yells.

He opens the garage door from the inside switch, and as it opens and reveals three feet of snow outside, he says, "I'm listening."

"Call the plow guy. He always gets here eventually!"

"I'm not too old to clear my own driveway. Same as you're not too old to do anything you do."

Gottfried walks to the snowblower and starts it. Marla tries to talk over it, but can't, so she goes back inside and starts cleaning the refrigerator.

I'm not too old to do anything I do? Why
would you say that? What do I even do
anymore? You don't take me to dinner. Never to a show or the symphony.
I make food for you to eat. I buy all the
holiday presents and remember all the
birthdays. I still clip coupons. I wash
your clothes. I put up with your baseball
games and I recycle your beer bottles.

Slip and fall for all
I care. Crack your
head open. Fifty years
together and the
only action I get in
bed is your snoring.

Gottfried comes in for lunch. He's only a third of a way done
with the driveway.

"It's good snow. Light," he says.

"Eat more than just half that sandwich," Marla says. "You'll
need your strength."

"The soup is really good, Marla."

"Your favorite."

They smile at each other. Gottfried can barely see her after
a morning in the bright snow. Marla can barely see him after
years of ignoring her cataracts. Sometimes when she looks at
him, she sees the young man in an ill-fitting suit on his way to
his first job interview, the man who was breaking away from his
family farm to go into business—the man she fell in love with.
Sometimes when he looks at her, he sees the girl who wore
white gloves to their first date and expected a corsage just to go
to the drive-in.

Gottfried never told Marla about the robins—it wasn't right for a man to cry in front of a woman like that. Not when they were young. Things were different.

Marla never told Gottfried about what happened after their last child was born. Back then, you didn't tell your husband about woman problems. And you kept the children as trouble-free for him as you could.

"I'm heading back out," he says after a stop in the bathroom.

"Be careful!"

Keeping the children trouble-free wasn't as easy as it sounded.

Marla had her own robins and sometimes she cried about them, too.

Jake & Bill go out for beer

Jake Marks wants to make a snow angel. He doesn't know why; he knows this makes him the biggest fag that ever lived. He's Jake Fucking Marks. King of in-school suspension. King of telling teachers to suck his dick. But he wishes for a minute he was just Jake, the little kid who could make a snow angel without his brother calling him a pussy.

Things haven't been the same since the day he and Bill had to drive to New Jersey. Sometimes he feels like he's splitting in two. Sometimes he can still smell the dirt and the wet leaves from the forest they drove to. Sometimes he wishes it was simpler. Like snow angels.

Bill starts the car and Jake jumps into the passenger's seat. "Goin' out for beer," Bill says. Jake nods. "Got any weed on you?"

Jake has a bag in his pocket along with some rolling papers. But his connection just got busted. "Nah, man. Smoked it all yesterday."

The snow never got all-the-way cleared last night. More of it fell. Bill doesn't care. He pulls out of the driveway through a foot of the stuff, fishtailing the whole way.

FREAKISH INTERLUDE!

The Freak is on the side of a hill in a forest, fully dressed. She's still thinking about *Solanum tuberosum* and going to college. She liked what the professor said about poison.

She looks down at the house—the house with the abundant skylights and the pristine deck that she can't see under three feet of snow. The Freak has been watching these people for a year and a half now. There are only two of them—an old couple. She wonders why they live in such a big house by themselves. It's got to be four thousand square feet. That's a lot of interior paint.

Flickers.

Lands next to the filing cabinets.

The Freak knows half-wit high school bitches are not the real problem. She knows what happened after she ran from the movie theater. But no one else does.

Some nights she flickers here, to the storage room of the police station, and reads the files. The files are mostly bullshit. Statements from people like Kelly Pointer. Lies. Rumors. Her gym teacher went on record and said The Freak was *"promiscuous."* Her father said *"she never listened."* Her ex-boyfriend in California said *"last time I saw her, she smelled like turpentine."*

Some days The Freak wishes she could accordion herself into the filing cabinets and pop out when they're opened. Maybe then someone might pay attention. Might ask her about how she loved to help her elderly neighbor. Might ask her about her favorite stuffed animal. Might notice that she was just a sixteen-year-old girl.

42

She thinks about what the professor said about history books. "A convenient narrative," he said. Same as The Freak's file.

What chance does a girl have when her dad won't shell out for a bra and tampons? What chance does a girl have when she can't learn about sex at school but can learn how to douche with turpentine on her phone? When her parents are arguing machines? When her father is a yo-yo and her mother can only think in oil paints? When she's moved all the way across the country because her family can't locate its owner's manual?

"Fucked if I do, fucked if I don't." That's The Freak motto. But if she could do it all over again, she'd just let Kelly Pointer punch her in the face.

Flickers.

The Freak lands in an empty office. She spins in a leather chair behind a desk crowded with papers and a nameplate that reads WILLIAM MARKS. The Freak shuffles through the papers to see if any are about her. She finds an invitation to a wedding—the kind with the tiny RSVP envelope and two choices for dinner: beef or chicken. No vegetarian option.

Bill and Ashley are getting married. The Freak doesn't know who Bill and Ashley are, but she pictures them tuxedoed and gowned up, surrounded by flowers and loved ones. She pictures a live band because it's much classier than a DJ. Maybe jazz. Hard-rock cover band, even.

Beef or chicken. Jazz or hard rock. Married or unmarried. Happy or unhappy. There are no variables anymore for The Freak, but she really thinks there should be a vegetarian option.

The Shoveler: Ma'am

Mike's brother's shitty snowblower isn't half as shitty as Mike said it was. Or, at least Mike makes it look easy. His goatee sticks out of his bright orange hunting coat and is caked with ice. He points to the places I should shovel by hand while he slowly makes his way between each parked car.

The one thing about Mike's brother's shitty snowblower is that Mike has to give it a rest every hour.

When we sit around his stove and warm up and he drinks a beer even though it's eleven in the morning, I struggle with what to say. I play one hundred different sentences in my head every second. I never find the right one. If my brain could do math at the same speed, I'd fill three chalkboards with equations every minute or so. Calculations. Each with its own set of variables.

"So you start school tomorrow?" Mike seems as uncomfortable as I am when he says this. Like he can't find the right sentence either.

"Unless they give us another snow day."

"Looks likely. A lot of ice under there."

"Yeah."

"That girl last night," Mike says. "She your girlfriend?"

"Did my mom tell you to ask me that?"

His face says yes. His mouth says, "You just looked happy to see her. That's all."

"Never saw her before. I just moved here," I say. I feel I can trust Mike, though. He's a guy. I'm a guy. "I wouldn't mind seeing her again, though. Mom thinks she's weird, but maybe I like weird girls. Who knows?"

"How old are you again?"

"Sixteen."

"Old enough to like whoever you want to like," he says.

"Yeah."

". . ."

Mike stops right after he takes a breath to say something.

"What?"

". . ."

He takes another breath but shakes his head. We sit for a complete minute saying nothing. I count it in my head because it's what I do. Six thousand sentences sprint through my mind and none of them get to the finish tape.

"I'm going to check in at home," I say.

Mike gets up and says, "I'm gonna take a dump."

As I walk across our adjoining yards, I think about telling Mom to butt out of my business. I see it like a movie in my head. I run different scenarios. In forty feet, I run maybe twenty movies. Every one of them ends with her yelling at me same as she did when I confronted her about shoplifting last year in Texas.

The movies are like the tunnels. It's all part of the same thing. I fuck everything up, pretty much. Before I ever open my mouth, I already pick the wrong thing to say. Brain moves too fast. Mouth moves too slow.

Mom's not home. I didn't see her leave, but I don't worry about her. The car is still out front, nearly cleared of its cage of snow, and she can't have gone too far.

When I check my phone, there's a voicemail.

> Hello! This is Marla Hemmings returning your call about the painting job. Please call me back. I'd like to have the interior done by Easter so we should get started now.

I've been to a few job interviews in my life. Never have I gotten a job by simply leaving a message on someone's old, warped answering machine.

By the time we're done clearing the cars and sidewalks, it's four in the afternoon. The sun is shining as if it had never snowed. Mike says he's going to take a shower. Mom isn't home yet. I decide to call the painting-job lady back.

"Hi. I'm returning your call about the painting job."

"Yes! My husband and I were hoping you could start this week."

I want to explain that she's never met me. I could be an ax murderer. I could be an arsonist. I could steal all of her jewelry. I could be a bad painter. A cannibal. A werewolf. The variables are endless, really.

She continues. "There are seven rooms in all. Two hallways. And all the ceilings. Can you give me an estimate?"

I want to tell her I'm sixteen years old and don't have an estimate because no sixteen-year-olds have an estimate. I say, "Um."

"Can you come out this evening?"

I want to tell her that there was just a blizzard and the roads are going to be frozen tonight. "I'm sorry. I can't make it out until Thursday night, ma'am."

I just said *ma'am*. I don't even know what to think of myself.

She says, "Thursday would be fine."

We say goodbye and I hang up before I get her address.

See? I fuck everything up.

The Shoveler: Au Gratin

Mom's phone dings while we're watching the late show. "No school again tomorrow," she says.

"The roads are still a mess," I say.

She nods. "I guess the temp agency can wait until Thursday."

"Yeah," I say. *Sure, Thursday.*

Snow Day #2. I wake up in the middle of the afternoon and find Mom in the kitchen, peeling potatoes.

Tonight we're having potatoes au gratin. I slice and Mom places the slices in the potato pot. She has twelve different au gratin recipes. This one is my favorite. Heavy cream, Gruyere cheese, and garlic.

We eat dinner with the TV on. Local news—weather; two schools have a mold problem; a missing girl still hasn't turned up; some guy robbed a grocery store with a gun; and more weather.

Mom doesn't talk to me about school. She never does. She never says, "Are you nervous?" or "Are you going to be okay?" or, even when I was little, "Do you know where you're going?" She just buys the backpack and leaves the rest to me. Fact: I'm nervous, not okay, and no, I don't know where I'm going and I'm a walker.

I go out back to the shed after dinner and smoke a nervous, freezing-cold cigarette. I look over at the back of Mike's house and his collection of snow shovels. There's an old one with a bright orange metal scoop—it's smaller than the others, but not child-sized. I walk through thigh-high snow to go get it. Once it's in my hands, I don't want to let go of it. It's like I'm a little kid with a teddy bear or a security blanket.

Mike shows up on his back stoop. "You stealing shit from me now?" He's smiling, so I know he doesn't really think I am. He's funny.

"I just—uh. I like this one."

"Take it. You can have it," he says. "And thanks for helping me yesterday."

"No problem," I say.

"Good luck at school tomorrow," he says.

I nod because I don't know what else to say. I look at him—his motion-sensor light shining in my eyes from behind him—and I smile.

I walk to the road, brushing the caked snow out of the creases of my jeans, and look up and down for the mystery girl who lights snowflakes on fire. She's not there. When I get back inside, I put my security shovel by the door and I sneak a sleeping pill from Mom's stash and get in bed. Except my pillow is soaking wet.

Mom and I place three pots under the three leaks. I move my bed. Mom tells me she'll trade pillows with me and puts mine in the dryer.

I sleep without moving once.

School. I walk without thinking, without worrying, without feeling my legs taking the steps they're taking. It's cold, but first-day numbness happens no matter where I live and no matter the weather. Here, in Pennsylvania, my shovel will keep me safe.

I fill my ears with my own voice. *It can't be as bad as that time in Kentucky. It can't be as bad as that time in Florida. It can't be as bad as . . .*

I go to my locker—the shovel doesn't fit inside it but that's okay. I plan on keeping it with me. And no one seems to care—not the students and not the teachers. New kid with a shovel. I guess they've seen everything.

The introductions aren't like elementary school—that awkward stand-up-and-tell-us-about-yourself shit that always left me with nothing to say. The homeroom teacher just explains that I'm here now, part of their homeroom, says my name, then goes on with his day. All the other kids turn in their seats and look at me.

I sit here with my shovel and I smile.

I'm given a buddy. Tenth grade and I've got a buddy. His name is Thomas. Thomas is a white kid with glasses and I can see through his backpack that he's carrying around three paperback books with their covers torn off.

"What's your name again?" he asks. I tell him my name.

"Where're you from?"

This is always the question that gets me. After the looks I got in homeroom, I decide to pick the least controversial state I can.

You think this is crazy. You think states can't be controversial. You're reading this in your own state thinking that your state is great, right? But everyone sees the world different from everybody else. If you're in the South, some people don't like the North because it's full of elites. If you're in the North, some people think if you're from the South, you're stupid or a racist if you're white.

50

If you're from the East Coast, some people on the West Coast think you're too uptight. If you're from the West Coast, some people on the East Coast think you're a weirdo whose parents probably smoke weed. You'd be surprised at the assumptions people make based on the answer to this question. I'm in Pennsylvania now, so I figure somewhere close by would be safe.

"New Jersey," I say.

Thomas says, "Wow. Bummer."

"Yeah," I say, as if I know why New Jersey is a bummer.

Day one ends and no one beats me up. Thomas stayed with me up until lunch, but never showed up again. I have some homework but not much. When I get home, Mom isn't there and the car is gone. I walk into my room and the snow on the roof is slowly working its way through the ceiling and into our pots. I call the landlord and leave a message. I empty the full pots and replace them. I look on my phone to see where Mom is. The phone finder app says she's at the temp agency, which is a miracle.

I text. Can I borrow the car tomorrow night?

She answers. Sure. Home in about an hour. I THINK I GOT A JOB!

I text her a unicorn emoji because it seems appropriate.

Marla & Gottfried Get Ready for a Guest

"Did you vacuum the living room?"

Gottfried can't hear well anymore. He hears this but doesn't reply. He already vacuumed the living room and the hall. And every room on the second floor. Seemed pointless—running the vacuum over the marks that were left from the last time he vacuumed.

"He's coming at five," Marla says.

"He's not the Queen of England. He's just a kid," Gottfried answers.

Marla purses her lips and tries to count how many times Gottfried has reminded her that the person who was visiting was not the Queen of England. There's nothing wrong with having a clean house, even if her grown children joke about how her kitchen floor is so clean you could perform surgery on it.

They don't come around much anymore, the grown children. Marla and Gottfried did it right—they raised independent kids who could do the same as they did. Work hard and save money.

Of course, Marla and Gottfried are somewhat delusional about things like this. Marla can often be overheard saying, "Our generation didn't have it any better!" And that's just flatly untrue. They were Baby-Boomer middle class and then Gottfried had his share from when the family farm was sold. They had money to go on vacations and money to store away in individual retirement accounts. Marla and Gottfried's children are not so comfortable. One married rich. Marla's favorite. The oldest girl. Makes her proud but rarely calls. The others are a salad of limp greens Marla won't touch with her fork.

Two of them could be dead, for all Gottfried knows. Gottfried wishes he'd have kept in touch more, but Marla had rules. *No contact with the children because we want them to thrive.* Gottfried thought of thriving children more like a thriving garden and felt calling them was like watering and weeding and making sure the patch wasn't overrun with voles. They argued about it.

Marla called Gottfried a simpleton.

Gottfried didn't call Marla anything.

Usually he just felt pity. For everyone. Inside, he was still the boy in the car wash who really cared that two robins would never live to sing another song or mate with purpose. He thought a lot about mating with purpose since that day in the car wash. Robins did it so they could make more robins. He wasn't sure why humans did it anymore. Seemed some sort of contest—but this wasn't polite conversation in any circle so Gottfried kept his thoughts about it to himself.

Gottfried had split in two, right there in the station wagon. In order to get through high school. In order to get through college fraternity brotherhood. In order to marry Marla in 1970. In order to do pretty much everything. The boy who cared about robins was always there, but he was a wart, a sore, a bad tattoo.

"You're not going to wear those jeans, are you?" Marla asks.

"They're my painting jeans," Gottfried answers, while storing the vacuum in the hall closet.

"There's a hole in the leg," she says.

"They're my painting jeans."

Marla sighs and shakes her head. Secretly she thinks Gottfried is the reason her children turned out the way they did. Secretly she thinks he's the reason they don't come around anymore. Except Easter. The Resurrection. Always a reminder that things once thought dead can rise again.

Except they can't, really.

Dead is dead.

And Gottfried knows it.

The Shoveler: Eyebrow

I didn't know what to expect but I didn't expect this.

Gottfried, Marla's old-man husband, walks me into their large, empty garage. In front of me is a can of white paint, a stir stick, a roller, a roller handle, a long extension for painting ceilings, a paint tray, and a two-inch paintbrush, all laid out on opened newspaper.

"Just anywhere on the wall there," Gottfried says. He seems preoccupied with a hangnail on the side of his thumb. He nibbles at it and makes small spitting sounds.

I open the paint can and stir it. I pour some into the tray, and before I put the roller in, I go to the part of the wall that I plan to paint. I run my hand over it. Gottfried says, "All prepped for you."

"Okay," I say. But I still check my hand for dirt. He's right. The wall is clean.

I cut in the top and bottom of the wall with the brush and then start with the roller. Only when I go back to the can to refill do I see another area of the garage wall that's been painted like this one—white over white.

I feel stupid for thinking I already got the job.

I keep painting until I've covered the wall in the area I chose—about eight feet wide by ten feet tall. It looks good for a first coat, even with thirsty walls. It looks better than the last guy's test patch.

Marla walks into the garage, clutching her arms due to the

cold. She smiles and says a bunch of weird grandma stuff to me that all blends into each other.

Gottfried is busy closing up my paint can, and Marla asks me to wash the paintbrush in the sink they have in the garage. She stands next to me at the sink, and I can feel her watching me wash the brush. I finish and ask Gottfried where he wants me to put it.

"He doesn't know anything," Marla says. "He's not the boss. I'm the boss."

Gottfried doesn't even look up from what he's doing. He must know he's not the boss.

"Leave the brush in the sink. Come inside with me while he cleans up the rest." Gottfried is not actually cleaning up the rest. He's fiddling with a golf bag and looking at his smartphone at the same time. I step up and walk into the house and close the door behind me.

"Would ten dollars per hour be enough for you?" Marla asks.

I'm realizing that Marla's trick is catching people off guard. I've known people like her before. One time in Florida, I knew a math teacher like that.

"I'd need to know how many rooms you want painted. If there's any wallpaper and what the prep would be like," I say. Marla raises an eyebrow. It makes me say, "But ten is a good starting rate for regular labor." Where did that even come from?

Her eyebrow is controlling me. If she lifts it, I feel I have to say one thing; if she lowers it, I have to say another. It's a magical eyebrow. As we walk around their huge house, I start to hear an echo in my head and I can't concentrate on what Marla is saying. I feel my heartbeat. I feel sweat dripping down the valley of my back.

Shit-shit-shit.

Not now.

Stop it.

I'm fine.

"We haven't picked any of the colors for the downstairs rooms," she says as she leads me upstairs. "But once you get the upstairs done, we'll figure it out."

Two of the rooms up here have high ceilings and skylights. I decide, through my sweating and my heartbeat, that those rooms will cost extra.

I remember there's a small notebook and pencil in my back pocket. I pull it out and make note of the two rooms with skylights. I look up a lot. I do not allow Marla's eyebrow to distract me.

This is a huge job. Seven rooms including ceilings. Marla tells me she's decided against the hallways because there isn't enough time.

"I want it done by Easter," she says. "Gottfried says I'm crazy, but I think it can be done."

"When's Easter this year?"

"First day in April."

That's almost three months. Eleven weekends. But something isn't right.

None of these walls need to be painted. None of Marla's color choices are that different from what's already there. There's no peeling or chipping or even scuffing anywhere.

"So what do you think, son? Nothing you can't handle at your age, I bet," Gottfried says when he wanders into the room where Marla and I are standing. The word *son* makes me want to throw up. Makes the sweat on my back cold. Makes me wish I had my shovel. *Son.* I feel the tunnels shift. I get dizzy. Blink.

"It's a big job," I say.

"Did she scare you off with the ten-dollars-an-hour thing?"

"No," I say quickly. Marla's eyebrow has no effect on her husband. She's moving that thing around like crazy, and he just chuckles and watches me squirm.

"Gottfried, stop it," she says.

"Wait her out. She'll get up to twelve," he says.

I want to smile at him but I stay controlled and try to work out how much extra I should charge for those big rooms with the skylights/for being called *son.*

I walk around and feel the walls. They're perfect.

There's no reason to paint this house.

It makes no sense.

The Shoveler: Placement Test

Friday after school, I stay late to take two placement tests because I'm apparently better at math than Pennsylvania kids. I walk out the front door of the high school, and there's this group of guys standing around this badass dude who looks like he's in his twenties. A kid from my homeroom—can't remember his name—says, "Hey, new kid!" to me, and I ignore him because I don't want any friends. I have Mike. I have the shovel.

"Hey, shovel boy!" he says and walks over to me. "You should come here. Meet this guy. He's smart."

I keep walking—down the long set of concrete steps toward the street—and don't look back. Three days of school so far and no one's laid a finger on me. No smacking up the back of my head, no kicking me from behind between my legs, no grabbing me, threatening me, or spitting. Not even an elbow to the ribs. This is a record for me, and I don't want to break it.

A hand on my shoulder. It stops me in my tracks and I nearly fall backward onto the steps. I use my shovel to balance. "I told you to come here," the kid says. He's chubby and white. Weird hair. His T-shirt is about two sizes too big for him. "You should listen when I talk to you."

"Sorry," I say. "I have to get to work."

"This'll only take a minute," the kid says, with a firm grip on my elbow.

He pulls me over to the group of boys. *This is it. This is the moment I get beat up. I can feel it.* The boys are different ages,

59

different heights, differently dressed—I notice one of them is in a pair of khakis and a button-down shirt. Another is in black canvas military pants and a T-shirt for some metal band I've never heard of. Some wear jeans. Some have winter coats on, some don't. Some have longer hair, some shaved bald. The only thing they have in common is, they're all white.

"New face!" the older guy says. He has a tattoo on his neck.

I nod.

"I'm Bill," he says. "Your new best friend."

I nod again. The kid who dragged me here says, "Have some respect, dude."

I say, "Hi, Bill."

"New kid, right?" Bill asks.

"Yeah."

"You like it here?"

I shrug.

"Where'd you come from?"

For some reason I say, "Texas." It's the truth, but I'd had a plan to keep saying I came from New Jersey.

"Southern boy!" Bill says.

The other kids laugh and say some stuff. One of them says something about how there are too many Mexicans in Texas.

Bill says to that kid, "You ever even *been* to Texas?"

Kid says, "No."

"You talk too much, Delaney. You should learn how to shut the fuck up," Bill says. He turns back to me. "How do we compare?"

"To what?" I ask.

"Texas, dumbass." That's the kid who dragged me here.

"Fucking cold," I say.

They all laugh.

"My girl's been in her tank two months now," Bill says. "Wait till spring and you can meet her."

"Cool," I say.

"You don't even know what he's talking about," one kid says.

"I have to get to work, man," I say. "Already late."

"Go on, working man," Bill says. "I'm here every Friday. You can count on that."

"Okay."

"Memorize these faces. Anybody gives you any shit, they can swarm on his black ass and do what I taught 'em to do."

I nod and walk down the steps, and it all makes sense now. But it doesn't make any sense because that shit never makes any sense.

When I get home, Mike is chipping away at some ice around his parking space with a big ice chopper. I wave and he walks over.

"Late from school—you find some friends?"

"Placement tests," I say. "I had to stay after."

"As if school on a Friday isn't a big enough drag," he says. "Wanna come in and have a beer?"

I've told Mike three times that I don't drink beer. Mom's car is gone and I don't start work at Marla and Gottfried's until tomorrow.

"Sure," I say. "Why not?"

"I got the 2016 World Series ready to go. Game seven. You seen it?"

"Nope."

"I'll make sure the hopper's filled with pellets," he says. He looks at the shovel, I look at the shovel, we both ignore that I'm carrying a shovel.

I go home and empty the pots that filled with water from the roof, replace them, pluck a bag of Doritos from my junk-food stash, leave my shovel in my room, and stop for a smoke in the backyard.

While we sit in Mike's living room and watch the seventh game of the 2016 World Series, I think about telling Mike about the kids after school and Bill with the weird neck tattoo but Mike is so happy being in 2016 I decide to join him there.

Control the brain and the rest is easy.

THE FREAK PICKS UP THE PHONE AND TALKS TO DIRT!

The dirt talks to The Freak. It calls her on the phone and tells her to warn her new friend. This isn't freshly plowed farm dirt. It's clay, mostly. Red clay.

The Freak doesn't like when the dirt talks. Sometimes she feels it all around her, wrapped like a tortilla around shredded chicken. Sometimes she can taste it in her mouth. Sometimes she can't clear her nose of it and can't breathe.

Warn your friend with the shovel. Things aren't what they seem.

The Freak has no interest in the boy with the shovel anymore. She got him a job. She told him about her dream brainman. She's done her part.

The dirt says there's something the boy needs to know. The dirt says there's an answer right next door. The dirt never lies. It's one thing The Freak loves about the dirt. It's the cleanest thing going. And look at the reputation it gets!

The Freak understands. *Been there, done that.*

PART 1.2: INTRODUCING MALCOLM

CAST IN ORDER OF APPEARANCE:

Malcolm

Malcolm's Dad

Random Fliers on Flight 860

The Flush Toilet

John the Old Friend in Scrubs

Marla

The Painter Kid & Gottfried

Malcolm Is Annoyed by the Basket

Dad refuses to go to the Margaritaville restaurant because he thinks Jimmy Buffett is a phony. It's the only sit-down restaurant in the Montego Bay airport, so we sit at the bar near gate 4 and I eat two bowls of bar snacks while he gulps down two fruity drinks and talks with the woman sitting beside him.

"Oh yeah," he says. "We come down about twice a month."

"That's amazing," the woman says.

Dad shrugs. "Business. It's boring, isn't it, Malcolm?"

I take the bar snack bowl and empty the crumbs into my mouth. Neither of them even looks at me for an answer.

"Amazing," the woman says again. She's still wearing her sunglasses and a beach wrap around her shoulders.

Dad runs out of things to say because he's not interested in women who think he's amazing. He taps his fingers on the bar top and looks around. Our flight is boarding, and the tourists are doing what they do.

Air travel turns normally sane people into animals. They block the small walkway outside the gate and won't let the American Airlines staff move wheelchairs to the jet bridge. They elbow one another. From my view, perched on a barstool only five feet from them, they look afraid, as if the flight were being piloted by kidnappers, and yet eager to get it over with.

I'm hungry.

Dad has half a drink left.

The Dairy Queen down the concourse has hot dogs and we

both know it. Only Dad has the money, and I have the stomach that never stops sending signals to my brain.

"Go get one," he says, and hands me ten American dollars.

We do this every time.

I look back and he's giving his card to the woman at the bar as she joins the animals in the great battle to board flight 860. He always gives them cards, even if they're uninteresting.

Business.

By the time I'm back with my two hot dogs, there are ten people left at the gate. Dad's just walking out of the bathroom and checking whether his fly is up. He runs his hand over his bald head, adjusts his sunglasses, and puts his hat on.

"Let's do this thing," he says.

He pulls out two pieces of paper and our passports from his leather man-purse, and the gate worker scans them and smiles at me.

"All set, guys." She hands the passports back to Dad and lowers her eyes at me. I walk behind him as we go down the jet bridge and he's not stumbling today at least. Sometimes he stumbles. It's not a big deal.

These are my father's last six months on planet Earth.

He can stumble all he wants to.

He can "do business" all he wants to.

Nobody knows what he's really doing this for—but I think I'm slowly beginning to figure it out.

He wants to find out the point of all of it.

He's trying to comprehend the meaning of life.

He's trying to finish the puzzle before it finishes him.

We end up in first class again.

No one in first class can figure out why the bald beach bum and his scruffy kid are in first class alongside them. Same every time. They think there are rules to first class. I hear Dad talking already to his seatmate—this time a guy from a suburb outside Philadelphia who likely has never smoked a joint in his life. My seatmate ignores me because I am a fifteen-year-old beach bum. They either think I'm so rich I can afford to look this ragged, or they think I'm some first-class anomaly, like a rotten cashew, a crying baby, or a lack of champagne. Never would they guess what I'm really doing on this plane two times per month.

I hear Dad say, "Oh no! You got rain every single day? Where were you staying?" This morning he had a two-hour-long conversation with Bradford, our friend and driver, about the obvious link between slavery, poverty, and mass incarceration. My dad is not a shallow conversation kind of guy, but he can talk about weather from wheels up to wheels down if he has to.

Judging from our last fifteen flights, I can tell you that poverty is not a popular conversation choice in first class. Or any class. In any plane. Going anywhere. Which is really handy for the people on the plane, I guess.

First class is a bummer on the afternoon flight. No warm meal, just snacks in a basket. I'm always annoyed by the basket—like, they pack that for the sake of what? The ten or twelve first-class passengers who would be offended being served out of a bag? We need baskets now in airplanes? This isn't my dad thinking;

it's me. I can't help that I'm like him. I'm trying to be more like him the longer time goes on. So maybe once he's gone, there will be one white, scruffy guy on the island left to talk to Bradford about real shit.

I go to the bathroom and look at my tongue. It's still black. As I walk by Dad on my way to my seat, I smile and he smiles back. I stick my tongue out and he mimics me and his tongue is still black, too.

We've had a long weekend.

And we already have tickets for the next trip. In between, we will wear sweatshirts and winter coats and fit in as well as we can in Pennsylvania but really our souls are still on Negril's seven-mile white sand beach. Dad won't be in the hospital getting treatments, he'll be on a sun lounger curled up sleeping, a Jamaican beach dog lying by his side. I won't be in class learning algebra for the third time, I'll be with Eleanor, weaving bracelets, talking politics, and trying not to look too long at her ankles.

Malcolm Ate Bad Shrimp

My tongue is black because Pepto-Bismol couldn't keep the bad shrimp down. It's the risk of the pink stuff. If it works, great; if it doesn't, the bismuth and the sulfur in stomach acid play chemistry class in your mouth. Probably the esophagus, too. I can only see my tongue, though.

I don't even know why Dad took it. He has special anti-nausea pills because he pukes a lot from the treatments. I think he was trying to make me feel better. Drank it right out of the bottle after I'd measured mine into the little cup.

Food poisoning was surprisingly freeing. The primal way in which my body purged the shrimp from itself was like a peyote trip. I've never had a peyote trip, but going on what Dad says about it, I'd say food poisoning compares. It was two nights ago and all my muscles are sore—the ones around my rib cage—my puking muscles. I sneezed today and it was agonizing.

But there was something about the way the vomit came—the way it pushed itself out of me before I knew it was coming—that made me feel free. Like Dad, I have no control over my body. Somehow, kneeling in front of the toilet, Dad's hand on my fore-head so I wouldn't slam it on the toilet seat as I heaved, made me see that he can't do anything about dying. None of us can.

I wasn't angry with him before then. I was angry at death and cancer and doctors. I haven't been angry at him during treatment. I was angry with bills and insurance companies and pharmaceutical companies and how nobody really cares that

Dad has cancer. That Dad is a man. That Dad is my father. That Dad has a son. Nobody cares. I was angry at all that, but I wasn't angry at him. Or maybe I was. Either way, puking my guts out in the middle of the night changed me. I woke up feeling wiser. I had black tea for breakfast instead of Jamaican coffee. I had plain toast instead of saltfish. Dad talked to the owner about our next stay, and I surfed the Internet on my phone to find out who invented the flush toilet.

Food poisoning makes you really think about some stuff.

It turns out flush toilets were invented over time. There's evidence that the concept of a toilet was around in the Stone Age, which I can't even wrap my head around, but the flush toilet, as we know it, started about four hundred years ago. Some dude named Harington—Queen Elizabeth's godson—invented the basic idea in the late 1500s. In 1775, a guy named Cumming invented the S bend so the sewer smell would stay in the sewer, which is handy as hell. Then, a guy named Crapper invented the ballcock, which is, without any doubt, the funniest word in the English language. Ballcock. Say it ten times. Hilarious.

That was in the late 1800s.

Frankly, I think they could have fast-tracked the whole thing. How did it take from 1590-something to 1890-something to improve on one of the best inventions ever? Three hundred years? That's way too long. What were they busy doing in that time? A few wars? Some genocide? Burning witches? None of that was worth ignoring the flush toilet.

Anyway. Food poisoning makes you appreciate things more. I recommend it to anyone who thinks their life is shitty. Believe me, when that fire hose of diarrhea starts, you will realize that up until that moment, your life was fine. Also, you will appreciate the flush toilet even more than you did twenty minutes before when you were puking your guts out.

I'm not trying to minimize your problems. Maybe you have big ones. Maybe you can't let go of some stuff. Maybe you have an uncontrollable body like Dad does. Maybe you don't care about the flush toilet. Maybe you had something really bad happen to you already. I'm just saying that in the here and now, food poisoning can help you prioritize things pretty quick.

I made some decisions.

This time when I get home I'm not going to stay with my grandparents. I'm staying with Dad.

This time, I'm going to tell him the truth about me. About *Malcolm*. When he dies, I'm getting out of Pennsylvania and going back to Eleanor and I'm staying on the island with her forever. He says he has my college tuition arranged in his will. He says, "It's all in the will, son."

He can write whatever he wants into his will. It's *his* will, not mine.

The driver is waiting for us at baggage claim. Dad walked with his new weather-obsessed buddy from the plane and handed him a card before he went into the men's room. He's still wearing sunglasses and it's dark outside. I wait at the bottom of the escalator and watch the driver wait for us. He looks up the escalator trying to figure out who he's looking for. He has an iPad open, facing out, with our last name on it. I'm standing ten feet from him and never in his life would he think I'm the one he's looking for.

Dad comes out of the men's room and is still wiping his

71

wet hands on his pants. He flags the driver and then we all walk out into the chilly Philadelphian night. By the time we're on the road, Dad rips off a bite-sized chunk from his business card, eats it, then cranks his seat back and falls asleep. I have the back seat to myself and I feel like lying down but I don't. Instead I watch the suburbs go by and then I close my eyes and listen to the rhythmic cracks in the turnpike.

Dad has to wake me up when we get home.

The apartment smells like cheese.

Dad turns the heat up to sixty-five and puts on dub reggae and starts making a grilled peanut butter and jelly sandwich. I say I'd like one, too. He says, "Marla will be here any minute to get you."

"I'm staying here," I say.

"Don't piss off your grandmother. Trust me."

"That's not the point," I say. "I want to go to treatments with you this week. I want to hang out."

He waves the idea off with his hand. "Nothing to see. Nothing to do. I can't have you hanging around while I'm being all sick and shit. Depressing. Plus, Marla loves you and she makes great pierogies and real food."

"I can make my own pierogies."

"Not like Marla's."

This is true. Marla does make the best pierogies you ever tasted. But mine are getting better.

"After the weekend you just had, I'd avoid eating anything exotic," he says.

"She's crazy with the food thing."

"Just steer clear of anything hard to digest until Wednesday. Tell her we caught a bug or something. Do *not* mention the V word."

"I know."

"She'll make you bathe in Lysol," he says. "Or spray you with furniture polish or something."

"I know."

He hands me a foil packet with pills sealed into it. "Take one of these if you feel like barfing. Should keep things down. Otherwise, head for the woods."

Jake & Bill communicate via brain waves

Jake Marks sits in the in-school suspension room staring at a book. It's a stupid book. It's a history book. It's a math book. It's a science book. Books are for pussies. Jake knows that because his brother, Bill, has explained it many times. Even when Jake was little, Bill said his picture book about underpants was stupid. That book made him laugh and he always tried to count the underpants, but Bill wouldn't do it with him so he stopped.

Bill's at work, baking pies. He's not some expert baker or anything. It's a factory bakery. All Bill does is put the pies into the long conveyor-belt oven. Some other guy takes them out. Another guy puts them in their packaging once they cool. Another guy loads them onto a forklift. Another guy loads them into a truck. Pies-in-transit. Bill thinks of Jake in the in-school suspension room. He's proud of his brother for being cooler than he was when he was in school. Bill Marks didn't get laid for real until after he graduated. He doesn't tell Jake that, though. He has a reputation he invented and he can't stray. Boxed in. Like the factory pies.

Jake thinks of his brother, Bill, at work. He can't wait to have a job. Get a car. Be free of this place. He sends Bill a mental message. *Let's get drunk again tonight.*

Bill, on his lunch break, drives to the liquor store and buys a bottle of Southern Comfort on sale. Thinks of Jake. *The kid has a lot going on. This'll help him forget.*

Malcolm Isn't Supposed To

Marla is an hour late and Dad can't stand it. It's like he has something to do, but he can't do it while I'm here. I don't know what that could be. I've seen him smoke giant ganja spliffs on the beach and veg out on pot brownies. I've seen him hit on women. I've seen him with his girlfriends over the years, and I saw his girlfriend Ruth in the shower once by accident.

"Her phone is going straight to that stupid answering machine," Dad says. "I'm not leaving a message. She should know by now how this train works."

"Okay," I say. Dad checks the time on his phone three times inside of a minute. He still hasn't taken off his sunglasses.

"I'm hungry," I say.

"She should be here by now."

"Can I have a snack?"

"I have a friend coming over," he says.

"Ah," I say.

"You can't be here."

"I can take a walk or something. The gas station has free Wi-Fi."

"She should be here by now."

"You said that."

"It's not like she has anything to do. She just watches TV all day."

That's not true. Marla does a lot every day. Mostly she cleans and tells Gottfried what to do. She makes a lot of food and stores it in the freezer. She volunteers at the animal rescue, even though I'm pretty sure she doesn't like animals. She's never rescued one, anyway.

The door buzzer sounds. Dad tells me to go to my room.

I hear mumbling. The visitor is a man. His laugh is real and I don't recognize his voice at all. Most of Dad's friends don't live around here. Or if they do, they're the ones who can't handle that he's dying so they've distanced themselves. That's how it works. Have no problems? Plenty of friends. Have problems? Friends suddenly have a lot to do. I've been planning what to say to them at the memorial service. I have a list of Dad's bad friends. But this guy seems like a good friend, and since I haven't met him yet, I think I should.

I'm telling you. Food poisoning dropped my balls for real.

I make sure Dad can hear me coming out of my room. Just so I don't piss him off, I say, "I'm grabbing some crackers and cheese from the kitchen. I'll be out of here in seconds."

"I tossed the grapes," Dad says. "Mold."

What a messed-up duality I live. Three days a week I'm eating food that requires me to pick bones out of my mouth. Chicken bones, goat bones, ox bones. But here I get cheese and crackers as if my American life is one giant art exhibit.

"Hi," I say to the stranger. He's wearing blue-green hospital scrubs with hippie sandals even though it's winter.

"Hey, Malcolm. Nice to see you!"

I have no memory of ever meeting him before.

"You probably don't remember John," Dad says. "He's a friend of mine from high school."

"Voted most likely to cure cancer," John says.

None of us laugh. Dad tells me to go back to my room.

Look. Dad doesn't need a pot dealer because he has a stash the size of Utah. John is clearly here to do business with Dad with a line like that, but Dad does business in front of me all the time. It's not like he's a druggie. He's helping people.

I think maybe Dad and John are more than friends. Dad's been known to do that. Back in art school he had a boyfriend and one time in grad school, he told his brother, Matt, he was bi. Matt didn't talk to him after that, and then my mom came along. They had me. And then Mom died. And now this guy, John, is in my living room and I really don't care why, but I'm not supposed to wonder.

That's how it's supposed to be. Dad's supposed to have a life and I'm supposed to not notice. He's supposed to have cancer and I'm supposed to not watch.

When Marla rings the doorbell, it's louder than when anyone else does.

Dad and John are watching *Monday Night Football*, even though Dad hates football. They're totally waiting for me to leave and I'm happy that maybe Dad is getting some love right now. These are trying times, the worst of times, and everyone needs love.

I throw some winter clothes into my backpack and grab my school bag. I look around my room like it might be the last time I'll ever see it. I don't know why, but that's how I look at it every time I leave.

I don't say it because I'm not supposed to.

I'm fifteen.

I have to take this like a man.

I stop in the bathroom for my bathroom bag. I look at the toilet and think of all the people who've gone before me who marveled at its construction. I stick my tongue out in the mirror and it's still black.

77

Malcolm Doesn't Eat Lamb

Marla talks the whole way to her house. About random bullshit.

Like her car. She acts like I haven't seen it before, but I've ridden in it a bunch of times since she bought it in January. "Your grandfather said I shouldn't splash out but I'm old. Why not splash out now?"

It's a BMW. She can barely see over the steering wheel.

"I bought two pounds of those sausages you like for breakfast.

"Your father said I should keep an eye on you after school. Says you're determined to fail tenth grade. Honey, you can't fail tenth grade. I hope you know that. We won't let you.

"Did you hear about James? The boy you went to pre-school with?"

I always liked James. I haven't heard anything about him. I almost speak, but I know Marla's going to tell me anyway.

"Malcolm, I'm so sorry to be the one to tell you but James is dead. He took his own life, poor thing."

Didn't see that coming.

I thought she might say that James landed a spot on one of those TV shows where people sing and win money. Or maybe that he won an award for going around to nursing homes and singing shows for them. He's been doing that since he was eleven. I thought James was fine.

"We're donating to the animal shelter in his name because his parents asked people not to donate to the gays. Did you know James was gay?"

This is a leading question because Marla can't figure out why I don't have a girlfriend. But yeah. Everyone knew James was gay. Just nobody seemed to know he was depressed.

This is the second preschool classmate I've known who's died. I can't figure out why death is following me like this and I decide I don't care. I'm ready to throw down if death shows up. I'm ready to kick death's ass.

"Young people taking their own lives," Marla says. "They just never see the bright side. Things are different now, I guess."

I don't think I can survive four more days with my grandparents. I've tried so many times to get Marla to see things from a twenty-first-century point of view, but she doesn't want to see anything. She just keeps the perks—her smartphone, her remote-start BMW, cable TV, and those plastic bags that steam vegetables in the microwave—that's all this century is to her. She will never wake up. She will never admit that Dad is dying of cancer, either. She says he's going to be fine.

Marla says, "You haven't said a word this whole time. Are you okay?"

"I'm fine."

"You're quiet."

"Just a little tired."

"I made lamb chops for dinner," Marla says and I don't know if she's been counting, but I have been, and I've told her I don't eat lamb twenty-four times. She says I should try it different ways until I find a way to like it. Fact: I will never like lamb. I just won't. It doesn't agree with me. And Marla makes everything too rich; so after a weekend of food poisoning, there is no way in hell I'm going to eat a lamb chop.

"I'm not that hungry," I say.

"You'll eat."

"My stomach's not right," I say.

"Probably have a T-worm from that awful food down there," she says. "You're too skinny. You should have some meat on those bones."

Emetophobes don't use the real words for anything vomity. Or wormy, I guess.

"I'm not eating lamb," I say. "You know that."

"I don't know why you're so picky."

"It's part of the package," I say. Because I refuse to explain one more time to Marla about how I won't eat lamb.

"What girl will be able to cook for you?" she asks.

"Marla, you're sixty-eight, not a hundred and eight. Please. I'll cook for myself."

"Don't call me Marla."

"Don't make me eat lamb."

"Don't tell me what to do after we open our home to you and give you all you need!" She's whining now—trying to get the tear machine going.

"I have all I need at Dad's house. I don't need your lamb chops or your BMW."

"You make us sound like elitists. We donate to the animals all the time. We know there are horrible things happening in the world. We're a lot older than you, you know."

"You donate to the animals and you eat lamb chops," I say.

"I'm being nice! Why can't you be nice?"

"I'm nice. I just don't eat lamb. There's nothing wrong with that."

"You make me out to be some sort of rich bitch or something!"

My brain reels. I have to bite on the inside of my lips so all my words don't come out. I keep biting my lips as Marla takes her final crazy turn into her cul-de-sac and we head for her driveway. There's a car parked at the end of the driveway that I don't recognize.

"Who's here?" I ask.

"A nice young man who would be happy to eat lamb chops, I can tell you that!" She clicks on the remote control for the garage door and speeds toward it a little too soon and almost takes the roof off her new BMW.

I have no idea how Marla managed to raise five kids with her temper the way it is. She really needs to take it easy.

Malcolm: White People

I don't know if it was hanging out in Negril or with Eleanor or being raised by my dad, but I've never understood white people who can't admit they're white. I mean, white isn't just a color. And maybe that's the problem for them. White is a passport. It's a ticket. The world is a white amusement park and your white skin buys you into it. A woman in economy argued with me about this once. She said, "I've heard this idea and it makes me uncomfortable."

"It probably should," I said.

Dad and I have been broke since he got cancer and sometimes he can't put the heat over sixty-two or put food in the fridge, but we were always white and he always made sure I knew that. Which sounds stupid because how can a person not know they're white, right?

You don't have to be racist to not know you're white.

But sometimes you do. And Marla has no idea she's white or that the whole world was made for people like her.

As I climb out of the BMW, the door to the laundry room opens and a kid walks out, two paintbrushes in hand. Gottfried is right behind him.

"Hey! You're here!" Gottfried says.

I half smile. "I'm here."

"How was island life?"

"Good," I say.

Neither of them introduces me to the kid who's now washing brushes in the garage sink, and he doesn't look up from what he's doing, so I can't give him a nod.

When we get inside and the paint smell hits me and turns my weak stomach, I ask, "Who's the painter?"

Gottfried looks at me blankly. "I've been paying him in cash."

I throw side-eye. "Did you forget his name?"

Gottfried nods.

"You can always just ask him again."

"Tried everything. I can't get it out of him."

"But you didn't ask."

"No."

"Forgetting the names of the hired help is very white, Pop."

"Stop it. You know I'm not like that."

I shrug at him. My pop can remember where the Dow Jones Industrial Average closed on any given day. He remembers the names of movie star women with nice legs. I go inside, and Marla passes me on the way to the garage. I bet you any money she doesn't know the kid's name either.

Marla & Gottfried's Grandson Is Not Acceptable

Marla pokes her head into the garage.

"He's already told me he's not going to eat the lamb chops," she says to Gottfried, who isn't listening because he's busy talking to the painter boy. "He has no respect for anyone. Harry is lucky I still say yes to this," she says.

Gottfried excuses himself from the conversation with the kid long enough to say, "Give the man a break. He's dying."

This hits Marla hard. Marla wants everyone to know how caring she is and how she places every Easter egg carefully for the grandkids and how she thinks all year about what might make the best Christmas gift for them. She goes back into the house.

She stands quietly at the kitchen counter and weighs her options. She could be nice about Harry dying or she could just keep pretending it isn't happening. She checks her lamb chops, which are marinating in the fridge.

She decides to let Gottfried deal with the painter kid, who's presently washing out brushes an hour earlier than he's supposed to. She resists the urge to mention this. *As long as the place gets painted by Easter, I don't care.* She goes to her bedroom and closes the door. She doesn't know where to sit.

If I sit on the bed, the quilt will wrinkle. If I sit on the chair, I'll have to move the pillows. If I sit on the hope chest, my back will hurt. I don't even have a place to sit in my own house. I can't sit. I can't sit. I have to get myself together and be a grandmother to a kid who hates me because I care so much about him that I make lamb chops and he won't even eat them. This generation are a bunch of spoiled brats. Harry failed with this kid. Harry is a failure.

He's even failing at staying alive, that's how much of a failure he is. He can't even stay alive to raise this boy. And there's nowhere for me to sit. Five kids and not one of them offers me a chair for dinner.

Marla looks at the footprints in her plush carpet. Her footprints. From the doorway to the space she's standing now. She takes a step forward and then peeks down to see if her footprints show up. She tiptoes. She does this all the way to her medicine cabinet and stares at herself in the mirror for a minute. Shakes her head as if she's disappointed in what she sees, and opens the latch. *If I took every one of these pills, I'd be dead in an hour or two,* she thinks.

But then she remembers the lamb chops. And the painter boy. And how Gottfried wouldn't remember to get his eyes checked if she didn't remind him. And she tiptoes out of the en suite and over the plush carpet and back into the hallway.

Gottfried has said goodbye to the painter and takes off his sneakers and puts them in the closet. Malcolm is sitting on the couch in the living room, doing something on his smartphone.

"Good kid," Gottfried says, after he closes the closet door. "A good work ethic."

"Go turn on the grill," Marla says. "The lamb needs to go on now or else we'll miss the news."

Malcolm says, "You can't miss news anymore, Marla. It's on all the time."

Marla either doesn't hear him or ignores him. Gottfried grabs his coat and slides the door to the deck and goes outside. He checks the gas line into the grill and lights it, then stares out into the woods and smiles. Talks to himself. Nods in agreement. Smiles again. Then he turns back toward the house and walks in, leaving his coat on the chair next to the door.

"Pop," Malcolm says.

Gottfried looks over and Malcolm gives him the silent motion for "come here."

"What's up?"

"I can't eat lamb." He points to his stomach. "I've been sick. I just need something plain," Malcolm says.

"Don't tell her that," Gottfried whispers.

"I know."

"I'll make you some toast."

Gottfried walks into the kitchen where Marla is now talking on her phone. Marla yells when she talks on it—as if she still hasn't figured out that a phone without a cord is not a lesser phone. Gottfried knows who she's talking to because she uses a certain tone when she talks to their daughter Missy. Missy hasn't been well in the head. That's how Gottfried puts it. Not well in the head at all.

"You should see the doctor for the itch, dear," Marla says into the phone. "No itch should last longer than a month."

Gottfried thinks about itches that have lasted longer than a month. He's had a few.

Marla is mixing a simple vinaigrette for the side salad. "Maybe it's bedbugs. How big are the bites?"

Gottfried scratches his arm.

"Have you checked Loretta? . . . You should . . . If you have them, she probably does, too."

Gottfried thinks about his favorite granddaughter, Loretta. Kid has spunk. Something different from the others. Smart as hell, mouthy, and a laugh like nothing else. He thinks about the last time he saw them all—years now—and how they looked indigent. Missing teeth, the ones left nearly brown. Natty hair. Old clothes. He thinks about how his daughter married a brute and how the little girl is probably in danger. He pictures the dying robins on the road again. Nothing he can do about it.

He sneaks two pieces of bread into the toaster and quietly presses them into toasting mode. Marla fiddles with the potato croquettes and puts them back into the oven. She keeps saying uh-huh to Missy, who is most likely rambling on the other end of the phone. She tends to ramble. Not well at all, that girl.

One time about ten years ago Missy called Gottfried and asked for money. She said she'd leave her husband and get to a place where he couldn't find her or Loretta, who was only in kindergarten at the time. She said he'd been beating them both for years and god knows what else. She said she'd try to pay it back, but Gottfried didn't want her to pay it back. He wanted her to be safe. He told Missy she could stay with them for a while. He said they could help her find an apartment. He said he'd help pay for anything she needed. Gottfried didn't have much in life, but he had money. He could have stopped it all had he just cut a check Marla would have never known about, but he told her his plan anyway. Marla was against it on pure principle. She said, "There is no way in hell we're giving her a penny. Girl has no skills and can't manage to marry right. What makes you think she'll know what to do with our money?"

Gottfried remembers looking at Marla that night and wondering how he married such a cold, razor-edged woman. One time he accidentally left the ice cream out on the kitchen counter. Marla left it there rather than putting it back in the freezer so he'd learn. He was sixty-eight when that happened. Only two years ago. He thought she'd grow kinder as she got older. But she only got here.

Gottfried always said that he'd live without regrets, but Marla changed all that back in 1980 when she sent him back to the farm. Before then, even. She tells Missy that she has to go because she's making dinner and hangs up. She doesn't acknowledge Gottfried standing in the kitchen, ready to help if she needs him.

"How is she?" he asks.

"Still doesn't have a job," Marla says. "Still won't go to the doctor for the bites. Says she doesn't have health insurance." She shakes her head. "I mean . . . who doesn't have health insurance in this day and age?"

PART 1.3: INTRODUCING CANIHELPYOU? AND LORETTA

CAST IN ORDER OF APPEARANCE:

CanIHelpYou?

Nancy the Guidance Gounselor

Pitiful Drive-Thru Customers

Len the Owner/Manager

Many Unnamed Clients

Ian the Best Friend

The Shoveler

Loretta Lynn & Her Flea Circus

Gerald, Cynthia & Dolly

You-know-who

Can I Help You?

I'm in a tunnel. It's like a submarine—a large, oval gunmetal-gray pipe just tall enough for me to stand up but confining enough so I have to hunch down to walk in it. There are beams I have to watch out for so I don't hit my head.

Sometimes the tunnel gets smaller. Sometimes I have to get on my hands and knees to get through the narrow spots.

Sometimes someone chases me and I have to run through the tunnel, crawl fast through the narrowness to escape. It's a stranger, but I know to run.

I've explained all this to my guidance counselor at school. She calls me in sometimes to talk because she thinks I'm a mystery. The day I told her about the tunnel I asked what she thought about it. She picked at her index fingernail and said, "Never get a manicure in Wichita." That's it. *Never get a manicure in Wichita.*

"Welcome to Arby's Drive-Thru," I say. "Can I help you?"

I work today. I work every day I can because it gets me out of my house and today is Saturday, so I'm working.

I'm the one you talk to through the little speaker at the Drive-Thru. You're in my head, cushioned by foam around my earphones. You say things like, "Gimme a cheeseburger and fries with a Coke." You say it like you're talking to the speaker and not a human being on the other side. You bark it sometimes. Windy night, busy inside with the din of eat-in customers, and I get your order wrong. You say, "No! I said LARGE, not SMALL!"

You ask me if I'm deaf sometimes. You lament the future of our country with people like me in charge.

In charge? Since when does running the Drive-Thru qualify me for being in charge? I want to say things to you—to all of you—but I don't. I like being nice to your face once you turn the corner and meet me at the window.

You never have your money ready. You check your change. You inspect your receipt. You feel ripped off when the order comes to anything over twenty dollars as if you didn't know that fast food is a racket when you pulled up to the little speaker. As if you didn't add up the prices on the enormous menu board. Not my fault you can't do math.

When I smile at you, I'm being sincere because I pity you.

I pity anyone who says *gimme*.

The world is going to be a giant disappointment for you.

All you'll ever get is the kindness of the Drive-Thru girl after growling your entitled order into my head. *Gimme-gimme-gimme*: the battle cry of millions of people every day. People who *want*.

You're a case study, an interesting specimen.

You don't scare me. Not even when you threaten to talk to my boss because your fries weren't the temperature you expected them to be.

"I paid almost thirty bucks for this and now the fries are cold?"

I only wish I could take you by the hand through life. I only wish to be there when the real disappointments come. The ones that don't involve a deep fat fryer. The ones that don't involve how much ice I put in your Sprite. You never hear a stranger chasing you. You don't even think you're alone in the world.

But we all are.

We're all products of convenience. I don't judge. I like potato cakes and curly fries as much as the next person. I understand you don't have time to make dinner. I see your kids in the back seat in their football gear, in their field hockey kilts, next to their pom-poms and their baritone cases. Parades and pep rallies and high school clubs. You parents do what you can.

Six Drive-Thru windows in a mile stretch. Maybe eight. Six pizza places, five that deliver. We've been ordering groceries on the Internet and getting them delivered right to our door for three years now.

Ian works at the Weis Market and shops for other people. One time he accidentally got the wrong kind of cat litter for some woman, and she tried to get him fired because she said her cat broke out in hives. This happens more often with Ian than the other personal shoppers at Weis. Probably because Ian isn't white.

"Why do people care so much about stupid shit?" he asked me last week.

"Maybe they don't have any real problems," I answered.

"Everyone has problems."

"Everyone," I echoed.

"The wrong brand of yogurt—that was today's drama." He shakes his head. "You know Gemma's dad? She's taking pills and shoplifting and shit, and he's worried about dairy?"

"Yeah. I know. Gemma's a client."

"Dairy," he said.

Ian is my best friend. Everyone thinks that one day we'll get married and have babies and live a happy life. But the fact is that

Ian and I are best friends. Since fourth grade. And neither of us can live a happy life. At least, not here. In this town when your mother is white and your father is black, people can only see the father's side—that's Ian's reason. My reason is different and not as easy to spot at the annual block party.

We're both off work at eight and he wants to go to a movie but I have to go see three clients before nine. Saturday night. Everyone wants to get wasted.

The beep sounds.

"Hi! Welcome to Arby's Drive-Thru. We have two new flavors of smoothies! Would you like to try a mango-and-pineapple today?"

"Gimme a Classic meal, large."

"What drink would you like with that?"

"Coffee. You got coffee?"

"Cream and sugar with that?"

"Black."

"Your total is seven oh five. Please drive to the first window."

"Seven bucks? Menu says it's five fifty nine."

"The coffee replacement for a soft drink costs a bit extra, sir."

"Why didn't you tell me that?"

"Would you like a Coke instead?"

"I want coffee."

"Okay, sir, drive to the first window please."

"No. I want coffee instead of the Coke. And I want it to cost the same thing."

"I'll arrange for the manager to meet you at the first window, sir."

"Fine."

I get Len. He's the owner and he usually doesn't stoop to work here but the actual manager called off, and Len has to fill in for two hours. It's impossible to pry him from the mirror behind the fry station. Every minute of his "shift" he smooths his hair and looks at it from every angle. If there is a god, I'd like to put my order in now for Len going bald before age forty, please.

"Guy wants coffee with his meal but doesn't want to pay for the change," I say.

"You told him it's policy?"

"He wants to talk to you," I say.

I stand behind him to see how he negotiates. I can't figure it out. I've been doing the exact same thing for a year and it never works for me. Men are always trying to talk me into things at the Drive-Thru window. Free stuff, usually. A guy asked me if I could give him a case of straws one time. He told me that ours were his favorite straws. He said, "The ones from McDonald's are too wide. Yours are just right." I told him I couldn't. He shrugged and said okay, and then he asked me for extra straws. Fifty extra. "Sorry, I can give you maybe ten." He pouted. Only after I threw in a wad of napkins and several handfuls of condiments was he happy enough with ten.

This guy isn't happy about his coffee, though. Len isn't helping. He's coming up with solutions that don't solve anything. He says, "I can give you a large coffee if you want." He says, "I can pour the coffee into a regular cup." He says, "Like iced coffee!" The guy just wants the menu to be fair to him.

My pity is enormous. It's bigger than a case of straws and a large iced coffee and our new mango-and-pineapple smoothie. Larger than the pile of dishes in the back sink that I'll have to do before I leave at eight.

In the end, the coffee guy yells at Len and Len doesn't

charge him for the coffee, and gets a large Coke for the wife so the guy doesn't have to pay for something he didn't get.

When he drives away, I see his bumper stickers. One says I LOVE MY RESCUED YORKIE! The other says SUPPORT OUR POLICE!

I get a half hour for lunch. I start with a cigarette break out by the dumpster because I started smoking again. It's something I do twice a month—quit then start, quit then start. I have an addiction situation. I was born with it. My birth canal was coated in cravings. And now I cater to my clients who were born the same way. In third grade I said I wanted to be a pharmacist. My dreams have come true.

I check my phone. Two texts from Ian about people who complained about him today. Three texts from clients. Coded. I need one page of chem notes. Can you bring me a large bag of cat food? How much for five more of those lollipops? An email from my mother—a forwarded email from the school automated system. The subject says *Missing Assignment Report*.

I don't need an email.

I know I don't do my work.

What's the point?

CanIHelpYou?: What's the Point?

We could all be shot dead by a crazy asshole with a gun because nobody really cares about dead schoolkids. We could all be kidnapped and no one would look for us. The chances of me getting raped before I graduate college are ridiculously high. The chances of me being abused by a future partner are about 40 percent. And there's no class about that at school.

I ask you: What's the fucking point?

The point of being in school is to graduate—switch the tassel to the other side of your mortarboard and then go to a party where there's a decent chance that at least one of your friends will attempt to drive home drunk and maybe die. Years of tying teddy bears and balloons to an electrical pole are ahead of you. That's the point.

You think I sound alarmist. You think I sound negative. High school isn't about graduating or getting out but learning. Learning a lot of stuff. Preparing for college. Being involved and doing the musical because it's fun. But you're the same one who argues with me about coffee and curly fries, eyes wide and angry. What did your hard work and memorizing lines and songs do for you? This?

Ian is the only one who gets it. We're not negative. We have a lot of fun. But we already know that adults are mostly assholes who think we're mostly assholes. Sounds dramatic to you, maybe, but at least I don't say *gimme-gimme-gimme* out of one side of my mouth while dishing life advice out of the other.

Either way, this email from my mom means something. She forwarded it to send a message. The message is: She thinks she's in charge. She has this bell she rings when she wants us to listen to her. It's an actual bell. My dad sits at attention as if she hypnotized him with the bell when they got married. I fidget, usually, and in my head I add up the money I made that day selling her own Benzos to her friends.

The bell is disgusting. You have to see it to understand it.

I don't want to tell you about the bell.

It makes me think about what else lined my birth canal the day I was born into this fucked-up family.

While I'm doing dishes, Ian texts about a white woman who lost her shit over him accidentally getting her acidophilus milk. I dry my hands off on my khakis and reply: Let's find a way to get really messed up tonight. Okay?

Jake & Bill eat old pie

"Saturday nights aren't supposed to be like this," Jake says. He's talking to the snake. Bill isn't there because Bill is out with his girl.

Jake is drunk for the twenty-ninth night in a row. Ever since Bill brought him that bottle of Southern Comfort, he's climbed into one after the other. There's only enough room for one there, so Bill can go out with his girl all he wants. Jake is fine. He falls asleep next to the snake's heated tank.

"What's up, fuckers?" Bill says, when he walks into the room. Jake wakes up and feels a bit sick but would never say it. Just keeps swallowing to balance his guts.

"What time is it?" Jake asks. His tongue feels like it fell asleep in the snake tank on the hot rock.

"It's pie o'clock!" Bill says. He's high and happy. *Probably got laid,* Jake thinks. Then he unthinks it because of the trip to New Jersey and the smell of wet leaves and pine needles and bourbon. Swallows again.

Bill produces four pies from the factory. Apple, cherry, peach, and shoofly. He pulls a box cutter from his pocket and starts to hack away at the peach pie. The blade goes through the aluminum pie plate and stabs him in the thigh. Blood soaks through. Bill laughs. Jake laughs.

Jake knows he has to eat a slice or else Bill will call him a pussy, so he takes the first slice of peach pie. It tastes like plastic and the crust is soggy.

"What's the expiration date on those?" Jake asks.

Bill mocks in a high-pitched voice. "What's the expiration date on those?" Bill takes a bite and chases it with milk, straight from the carton. A single white dribble runs down his chin.

This acts as a paddle inside of Jake. It stirs. It stirs.

Never once has Bill helped Jake throw up. This time is no different.

CanIHelpYou?: Healthy Bacteria

In Ian's back pocket are three things.

A fat quarter ounce of weed that tastes like lemon meringue pie, a baseball-card-sized vaporizer, and two tabs of pyramid gel.

"You always said you wanted to try," he says.

I do. I do. I do. I move the shit like crazy, but I've never tried.

We go to the park because that seems like the right place to do our first hit of acid. The place is empty in the dark aside from a few walkers-by.

"Do you even know what acidophilus milk *is*?" Ian asks me.

I say, "It sounds gross."

"I looked it up. It's got healthy bacteria in it. I'm gonna try some."

The shoveler is here, walking along with a snow shovel like it's a completely normal thing to do in a public park. It's been a warmer-than-usual February and all the snow has melted. He's a new neighborhood crazy—everyone has heard about him and they talk because there's nothing else to do here. I don't know his name or anything about him. He lives in the city and carries his shovel with him everywhere, that's all I know. I wish I knew why he walks all the way down here to be crazy. Maybe it's safer. Mom says the city isn't safe anymore because—just because. Her logic is faulty, so her reasons don't matter.

My phone dings with a text. It's a link from my mother. A *Teen Vogue* article called "Here's Exactly What to Do If You Think You're Being Kidnapped." She's sent it to me six times before.

This time she adds, "PLSE DON'T GO TO THE MALL." It's always the mall, as if that's the worst place anyone could go. She says it's because a friend of hers had their kid kidnapped from a mall in California. Then some girl went missing here, too. Whatever. She probably doesn't really care. She's just trying to control me.

Ian says, "You okay?" after I'm lost in the article for a minute.

"I had a dream last night about a giant owl," I say.

Ian's sitting with his chin on his hand, looking at me the way he does. He seems to think I'm interesting. I have no idea why. "Giant? Like how big?"

"When it landed and spread its wings, there were billboards inside. So probably really big." I spread my arms as wide as they can go. "I was here. At the park."

We both look around the park. No giant owls.

"What did the billboards say?"

"They were billboards for Idaho potatoes."

"What time is it?" he asks.

I check my phone. Three texts from my mother. I don't read them. "Eight fifty."

"Let's do this," he says.

I look around the park. There's an older couple walking, holding hands, heading for Main Street. The shoveler is shoveling over by the fountain, his shovel bucket a centimeter off the ground, like a mime with a prop. When I turn my attention to Ian again, he's already put the tiny piece of gel acid into his mouth and he's handing me mine with his other hand. I take it. Look at it. A tiny green pyramid. I wonder what the billboards under the owl's wings will say tonight.

I put it on my tongue and let it dissolve. Ian hands me a

bottle of water and I take a swig, and then I ask him for a cigarette. He lights two and hands me one. We wait. Time stretches. I can't keep my mind focused. My mother's texts fade into the clouds. The Drive-Thru customers fade. The missing mall-girl fades.

We decide to walk up and down Main Street. We trade coats in case people recognize us, as if this makes sense. It's Saturday. (*I think. Saturday, right?*) Main Street is empty except for drunk adults outside our faux-British pub, smoking. I look at one woman laughing and she's a cartoon witch and I want to ask Ian if he sees it, too, but when I look over at him, he's staring into a streetlight, smiling.

Main Street was probably a bad idea.

"I'm going back to the park," I say. I grab his hand.

"Okay."

I cross the street and head for the pavilion and lie on a picnic table. Ian lies on the picnic table next to mine and we're quiet for what feels like a half an hour. Everything is quiet. The body rushes are overwhelming—like I'm on a roller coaster but I'm lying as still as I've ever been.

My phone rings and it's my mother's ringtone. I don't answer it because I have nothing to say to my mother. Not now. Life is too happy here. Life is never happy with her.

You probably think I'm some cliché kid who hates her parents. I don't. I have reasons I don't like to spend time with them. For one thing, they hate gay people. And Jewish people. And black people. And Mexicans. And Muslims. My mom doesn't even know a Muslim from a Sikh. She just talks about how great it is that their god makes them wear "turbans" so she can pick them out in a crowd. She thinks this is funny.

Shocked? I bet you aren't. All you *gimme-gimme* people have met someone like my parents.

It's not just a passing comment or a racist quip in the hallway. My whole house is wallpapered with hate. My dinner is made with hate. My Christmas gifts are bought with hate. I started doing my own wash when I was ten just so my clothes can feel clean when everything else feels dirty.

It's not like they burn crosses, no. And people still do that around here. But they wouldn't go out of their way to put the fire out.

I've never known what to do about it. I can't argue with them because they don't listen. I can't reason with them because you can't reason with people like that. I wish there was a healthy bacteria—like in acidophilus milk—I could put in their food that would change them.

I try to be the healthy bacteria.

CanIHelpYou?: They Always Call Back

"My parents are in there," Ian says, pointing to the faux-British pub. "I should go see them. I bet they're beautiful."

My phone is filling up with texts from clients. I can't even read them. I couldn't do business now anyway. Can't even understand money. Clients can wait. They always call back.

Ian wants to walk around the neighborhood so we do, but I make sure we avoid Main. Block by block, street by street, we look at people's rough pre-spring lawns and flower gardens. We trip over uneven sidewalks and go single file to avoid late-night walkers. I have no sense of time. I don't know whether Ian and I are talking to each other or whether we've become telepathic. I don't hear sounds the way I usually do.

There's a grin plastered on my face like I love the whole world. Ian has it, too. It's almost creepy how we can't get rid of them. We hold hands sometimes because it explains our late-night walk to people who see us even if it's a lie. Ian even kisses me once just because it seems like the right thing to do. Somewhere on Elm Street. I won't find out until Monday if anyone saw it.

"I'm inside your tunnel," Ian says.

"Are you?"

"It's scary. Everything echoes."

He can't be lying because that's a detail about my tunnel that no one else knows. Everything echoes. His mention of it makes me hear it. I listen closely to what's echoing now. Everything is echoing now.

"You okay?" He bends his eyebrow down.

Ian is looking at me and I'm looking at him and his eyes are beautiful. Pupils dilated almost completely, he looks like he has black irises and I know I must look the same way and I don't know what time it is.

"Is anyone home at your house?" I ask.

"Trivia night," Ian says. "They won't be home till the pub closes."

We walk.

Ian's house is layered in books—all kinds of books from picture books for little kids to huge books about art that Ian and I used to press flowers in when we were young enough to care about pressing flowers.

We sit in his living room and he puts on some music and it sounds like a painting in my head and my chest. It's hard to explain. It's as if I've lived my whole life underground and just found the hole to the surface.

My parents don't like me hanging out with Ian. He's not allowed to hang out at my house. Not even when we were little. My mother rang her bell once, and she and Dad tried to talk to me about it. How maybe I shouldn't *get too close*. How maybe it looks bad for our family for me to be friends with a *boy like him*. Now, Ian gets good grades and leads the debate team. I'm growing my client list to nearly sixty and will scrape through junior year with my worst grades yet. I'm pretty sure having Ian as my best friend is the only good thing I have going for my reputation.

I check my phone. I look at the numbers on the clock but they still make no sense to me. Ian is lying on the couch with his eyes closed.

I decide to lie next to him.

We kiss and it's a longer kiss than when we were on Elm Street. I can feel every nerve in my body. It's like Ian's kiss is a million times more powerful than my mother's stupid bell. I'm breathless when we finish.

"Wow," I say.

"Yeah," Ian says.

I am out of my tunnel here, lying in the crook of his arm, curled in on his body. I can feel him breathing. I can hear his heartbeat. The grin on my face won't calm down. It may be bigger than ever.

I don't know what I'm doing. He's just lying here and I'm just lying here but something makes me reach down and touch his penis. I think of the word *penis* and start laughing slowly. The laugh builds and I don't take my hand off, but I squeeze it with each giggle and Ian laughs, too, and we're lying on his couch, me with my hand on his penis, laughing, when my phone rings again. My hand hesitates. In order to reach my phone I will have to take my hand off Ian's penis and I really don't want to because it's growing in my hand and that's far more interesting than anything anyone could tell me on my phone.

"You getting that?"

"No."

We fall into a hysterical fit and Ian nearly falls off the couch but I hold him steady by his penis. The phone rings again and it makes us laugh until I feel like I'm going to pee in my pants and I leave the ringing phone on the coffee table and make my way to Ian's downstairs bathroom.

"It won't stop ringing!" he screams as I'm peeing. I try to block it out and stare at the two green hand towels on the rail in front of me. The towels breathe as I breathe. The floor is a sea of movement and I glance up at the towels and then back at the floor and I realize that I'm tripping my balls off—the way my clients have described it to me. And then I remember touching Ian's penis and I laugh so hard I fart and that makes me laugh even harder, so I pee more.

I finally finish and wash my hands for what feels like twenty minutes, and I come back to the living room and my phone is still ringing and Ian's hard-on went away because he's holding my phone, staring at it.

"I think you should read your texts," he says.

"Your towels breathe," I say.

"No. Seriously," he says, but he's laughing while he says it so I don't take him seriously.

I can only read one text. The latest one. It's from my mom. It says: When u get home we have to talk about spending time with that boy.

I read the last part aloud in a white dickhead voice. "We have to talk about spending time with *that boy*."

Ian and I fall off the couch laughing even though nothing about this is funny.

Loretta's Ticket Is a Flea Circus

In a dark corner of her bedroom in her family's traveling wagon, which is parked in a back lot at the RV camp, Loretta Lynn, named after the famous Loretta Lynn of country and western music fame, talks to her fleas.

"You have to sit still while Gerald does his train act," she scolds. "And, Gerald, you need to go offstage the minute that set is over so you can get ready for the band act. I've told you all before. This isn't just any act. It's the act that will get me away from You-Know-Who."

Loretta listens as her flea troupe talks to her about the issues in the show. Dolly complains that Gerald hogs the spotlight. Cynthia cries when Gerald tells her she sucks at trapeze. Dolly comes to Cynthia's rescue when she says that Gerald's father, Holloway, was a better performer than he'd ever be.

Holloway was the best train-pulling act anyone ever saw.

"Stop picking on Gerald," Loretta says. "And, Gerald, go practice the train act."

Loretta hoists herself up and walks to the bathroom and closes the door. Before she can get the door all the way closed, she puts her hand down her pants and touches the spot she's been thinking about since she was last able to touch it. She's silent so the fleas don't hear her. When she's done, she waits and catches her breath. And then she does it again. Because she can.

CanIHelpYou?: Us & Them

Ian and I are still on the floor next to his couch, but we've stopped laughing. I close the text app on my phone and stare at the clock. I see the glowing numbers but they don't make sense. 1:32. It just seems like someone was counting and got 3 and 2 mixed up.

"Are you okay?" Ian asks.

"Doesn't that bother you? That my mom is such a fucking idiot?" I say.

Ian nods and says, "I'm going for a cigarette before my parents get home."

"I can't see your parents like this."

"I can't see them either," he says.

We stare at each other and then crack up laughing again.

"Let's go back to the park," I say. Ian looks like he doesn't want to go to the park, but he walks with me anyway. We take the back alleys behind garages littered with basketball hoops and wood piles. We're quiet and we hold hands again.

I think about how I had my hand on Ian's penis. How he kissed me the way I've always wanted to be kissed. How he laughed at my mom's text. How he looked like he didn't want to come with me on this walk.

I think about how my grandmother once told me that black people have different blood than ours. How it's got disease in it. I was nine years old. "They're not like us," she said.

It was my birthday party. I'd invited eight friends from

school to the local roller rink and two of them were black—it was the year I met Ian, and I'd already known Talia since first grade. I watched them skate in circles, and I looked over at my grandmother and my parents, who were eating half-burned pizza and french fries. I skated toward the opening into the rink and then stepped out to join my friends going in circles. When I looked at Talia and Ian, I saw them differently. I didn't think what my grandmother said was true.

They weren't like us, no. They were better/stronger/smarter because they had to live in the same world with people like my grandmother.

They didn't know anything had changed that day, but I did. And as I skated around in circles and played an endless game of roller-skating limbo, I felt the tunnel building itself around me, the way a shell grows. Layer by layer, I was part of *them* and the shell would protect me from *us*.

Except the older I get, I realize it's not that simple.

THE FREAK HATES YOUR IDEA OF A PARTY!

The Freak has landed.

There's is a haze over the room. It's pot haze. She's at a party, except people at this party think having a party means smoking pot and playing *Call of Duty*—or watching people play *Call of Duty*. This is not The Freak's idea of a party, but she could sure use a joint right about now.

No one's even noticed she's here, standing in the kitchen. She sneaks over to the living room and slowly coaxes a boy's stash bag off an end table and sticks it in her pocket.

"Don't you guys have anything better to do?" she asks.

"Who the fuck are you?"

"What the fuck do you care?"

"Where the fuck did you come from?"

None of them actually take their eyes off the screen to look at her. She walks to the window and looks into the night. It's cold out there. Some snow on the ground, but not nearly as much as when she met the boy with the shovel last month.

There's mail on the kitchen counter, and she looks at the address. The Freak is in Wisconsin. She closes her eyes. Flickers.

The Freak is in another lecture hall at Potato University. *Go Spuds!*

The professor is a tall African American woman. Every student is white.

"*Solanum tuberosum*, our modest friend from the Andes, saved

111

you from certain mediocrity. Grew your population while others withered—doubled it in some places. Rose you up. Rose up your children, your servants. Starched you rigid into your beliefs. The key to the kingdom was yours for the taking. Who wouldn't take that key?" The professor adjusts her glasses with the back of her index finger.

"Your ancestors arrived in the New World, strong and ready," she says, "to wipe out whatever and whomever stood in their way."

The Freak raises her hand.

"We didn't do it on purpose, though, right?"

The professor smiles. "All depends on your definition of purpose." The Freak waits for an easier answer. "I mean, accidents are usually fast, right? Can't say the last four hundred years counts as fast. Can you?"

The Freak closes her eyes. Flickers. Underground.

The Freak is in a tunnel. It's like a submarine. There are people here. She feels a lot of them, but can only see one at a time. She sits on the floor and pulls out her stash from Wisconsin. Rolls it into a joint. Lights it with her lighter.

The Freak looks up and the ceiling is made of glass. Everything on the other side is roots. White filaments searching for water and nutrition. The longer she looks, the more roots she sees.

The Freak is sad. She feels the roots working their way toward her—as if she is water and nutrition. As if she is dinner.

The Shoveler: Existence

Mom got a job at a used-car lot two weeks ago. She gets off at four on weekdays and she has weekends off. We've been able to share the car so I can go to Marla and Gottfried's house to work, but she's getting fed up with it, even though I'm the only one who puts gas in the tank. All I want is a shower after a long day. She seems to want to complain about how we need to figure out what to do about the car.

"Maybe one of the guys at your work can find me something cheap," I say.

"You'd need insurance."

"I can pay for insurance," I say.

She doesn't like that I make enough money to afford insurance. I'm not even sure if I can. I'm not even sure if *she* can. I'm just trying to find a solution to her being pissed off that I take the car the minute she gets home. It's not like she goes anywhere at night or on weekends. Mostly, she texts Mike next door even though he's right there, in his house, watching baseball and controlling his mind.

I decide to take a walk.

I've been painting Marla and Gottfried's house for three weeks now. My arms hurt, but I can feel them getting stronger. I like the relaxing art of house painting. I like to think it's helping me somehow. I don't realize how fast I'm walking until I get ten blocks away inside of what feels like five minutes. So much for being relaxed.

Slow down.

Take a deep breath.

I pretend like Mom being mad at me doesn't affect me, but it does. Not just her, either. If a stranger was mad at me, I'd feel something deeper than I should. Like shame or something. I can't explain it. I'm guessing it's my father again, like a part of me is always going to be nervous and ashamed of him and me and Mom. But mostly me.

I turn around before I get to the center of town and I start walking back toward our apartment. There's a sound I can't figure out, but I'm walking toward it. It's too late for anyone to make this much noise. Sounds like someone digging.

"Can you help me out of here?"

This question comes at me from the rain drain at the bottom of our block. I'm hearing things. Clearly. I keep walking.

"Come back! It's me!"

I look around. The people who live on the corner have a big hedge. I look behind it. No one.

"In the drain!"

I look into the drain grate and she's there. The girl who tried to light snowflakes on fire. She says, "Can you lift this?"

I lift it and she climbs out.

"Thank you so much," she says. "That place is fucked up."

"The sewer?"

"It was like a submarine," she says. "Lots of people down there."

"Okay."

"I'm stoned. Sorry," she says. "It's been a while and what do I have to lose, right?"

"If I was trapped in the sewer, I'd probably get stoned, too," I say. "How'd you get down there?"

"How do I get anywhere?" she asks.

She grabs my hand and it instantly starts sweating. I try to make it stop, but it just gets worse. We walk toward my house.

"Can't go to my house. My mom's in a mood," I say.

She keeps walking.

"It's nice to see you," I say.

"Stop being so nervous," she answers. "It'll all work out fine."

I want to ask her what "it" is, but I just follow her up the road. She still doesn't use sidewalks, it seems.

Mike's house glows with TV light—probably more baseball.

"What's your name?" I ask.

"Don't have a name."

"Everyone has a name," I say.

"The Freak," she says.

I don't know what this means. She notices.

"My name is The Freak. Or just freak. Or The Freakish one. Lady freak. Whatever twist you want to put on it. Freak. That's me."

"Okay."

"I'm The Freak and you're the shoveler."

I'm embarrassed now. Carrying a shovel around with me like some crazy person. She obviously heard.

"You'll find a lot underground if you keep digging," she says.

I'm puzzled. "I'm not digging. It's a snow shovel."

"Shovel's a shovel."

I never really liked stoners. This is why. "Okay."

"You can do whatever you want. You've got arms. You've got legs. You've got existence. Don't waste it. Trust me."

I have *existence*? What the fuck is that supposed to mean? I'm suddenly sweating all over my body.

"Got a smoke?"

I smile. I nod. I grab her hand this time and we walk to the bench in front of the church—the one on the opposite side from my house.

She sits with her legs out and leans back so relaxed and I envy her. She truly doesn't give a shit about impressing anyone. Her feet are splayed out. She doesn't push her chest out like most girls do; she lets it sink into the gap between the sky and the bench.

I'm surprisingly relaxed by this, but my brain won't stop the variables. Why did she wait three weeks to show up again? Where did she come from? Where does she live? Why is her name The Freak? How do I show her that I'm a brain man? The movies I make run one after the other. All the variables. "What did you mean when you said I had existence?" I ask. Sounds smart. Brain-man kind of thing to say.

She inhales from the cigarette and holds it in and then exhales while answering so the smoke escapes her mouth as she forms out the syllables. "Existence is wasted on the living."

"You're stoned."

She takes another pull off the cigarette. "What do you think happens when we die?" she asks. "You believe in Heaven and Hell and all that shit?"

We're outside a Catholic church, sitting on a bench next to a statue of Mary. "This is the closest I ever got to a church. Wasn't even baptized," I say.

"So?"

"So, I don't really believe in Heaven and Hell, no."

"So, you're an atheist."

"I don't know. I don't think so. I believe in something but I don't quite know how to explain it."

I try to ignore the feeling inside me. I can't breathe. My chest is tight and there's sweat running down my back. I try to take a deep breath.

"You ever know anyone who died?" she asks.

"Yeah." I think of my dad. I don't know if he's dead or not, but he may as well be. Dead. Never existed. Existence is wasted on the living, I guess. At least for my dad.

"Wanna know what I think?" she asks. "I think when we die we all become part of a larger thing—a place where everyone who ever died lives. Not like Heaven. Not like Hell. Nothing really exists there. There's no beer or anything. Or swing sets or shovels. It's just thoughts. Ideas. Like a big bubble of ideas."

"I like it," I say.

"You'd better," she answers and flicks her cigarette into the bush next to the statue of Mary.

"I really like you," I say. My eyes are closed and my sweat is soaking now, through my sweatshirt. I flick my cigarette toward the same bush she flicked hers into. I wait for her to say what she said in my movie. Same movie's been running through my head for three weeks. I say *I really like you* and she's supposed to say *I really like you, too.* But she isn't saying anything at all.

I don't want to open my eyes now. But I do, and I find I'm sitting on the bench alone.

Look left. Look right. No one. Just the statue of Mary.

I run around the church. No one. I run home and grab my shovel from the front porch and go to the sewer drain. I try to take the grate off it again, but it's bolted down.

This makes no sense.

So much of my life makes no sense.

I think about going to watch baseball with Mike. We've been doing it pretty regularly and I was right about him being my only friend here. I don't want to see Mike, though. I want to find The Freak.

I walk my shovel back to the nearby rich area—it's a little town on the edge of this city with a fountain on its Main Street and a big park. *Maybe she's here. Maybe she's rich.* I walk around for a few hours, and when people look at me sideways because of the shovel, I just start pretending to shovel with it. Why not, right? I have existence. I can do whatever I want.

Gottfried's Big Decision

Gottfried and Marla had three kids and one on the way. It was 1980. Not a great time for Gottfried's business to fail, but fail it did—after six years of hard work. Businesses fail. That's what Marla kept telling him. *Businesses fail. It's not anyone's fault. It's always a risk to be self-employed. It's nothing to be ashamed of.*

But Gottfried felt shame all over. They needed a bigger house and a bigger life. Marla was sick a lot with this pregnancy and he had to provide. He didn't tell her that he'd pissed away most of his savings trying to keep the business going. He didn't tell her that he hadn't saved for the tax bill. Bankruptcy was a word he didn't want to think about, but there was no way he could pay the bills he'd racked up.

He hovered around the house like a ghost for a whole month before Marla made him tell her everything. It was worse than the robins. Worse than anything Gottfried had ever witnessed—the death of everything they'd worked so hard for.

"You spent the savings?" Marla said.

"Yes."

"You got a second loan on the house?" she asked.

"Yes," he said.

Marla picked up the nearest thing to her—a tea towel with exotic birds printed on it—and started to hit Gottfried over the head with it. "You stupid man. You stupid, stupid, stupid man!"

"I can figure this out," he said.

She kept hitting him with the tea towel and she started to cry.

This went on for some time. In Gottfried's mind, Marla hit him with the bird towel for what seemed like twenty years. In reality, it was only until four-year-old Harry arrived in the kitchen.

"Why's Mommy crying?"

"Don't know, son."

"Mommy?"

Marla kept crying and hitting, though Gottfried had moved out of range and the tea towel was only hitting the table now.

Finally, Marla said, "Harry, go get your sisters."

Harry left the room and Marla turned to her husband and said, "I guess starting tomorrow you're a potato farmer again. Call your father. Call your brother."

"I can't do that."

"Yes. You can," Marla said. The rest of the sentence went unsaid. The rest of the sentence was the same threat Marla'd been rightfully issuing since Gottfried's business started its downward turn two children ago.

A week later, Gottfried was in a barn full of harvested potatoes. The smell made him gag. Dirt made him gag. Wearing blue jeans and boots made him gag. Knowing his farm-loving brother had more money saved than he did made him gag. Looking at the old farmhouse that could easily fit four children made him gag. He kept telling himself that men did what they had to do to survive. But even that made him gag.

He couldn't tell Marla about the deal he'd made with his brother and father. He lied and said he had part ownership of the farm—a rightful share. Really, he was earning a higher-than-usual wage for being general manager. Gottfried wanted a better position. More responsibility. More money.

"Things have changed," his brother said to him. "You need to work here at least a month. It's not like it was when we were kids. Things were different."

This was true. His brother, John, had purchased equipment for harvesting and packaging that didn't exist when Gottfried had last worked the family farm as a teenager. He almost caught his fingers in the new packaging machine the day John showed him how it worked.

Both brothers knew the whole thing was a bad idea.

In only two months, Gottfried took over as head bookkeeper.

In only one year, he'd made so many intentional mistakes that the business was approaching legal trouble. He "forgot" to pay the right amount of tax. He "forgot" to pay into the state's unemployment. He got letters from the government and threw them away without opening them—gagging the whole time. Never throwing up, but always gagging.

Gottfried had wanted to be a good businessman. He'd wanted to be a good son. But he tossed both things aside to be a good father and a good husband. He told himself, *A man can't be good at everything.*

By the time the government came to the farm, Gottfried's fourth child was a year old. By the time the government came to the farm, Gottfried's brother had started an affair with the girl who worked in the shipping department.

When their father called him on the loud intercom that ran throughout the farm buildings, Gottfried knew what it was about. He arrived to the office where John and their sister, Gretchen, were already sitting. And his mother, too, uncontrollably crying.

"What the hell are you trying to do?" his father asked.

Gottfried shrugged and played stupid.

"A man can't fuck up the books this bad and not mean to."

He shrugged again.

"John worked his whole life on this farm. You just piss it away like it's nothing?"

"John's fucking the Mexican girl from shipping. What's her name?" Gottfried said. He sighed. "At least I can keep my marriage in order."

John looked at the floor. Gretchen looked at Gottfried. No one said anything.

A week later they all decided it would be best to sell the farm. They split the land four ways—150 acres apiece—so each could choose to do with their cut what they wanted.

Gottfried felt successful in business for the first time in his life.

CanIHelpYou?: the Shoveler

The alleys are dark and no one is around this time of night pretty much. The pub has closed and the faux-British people will crawl back into their beds and sleep it off and then wake up and post their selfies from the night before on their social media pages and say what a great night they had. They will eventually stop at my Drive-Thru window and use the word *gimme*. They will eventually yell at Ian for buying them the wrong size container of organic heavy cream.

We get to the park, and I see the shoveler again.

"Does he ever stop?" Ian asks.

"I want to talk to him."

Ian laughs. It's a giggle, really. High-pitched and laced.

"I'm serious. I want to find out his deal."

"Dude. No. Trust me."

"I just want to talk." I don't know what I'll say, though.

Ian keeps walking toward the park. I stop and watch the kid with the shovel.

When I get about ten feet away, he looks up and says, "You're not her."

I don't know if he really said that because part of me is still hallucinating quite a bit. I say, "Hi."

"Do you know her?"

"Who?"

"The Freak."

"I'm a freak."

123

"You're not her."

I nod as if what he said makes sense even though it doesn't. "Can I ask what's with the shovel?"

He looks down at the shovel as if he'd forgotten he was holding it. "I'm tunneling."

I stare at him. He stares at me. Locked eyes.

"Me too," I say, but I've never tried a shovel. Maybe it's the way out. Maybe I should carry a shovel.

He says, "If you see her, tell her I'm looking."

"Okay," I say. I back away and over toward Ian.

"See you around," he says.

"I hope you find her," I say. But really I hope he finds me and I can be his freak. It's not that he's super attractive or anything. I mean, he's okay. It's not about looks. I'm on acid. Everyone is beautiful. This was deeper. Something deeper than anything.

He's tunneling.

I'm tunneling.

We're bound to meet again. Probably underground.

Loretta Likes Scabs

Flea bites are a doddle. That's how Loretta Lynn sees it. A few little scabs are worth the joy she gets from the circus. She lets them feed on her twice a day, every day, arms, legs, torso. She encourages them to mate and lay eggs. More performers. A bigger act. She has enough blood to feed them all if they can get her out of there one day. And when she picks the scabs, she feels a sort of relief she can't describe.

Gerald has refused to rehearse since the rebellion. Tomorrow is school, and Loretta doesn't look forward to that. She can't touch herself in class, and the bathrooms aren't really great for that sort of thing. Sometimes she goes to the nurse's office and lies on the cot to get her fill. It's not easy having needs like this.

Fact: If Loretta Lynn doesn't orgasm at least four times per day, then she will probably die.

Her flea circus is locked up in its lunch box. The speaker Loretta got for her birthday—the Bluetooth kind—is still turned on and from the bed Loretta can see the blue light. Rather than get up and turn it off, she reaches for her knockoff iPod and finds her favorite song. It's the closing song for the act, and she hopes that inside the lunch box the performers are rehearsing just by hearing the bass line. Reggae is Loretta's thing. Her parents—clearly country and western fans—are not fans of reggae, which makes Loretta happier to play it. They don't know about the circus. They have scabs, too, but Loretta pretends she has nothing to do with it. They never look inside her lunch box. They've never asked.

They blame the RV camp for having bugs. The landlord comes to fumigate once a month. This is why Loretta takes her lunch box to school every day. Just in case.

CanIHelpYou?: Acid Hangovers Are the Worst

Ian calls me on Sunday afternoon.

"Acid hangovers are the worst," he says.

"What time is it?" I ask this because my eyes are still closed and I don't plan on opening them any time soon.

"Three."

I try to remember if I'm on the schedule today. I think I am. Four to eight. "Shit. I have to work."

"Call off sick."

"Can't." I have clients. Clients come to the Drive-Thru on Sundays.

"I have to write that comparison paper for English," he says. "But that's not why I'm calling."

"Me too. Shit."

"You'll get it done. Anyway—"

"I didn't even read the fucking books, dude. How can I compare them if I haven't read them?" I ask. "Look. I gotta go. I'll call you later. Fuck."

I hang up and go to the bathroom. Pee. Stare at the towels and they don't breathe. I brush my teeth, but my mouth still feels wrong. I floss the shit out of every single tooth. I now have the cleanest teeth in the universe.

Did you know plaque is considered a living thing?

Not kidding. It fits all the criteria to be a living thing. Plaque. It's millions of tiny bacteria living *in your mouth*. They shit on your teeth. *They shit on your teeth.*

And people think I don't listen in class.

Mom and Dad are nowhere in the house when I finally get downstairs. I need a ride. It's raining.

There's no note on the kitchen table. There's no texts on my phone. Mom and Dad may have finally given up on me. I can't stop thinking about Ian and me kissing last night. Probably good that my parents have given up on me, then.

I weigh out my Sunday sales and bag them. Mostly eighths, which is the stupidest way to buy weed, but people are people and who am I to judge? They're helping me save for a car so I can be free of this place. I dig through the hall closet for an umbrella. I find the only coat I own that will repel water—something Mom bought me years ago that's too girly and too preppy. But it'll keep the rain off.

"You're late," Len says. He looks like he has an acid hangover, too. But it's probably just a regular hangover. He and Nelle, the co-owner and his wife, drink a lot. If there is a god, I'd like to put in my request now for bald Len at forty to be abandoned completely by Nelle, who is actually pretty fucking cool.

"Hangover. Be nice," I say.

He smiles and shakes his head. I am his Drive-Thru guru. He knows I'm only a few minutes late. He knows I walked because I'm in his office to drop off my soaking umbrella and hang up my stupid, wet preppy coat.

I have my station ready in under a minute. First customer is a Gimme.

128

"Yeah, gimme a turnover and a milkshake."

"Apple or cherry?"

"Apple."

"What flavor milkshake?"

"Vanilla."

"Your total's four sixty." I don't even add something snappy. It hurts to reach up to the turnover shelf. I nearly drop the turnover on the floor because I don't have enough strength in my hand to pick it up with the pair of plastic tongs. I'm slow making the shake, too. I need to get my shit together before dinner rush. Sundays can be hell. Sometimes buses stop here on their way back from Philadelphia.

I finish the order and no one else is waiting. I stand with my back to the Drive-Thru window and look out to the registers. Barbara is working #1 and Young Jack is working #2. We call him Young Jack because he's our baby here at fifteen. I'm supposed to train him into Drive-Thru in a few weeks and I don't think he'll be able to handle it. I look farther into the restaurant—people eating their early dinners or late lunches or just a dessert.

Something is different today.

I'm different today.

Young Jack says something to Barbara about the kid with the shovel. About him walking around town last night. "Kid's a freak," he says.

"He's not a freak," I say.

"You know him?"

"Kinda."

"My dad says he's crazy. Like for real."

"He's not crazy."

Len walks through with his can of hairspray headed for the men's room. "Why isn't anyone making coffee?" he asks.

Young Jack says, "I don't know how."

"I'll teach him," I say. Len nods.

As I show Jack around the coffee machine and explain that he always has to use cold water, he says, "You should stay away from that kid. Seriously. You have to be safe."

Our Young Jack is so kind. "I'll be fine. He's not dangerous. Your dad is paranoid."

"He's a cop."

"Yeah. Paranoid. Gotcha. Now all you have to do is press that orange button."

He presses the orange button. I make a mental note to never offer Young Jack a joint or anything else like that. Cops' sons are usually badasses, but sometimes it takes a while.

My regular Sunday clients arrive right on time between five and six thirty.

They always say please and thank you. It's a rule. Manners in trade for Drive-Thru weed convenience. Always a meal with potato cakes so they take a while because we always run out of hot potato cakes during dinner hour. I slip their orders into their bags. They slip the cash into my hand, and I make it disappear into my bra before I get to the cash register to ring up their food.

Young Jack nearly catches me one time, my hand still down my shirt. I clear his puzzled face by saying, "Bras, man. Be happy you're a guy."

Jake & Bill score convenient weed

Bill Marks is skeptical.

"I'm serious," Jake says. "The bitch works the Drive-Thru and all you have to do is order potato cakes and say please."

"Can't be true," Bill says. "She'd have sold to a cop by now."

"I told you. You have to arrange it first."

"And you arranged it?" Bill asks.

"Yeah. She said to come today between five and six." Jake looks at his brother like he's losing patience. Bill always treats him like some sort of kid, and yet Jake is the one who's been scoring the weed for two whole years. It took him three weeks to find a new connection and Bill doesn't seem to appreciate the struggle.

Bill pulls up to the speaker and it says, "Welcome to Arby's Drive-Thru, would you like to try our new mango-and-pineapple smoothie today?"

"Gimme potato cakes," Bill says. "Large."

Jake yells, "Please!" from the passenger's seat.

"Is that all?"

"Yes, *please*," Bill says. He rolls his eyes.

"That's two forty. Come to the second window."

Bill looks at Jake and then beyond him to search the parking lot for cops.

They do the deal and Bill looks in the bag before they drive away. Got what he paid for. Can't wait to tell his friends about this girl. She's clearly a genius.

He hands the bag to his little brother. "Roll some of that up and see if it's any good. Girls don't know shit about weed, man. If she fucked us, I'll have to go back."

CanIHelpYou?: You

By seven thirty, I already have everything stocked and ready for the morning. No dinner rush. No buses from Philadelphia. The Drive-Thru was hectic for about twenty minutes but since then, nearly dead. Rainy day in February. People probably made dinner after a good day of sitting around watching TV.

I texted *OMG this fucking hangover* to Ian about an hour ago. I asked him how the comparison paper was coming. He never answered.

Once I clock out and get my umbrella from the office, I go outside to walk home but Dad is in the car, waiting.

Dad doesn't say a word as we drive the six blocks home. He has the radio on. Politics. Dad is happy about politics. His guy won. We don't talk about it because he's a condescending jerk about the whole thing and thinks I believe he voted with his wallet. "Economics" are the source of his anxiety.

Bullshit.

Dad pulls into the driveway and parks. He hasn't said a word yet. Tomorrow I go to school. Tomorrow I will not hand in my comparison essay and I will fail a chemistry test. He's never asked me anything about why I'm doing this to myself. He's never said much of anything about anything, really.

"Just who do you think you are?"

That's my mother talking. She's on the couch and she's muted the TV in order to ask me this question.

I don't have an answer. After last night, I'm pretty sure I'm someone else.

"Grounded. Two weeks. You go nowhere with no one, and one of us will drop you off and pick you up from work. After school, we'll track you with your phone. If you step one foot off the walk home, we'll see it and add another week.

"I don't understand you. We give you everything! And you stay out all night with your *friend* and don't answer our texts and don't care if we worry. You could have been kidnapped! And you don't do anything at school. You're blowing your whole future," she says. "I've just had it with you. I'm done. You'll do makeup homework for two weeks until every class is above a C."

The tunnel protects me from the real effects of this. The tunnel protects me from politics and parents and impossible possibilities. Grounded? I've been grounded since the roller-skating party when I was nine. Grounded? I've been grounded since my mother sat me down and told me about the missing girl and how I wasn't allowed to go to the mall anymore. Grounded? I've been grounded by having a mother who thinks I'm naïve for not hating my best friend because of the amount of melanin in his skin. I can't imagine what she'd say if she knew that I'm falling in love with him.

She tells our extended family—my grandmother, the only one who talks to her—that when I graduate I'll probably get some job helping people get on welfare. I heard her say that. She doesn't hush herself when she talks about me. I've heard her say worse things. It's not a big deal. I'm a disappointment.

My mother did well for herself. She went to college and met my dad. He's from a rich family outside of Philadelphia. Like, rich-rich.

Like, my mom had to sign a prenuptial agreement and everything.

Hasn't worked a day in her life.

And yet she's never happy. And Dad isn't happy either—just playing along with the part he was given when he was born with a penis and a silver spoon.

They're the reason I pity you. My parents. You remind me of them. You have dumb ideas and think you're smart. You have no inclination to listen because you already know everything. And it's all *gimme-gimme-gimme*.

You want more. You had kids too young. You miss your college days. You reminisce about your girlfriends while you talk to me. You say I remind you of them. You say I'm likeable. You commend me on not stiffing you a gram. You tell me about how in high school you could buy a quarter for thirty bucks. You look at my chest and think I don't see you. You look at my legs. You comment on my tan. I don't even have a tan.

I have what you need. I have your youth. I have the euphoria you checked at the door when you stood at the altar, defended your dissertation, said yes to that job you never wanted. Not my fault you can't move forward. Not my fault you made promises you don't feel like keeping. My legs can't save you. My weed can't save you. Even when I go looking for your special orders. Your coke. Your oxy. Your ecstasy. I make my trades and I bring you your goods. And still, you can't be happy.

You won't find happiness inside that bag I sold you. You won't find it in a night out with your pals. You won't find it in your cold bed with your cold wife/husband who doesn't even remember who you are anymore.

You think you don't seem desperate? You think because I'm seventeen I'm stupid?

Drooling, you tell me about your grueling day at the office. You think I care. You ask me if I've done my homework like you're my parent. You ask what I want to go to college for. You say I save your ass.

I'm not saving your ass. Your ass is your responsibility.

I'd tell you if you asked, but you never do. You know me but you don't know me. I'm just your convenience store. I make life more palatable. I make it livable. I make it numb. I help you forget about bills. About anniversaries and your kids' birthdays. I help you forget everything you are.

You never ask this.

And I never tell.

But if I told, I'd tell you that your wife/husband knows me, too. And your kids. They all know me. I'm CanIHelpYou? I'm here to serve. Whether it's joint by joint, a random hit of something harder, or just some Xanax so your wife/husband can handle your man cave/girls' night bullshit, I can help you.

The only one I can't help is me.

You have no idea how lucky you are to be aboveground. Breathing fresh air, oxygen, pure. You think my life is easy. You think I'm a careless teenager with a shitty job and a side hustle.

But I'm in this for life.

Because you need me. You need me more than I need you. Unless you can tell me why I'm stuck in this tunnel. Unless you can show me the way out.

PART TWO: OUR CAST
IN A BLENDER

Loretta Knows Her Lines

Loretta thinks back to the days when Holloway would haul six train cars behind him. Amazing animal. Strong. Determined. Never complained. Always loyal. Died in his sleep a year ago while Loretta was in the bath, doing what she does.

She felt it was part of the curse. You find joy in life and you lose something special, as if a constant balance would always hold her back from full happiness. Of course, Holloway was due to die. He'd outlived his friends and fellow performers. Not many fleas can brag two whole years on the planet. And he gave her Gerald, who's nearly as good as him at pulling the train.

The wagon is cold today—it's been a warmer-than-normal February—but Loretta wears three sweaters over her blue-chiffon circus dress to stay warm, the last layer a sequined green sweater that makes her look a bit like a Christmas ornament. Her parents are rehearsing their act, which isn't a difficult act and it isn't funny or entertaining. Loretta can't understand how her parents even survive anymore. They don't talk to each other. They don't have sex. They don't eat very often, and they don't go anywhere.

The act is played out in the living-room portion of the wagon—matinee at two, dinner show at five, and a late show in case there isn't a good movie on TV, at around nine or so. They juggle, not things but words. They dare to leap through the ring of fire that is TV news. They are contortionists of ideas. They know nothing else but this act and how to work a toaster oven.

They don't understand why their ankles are covered in scabs. They don't own a vacuum cleaner.

Loretta sets the train cars up the same way she used to when Holloway would pull them. She says their numbers as she assembles it.

"Four . . . five . . . six. Caboose!"

Once she has the cars connected, she tests that the wheels are still working—pulls it slowly with the tip of her finger.

She produces a roll of thin copper wire from her bag and cuts three pieces of different lengths and then ties a loop into the middles of each. The loops are so small you'd never know they were there unless you looked really hard. Loretta puts on a pair of high-powered reading glasses. +2.00. She squints to make sure the loops are the right size.

She takes Gerald from her matchbox of fleas inside the lunch box. The matchbox is decorated with glitter and sequin stickers that look like gems. On the lid it reads THE BEST FLEAS IN THE WORLD! The box is orange, which was her favorite color from the ages of eight to eleven.

"Loretta Lynn, get your ass in here and eat your sandwich!"

She often wonders if she had siblings, if they would help her understand her parents. She doubts it. But she knows kids at school who have sisters and brothers and they stick together. Loretta can only stick to her fleas. She leaves the train assembled but closes Gerald back into his box.

"I'll be back in five minutes," she says. "Do your strength exercises."

The sliced roast beef smells wrong. The cheese is processed. The bread is stale on the edges. The only thing this sandwich has going for it is the mustard.

The TV is set to some show with a preacher. His head is as

139

big as the screen and it makes Loretta feel claustrophobic for the man. He seems pained. He says, "The Lord Jesus Christ knows you want a better life. He is saving a place for you in his palace in Heaven. Consider what I'm asking you to do as a down payment. One hundred dollars isn't too much to ask for a place in Heaven, is it?"

Loretta's mother starts the act. She picks up her cell phone, flips it open, and starts to dial the number.

Loretta's father sits still and waits for his cue.

"Hello? Yes . . . yes!" her mother says. "I do! I accept him in the fullness in my heart."

Loretta stops eating her sandwich and opens it. She pulls the roast beef out and slips it into a fast-food napkin. She looks across the breakfast bar and notes that they are running low on straws, which can only mean a drive to Arby's soon—maybe before Wednesday.

"One hundred dollars," Loretta's mother says. "That's the cost of my ticket . . . that's what he just said. I heard him. One hundred." Loretta's mother listens for a few seconds and adds, "If I had a thousand, I'd send it but I only have a hundred. And no, I don't care if there are bigger rooms in the palace. I'm used to living small anyway. In fact, keep me away from the people who can afford the bigger rooms. I hate rich people."

Loretta's father turns up the volume on the TV. The preacher says, "The pool at the palace is filled with unconditional love. Your brothers and sisters will join you here and you can bathe together in His light."

Loretta thinks this part is creepy.

"A hundred . . . yes. I can send it to you in cash," Loretta's mother says. She nods as she listens as if she's never made this phone call before. "I don't have a credit card or a bank account. I told you, I hate rich people."

The next scene starts with a drumroll and cymbal crash, and Loretta's father appears in the spotlight. The crowd goes wild. He gets up out of his chair and grabs the phone from his wife's ear and says, "Hello? Hello?"

Loretta's mother tries to get the phone back, but he shoves her back into her chair with a stage-push. Doesn't hurt. It's all for show.

Loretta reaches for another packet of fast-food mustard and puts it on the processed cheese left on her sandwich. She opens a packet of horseradish sauce, too, and applies it to the hard crusts.

"What kind of Jesus doesn't accept cash?" her father asks. "What kind of Jesus asks us to give our money to a bank? What kind of whore are you for trying to get my wife to apply for a credit card? You work for the Devil. Have a nice day."

He presses the hang-up button and hands the phone back to Loretta's mother. Then he looks straight at Loretta, who, out of nervousness, shoves the last of the sandwich in her mouth at the same time she checks to make sure the napkin with the roast beef is hidden in her green-sequined pocket.

"You have school tomorrow. What are you doing out here? Don't you have things to study for?"

"Yes."

"Go back to your room," Loretta's mother says.

"Did anyone ask you?" he says to Loretta's mother.

Loretta doesn't want you to read any more about what happens next, so she goes back to her room at the end of the hall and she locks the door behind her. She doesn't want to touch the magic spot. She doesn't want to think about that right now. She puts on the reggae music for the train-pulling act and picks up the orange matchbox.

She can hear the screams between the bass line and the *chicka-chicka-chicka* of the guitar, but she knows it's all an act. The police have come a few times and her mother says everything is fine. The neighboring campers just don't understand. They're too quiet anyway.

"Our family is just loud and fine. We're like any other family in show business," Loretta says to Gerald as she places him on the white felt and loops the copper wire around his torso. It's easy. He walks into the loop headfirst and she just has to pull the ends of the wire at the right time. "Not too tight, now. We don't want this to be a half-flea circus."

Holloway would have loved that joke. He had a great sense of humor.

Once Gerald is in the harness, Loretta tests to make sure he's okay. She puts a tiny ball in front of him, and he kicks it out of the lunch box. "Strong legs," she says. "Just like your father."

She pulls the six-car train onto its track and places Gerald in front, attaches his harness, and opens the four sides of her circus box so he can pull it as far as he wants. Nothing happens.

She gets her magnifying glass. Through it she can see Gerald working so hard to walk, he stumbles. He moves his head for momentum. He tries using all six of his legs at the same time as if he were running in place. Nothing will move the train.

CanIHelpYou?: Never Get a Manicure in Wichita

So maybe I'm in love with my best friend. So what?

This is what I think during homeroom. During math. English. Lunch. *So maybe I'm in love with my best friend. So what?*

Then I'm in my tunnel. There's graffiti everywhere. It says, HE HATES YOU/YOU'RE A RACIST. There's a clever one in red paint: IAN + ANYONE WHO'S NOT YOU.

I can't figure out what I'm supposed to do.

In my house lives a bell. It's a disgusting bell. It's a bad bell. It's never been used for anything good since it's been in my house. All it does is announce the speaking parts of my mother, the racist who owns the bell. Cherishes the bell. Thinks the bell is "tradition."

Tradition gets away with lots of shit around here.

Like, we had a racist incident at our high school a few years ago. By *incident*, I mean a large group of people celebrated the "tradition" of being assholes to the kids who aren't white. Yelled stuff at them. Waited outside school every day—morning and afternoon—and threw things at them from their trucks adorned with Confederate flags. They didn't throw rocks, no. Balled-up pieces of paper. Snot loogies. Paper clips. Things that don't count as dangerous. Safe things. Safe hate.

Tradition. You can say what you want so long as you're not throwing anvils, I guess. They call it freedom of speech or *traditional family values*. The louder ones call it heritage—as if it were in our blood to be assholes to other people, as if we'd inherited it. The best the administration ever did is ban Confederate flags on cars in the parking lot. Sure, you can go to my school if you have a Confederate flag on your car—you just can't park in the parking lot. That was the solution to the incident a few years ago. Nothing about the subtler white supremacist bumper stickers—an Iron Cross decal or that weird Rhodesian flag sticker that a kid from down our street has on his BMW. Not an assembly, not a single suspension for any of the kids who took part in the incident. Just a parking lot rule. Freedom of speech. Freedom of family values. Even if your family values suck.

So maybe I'm in love with my best friend. So what?

I can't stop thinking of kissing Ian even though we haven't kissed since that night. I feel like an idiot. I'm usually far cooler than this. The tunnel is eating me.

Then magically, mid-history class, I am summoned to the guidance office to meet with Nancy. Mrs. Waters to you. Nancy to me. She wants to make a plan so I don't fail junior year. My mother called her.

Nancy says, "From what your mom told me, you don't have any friends."

I look at Nancy. I sigh. "My mom lies."

I tell her about Ian. I tell her about roller-skating. I tell her that my mother doesn't approve of anything I do since Ian is my best friend and because she and my dad are *traditionally conservative*. I put air quotes around it and mouth the word *racist*. Nancy sits with this for a while.

"Let's unpack this," she says.

"Okay," I say. This'll be a challenge.

"Does she use words that make you uncomfortable?"

"All the time." I shake my head like I should be ashamed to admit this even though I'm not the one who uses the words. "And she has this bell," I say.

"A bell?"

"It's like, an heirloom or something. I think it was a souvenir someone got down south. It's a slave bell." Nancy looks at me like she doesn't understand, and I realize that most people wouldn't. "I have a picture," I say, and scroll through the pictures on my phone.

When I show it to her, Nancy makes a face like she'd do anything to unsee the bell—even if her only other choice was getting a manicure in Wichita.

THE FREAK HEARS THE ENTIRE POPULATION OF EARTH TALKING AT THE SAME TIME!

The hallway at any school on any given Monday morning is loud, but today it's louder. Like the entire population of Earth talking at the same time.

The shoveler is swinging his shovel at a group of boys who have tried to take it from him.

"Get the fuck away from me!" he screams.

A discipline employee is running down the hallway, but he won't get there in time.

The Freak saw this coming. She can sometimes hear the movies in the shoveler's head and it wasn't going well lately. Everything ended in anger. Everything caused frustration. The kid wasn't doing well socially at his new school. Not like he'd tell anyone about it. Who does he have to tell?

His mother?

Mike the neighbor?

Marla and Gottfried Hemmings, who're too distracted by paint color charts to give a shit about their own messed-up kids, let alone the social life of the cheap labor they hired to paint?

The Freak feels like she's failed him as she watches the shovel graze a boy's cheek—as she watches the shovel nick another boy's arm. By the time the discipline guy gets him in an armlock, the boys grab the shovel from the hallway floor and start running with it.

That's when The Freak steps in.

She holds the boys by their hair. She says, "Give me the shovel."

"Who the—what the fuck are you?"

"Just give me the shovel."

A boy approaches from behind her, and she lets out a kick that makes him tumble toward where he came from. The two boys in her hands try to squirm free, but she tightens her grip on their hair.

"Drop the fucking shovel," she says one last time.

They drop the shovel at her feet. She tosses them, like two dolls, across the hallway. She picks up the shovel and walks slowly toward the main office.

Teachers try to get students into their rooms. Try to get the place to quiet down. None of the students listen. They mill around in circles like they're in an enormous, angry blender, looking for more ingredients.

"It's like a fuckin' prison riot," one teacher says to another.

"I don't know how I do this anymore," the teacher replies.

The Freak can't flicker now. She's got the shoveler's shovel. She's already underground and has nothing to lose. She walks into the main office, past the protesting secretary, and into the principal's office and hands the shovel to the shoveler.

He looks up at her and says, "I've been looking for you everywhere."

The principal nods at the discipline guy who's still there.

He walks toward The Freak and she closes her eyes slowly.

The shoveler yells, "No!" but she's already gone.

The adults in the room all look like they need Easter break to come a lot sooner than a month from now. The principal is the only one who looks concerned for her own mental health. None of them ask the obvious question.

The Freak finds herself back in the tunnel she was in more than two weeks ago. Gray, rivets, lit only where she stands, and the sound of someone writing.

Scribble-scribble-scribble.

The Freak walks toward the sound. Everything in front of her is dark. Everything behind her is dark, but she trusts. Two right-hand turns later, she finds a lit piece of the tunnel ahead. A girl.

"Who's there?" the girl yells.

The Freak stands still.

"Leave me alone!" the girl screams.

The girl gets up and starts running—in the direction away from The Freak.

"This is MY fucking tunnel! Stop chasing me! You're not welcome!"

The Freak doesn't know what to say. She's never wanted to scare anyone, but she suddenly feels at fault for everything that's happened today. The shoveler in the principal's office. This girl, freaking out.

"I'm sorry!" The Freak says. Then she closes her eyes.

Lands in her bedroom again.

To the same old note.

You can't just disappear without telling me where you went. I know your dad leaving has been hard on you, but we have to be a team now. I want your car keys on the kitchen table before dinner.

The Shoveler: Some Shrink

Mom is not impressed. She had to leave the car lot an hour early and mutters something about how she might get fired on our walk from the office to the car.

"I'm really sorry," I say.

"Doesn't sound like it was even your fault," she says. But then she shakes her head and has that look on her face. "Can you explain again why the hell you're carrying a shovel around?"

I can't tell her. How do I tell her?

Safety is a lie. I'm floating in space with no tether. I'm underground and existence is pointless until I find the right roots to the right plant. It's hard to breathe here. It's hard to see here. I just keep living, but I don't know what for. I make movies. Movies in my head. I plan everything. Every step. Every word. Mostly I plan to avoid. Avoidance is the only way to live like this. You never told me who my father was. You never told me where I got half of me. I'll always be half lost. Half here. Half real.

What if he was a bad guy? What if he was some guy who hurt you? What if he was someone who didn't know how to take a no? What if he was someone you don't remember? What if he was someone you don't want to remember? What if he comes back one day and wants me to visit him? What if he finds me on the Internet and asks me to go fishing? Will he drown me?

Will he drown you? Will he blow
up our house? Will he steal our
TV? What do I do then? What
do I do when he comes for me?
Do I even want to meet him?
What if he's rich and can help
us out? We could buy a house.
We could afford more food.

That's why I carry
the shovel. I can't
stop the variables.
I can't stop asking
because I haven't
found the answer.

I don't answer her. Instead, I say, "Do I have to see that shrink?"

"Yes."

The school said they'd give me a break if I saw the school
shrink. Mom didn't even fight it. "You think I need to see a shrink?"

"No," she says. "Maybe. I don't know. They're not all that
bad. And this makes us look compliant."

"Those guys were going to steal my shit. Probably beat me
up, too."

She sighs. "Life's not fair, kid. Life's not fair."

"So now I have to see some shrink."

"Right."

"You don't seem upset about this. You're my mom. They're
saying I'm crazy."

She pulls the car over to the side of the street. Turns to me.
"Nobody said you're crazy. I don't think that at all. Stop being mad
at me because you got in trouble. I wasn't the one who brought a

shovel to school," she says. "And you know what? Maybe it'll be okay for you to talk to someone. You sure as shit don't talk to me, and you don't talk to Mike even though he's tried. He likes you, and I thought you two could hang out. He's a good guy."

My brain's flying. Movies. Most of them with Mom and Mike and things I don't want to describe.

"You got this job and that's great. You're doing great. But you really need some friends. I mean real friends, too, not like Texas or Nebraska. Those boys just used you to do their homework in exchange for teaching you how to smoke cigarettes," she says. "You think I don't know? I know plenty. I was your age once, too."

The only word on my lips is *shoplifting*, but it seems so petty. I'm not handling this well. More movies. More movies with Mom and Mike and how familiar they are.

I take a deep breath. "Can I ask you a question?"

"Sure."

"I mean, can I ask you a question and can you give me an answer?"

"I'll try."

"You've known Mike a lot longer than since we got here, haven't you?"

She nods.

"What's your old business? Was it Mike? Are you guys gonna get married or something?"

She laughs like I just told the funniest joke, but it's not the kind of laugh that pisses me off. "Oh, boy! Your imagination! Look." She smiles. "I've known Mike since I was about nine years old. We're friends. That's all. He helped me out a long time ago.

A few times," she says. "Remember the Christmas you got your first phone? That was Mike. Good guy. But I'd never marry him."

This makes me happy. But her last claim makes no sense to me. "So he's the nicest guy alive but you wouldn't marry him? Why not?"

She shakes her head and makes that sound: *ffffft*. "You don't know Mike like I know Mike. That's all I'll say."

I can't think of Mike as anyone other than a guy who watches old baseball games and apparently uses a lot of kitchen appliances. And he's even nice to his mom. Can't see what's so wrong with that, but Mom's already pulled back onto the street and is driving us home.

When we get in the house and I change into my painting clothes, she says, "I miss you these days. You're working so much."

"It's a short-term thing. I'll be done by Easter."

"Doesn't make me miss you less. Soon you'll be out in the world and I'll be on my own."

"Maybe rethink marrying Mike, eh?" I say. We laugh. "Thanks for today. I know I nearly got suspended. I know you're the reason I didn't."

"I still want to know who the girl was that they talked about."

"No girl. They must have been hallucinating."

"Are you seriously still going to take that everywhere with you?" She's motioning toward my shovel.

"Um. Yeah. If that's okay."

"Whatever gets you through."

On my drive to Marla and Gottfried's house, shovel lying across the back seat, I think about that. *Whatever gets you through.* That's why she shoplifted pork loins. It's why she

Gottfried Thinks Marla Is the Grim Reaper

Gottfried is impressed with the painter kid. He's a bit weird—always has a snow shovel in his car, even now, when Marla's crocuses are blooming and the tulips are starting to bud—but he's got a good work ethic.

Gottfried respects a good work ethic. His father did, too. And probably his father before him. Gottfried wouldn't be worth so much if he'd been lazy. He gets pride butterflies whenever he sees the total. Sold off those hundred and fifty acres slowly, developed them with the right builder, grew them with the right houses, rented them to the right people, collected check after check after check.

He's intrigued by the kid. Doesn't say much. Hasn't even talked to Malcolm, the grandson living there. Malcolm isn't hard to get to know. He's a good kid, too, for the most part. Different from the painter kid, though. Reminds Gottfried of his sister. Just one sister, dead now, and a brother, who hasn't talked to Gottfried in decades, the three of them completely different from one another.

Marla is working on her checklist. It's the last day of February and she's planning Easter. The dinner. The eggs. The flowers. Even the place mats. One month to go.

Gottfried doesn't know what to do with himself in the evenings. Malcolm stays in his room for the most part, sometimes coming out to watch TV. Marla sits reading or making her list or using the iPad she got for Christmas to look for new recipes. Not like Gottfried minds. He never learned how to cook like that.

The painter kid had the second floor to himself for the last four weeks and he did the first four rooms quickly. Started small—the bathroom. Moved into the guest room, then the office, and he's finishing the other guest room now—the one Malcolm lives in. Marla picked the ugliest color for that room, a pastel sea-foam green. Malcolm hates it. He told her. She said, "Tough noogies, kid."

It's as if Marla doesn't see what's coming.

One day their son Harry will die.

One day their grandson Malcolm will be theirs.

Gottfried's had to talk to her three times in the last month about making lamb chops when Malcolm is here and she doesn't listen.

And every night she serves dinner while the painter kid is here and she never offers him any. Kid's skinny. Could use some of her cooking. She used to love feeding people—the compliments and the clean plates.

Gottfried watches the kid drive away, then closes the garage door and walks into the house, landing in the living room, where Malcolm and Marla are fighting about nothing. Marla's just picking again. Malcolm can't do anything right.

"Marla, stop it," Gottfried says.

"Shut up," she says. She turns back to Malcolm. "You can't live here and disrespect me. Do you hear me? You have to live by my rules."

"Marla, stop it," he says again.

Malcolm looks at his grandfather as if he might cry. Gottfried can see Harry in the boy's face. Marla didn't want Harry to be Harry, either. She's just repeating herself—going to give this boy cancer, too, if she doesn't stop.

Marla stands there for a few seconds and looks from Malcolm to Gottfried and back at Malcolm again. Then she storms out and into their bedroom.

Gottfried thinks of the robins. He walks to Malcolm and hugs him. Not just some small hug, either. This is a real hug. And Malcolm cries, finally. Just sobs into his chest and Gottfried finds himself crying, too. He's not sure what he's crying about, but he's pretty sure he's crying about everything.

Malcolm in the Consciousness

Marla fights with me about everything. World news, national news, local news. She's the most entitled woman on Earth. It's almost spring, so Marla is in full-on Easter mode and it bothers me.

Marla and I have differing views on Easter.

I'm not even sure why Marla is so into Easter. She doesn't go to church or do anything religious, really. I'm not even sure she believes in the resurrection. Or Jesus. Or anything. Marla's religion is her kitchen. Her freezer. Her flower beds. Interior paint.

Dad and I believe in the Consciousness—a huge ball of energy formed by the energy of people who've died. It's like a giant resurrection, really. Picture it as big as the Pacific Ocean. As big as Jupiter. As big as the galaxy. How big does the pool have to be if it has to fit the ideas of everyone who ever died into it?

I'd be lying if I didn't say this is a seriously white belief system. New Age bullshit, probably. But it means my mom is here in every moment, and it means Dad will be, too.

When I talk to Marla about it, she seems to think the only people in the Consciousness are either people she knew or famous people. She says she can't wait to see her mother again and meet Elvis Presley.

I say things like, "All the people from India will be there, too."

And she rolls her eyes at me. "They're Hindus. They'll go somewhere else."

Marla's grasp on the afterlife and Hinduism is tenuous. "The Consciousness is all-inclusive," I explain.

She really thinks about it. "So murderers and rapists and dogfighters'll be there? I'll take a pass, thank you. It's scary enough to live with those people. I don't want to die with them!"

"Maybe that's the challenge," I say.

"No one wants a challenge after they die, Malcolm. This is a depressing theory. No way I could go there."

"So Heaven and Hell work better for you?"

"Absolutely!"

"And what makes you think you'll end up in the right place?" I say. "I mean, away from the murderers and stuff?"

"I'm a good person."

Marla is resolute in this idea. Marla Hemmings is a good person. She looks after me while my father dies. She gives money to the animals. That's her convenient ticket to Heaven. It's Marla's flush toilet. The septic tank is underground, just like Hell. She never has to think about it once she presses the handle.

She has no idea how her shit affects what she's planted above it. No idea that her grown children, my dad and his siblings, resent her for good reason—that each flush douses them in the knowledge that they're failing at mere survival while she marinates top-cut lamb chops.

Loretta, Act Two: Classic with Cheddar

Act Two is always a struggle. Act Two is always a surprise.

"Hurry up! We'll leave you here if you don't come out in five seconds!" Loretta's father is yelling this into the crack of the bathroom door. There's no need to yell, but it must say in the script that this line should be yelled. It's a very good script, and he's a very good actor.

From behind the door, there's the sound of weeping. Loretta thinks the critics will give them a rave review. Never has an act been so convincing.

The actor who plays her father grabs Loretta by the arm and says, "Forget it. Your mom mustn't be hungry enough." He pulls her out the door of the wagon and Loretta stumbles a bit on the steps, but manages to get herself into the back seat of the car.

"Why are you sitting back there?" her father asks.

"I always sit back here."

"Sit up front."

Loretta doesn't ask any questions. This act is serious, and she knows her part. She moves to open the car door to get out.

"Just climb! Don't make more noise."

Loretta used to climb in cars when she was little. She's not little anymore. She tries to calculate the act and pretends she's the contortionist from Prague. The contortionist from Prague was very bendy.

"Don't get dirt on the seat!"

She takes off her shoes.

"Jesus, hurry up!"

Loretta stumbles into the front seat, and before she can fasten her seat belt, the car takes off down the small driveway, tiny bits of gravel flying under its tires.

"You don't need a seat belt," her father says, as she's halfway to buckling it. She buckles it anyway. He reaches over and clicks the belt free.

"I drive just fine. Don't be so over-reactive."

The drive is five minutes long, and her father sings along to a song on the radio even though he doesn't know the words. He pretends to be a normal dad. He seems happy. The audience is tense because when characters change like this, it's a bad sign.

They pull into the Arby's Drive-Thru lane and he doesn't ask her what she wants to eat. Loretta always gets the classic with cheddar cheese and an order of potato cakes.

"Hello. Welcome to Arby's! Can I interest you in our—"

"Just gimme a number one meal large with a Coke. And an extra order of fries."

"Large fries?"

"Large curly fries."

"That all?"

Loretta puts her hand up inside the car as if it were some sort of classroom.

"And whatever she wants," he says.

"May I please have a classic with cheddar cheese, the gooey kind? And an order of potato cakes?"

"Small potato cakes?"

"Yes, please," Loretta says.

"Twelve forty-eight," the Drive-Thru girl says. "Please come to the second window."

There are two cars ahead of them. Loretta's dad doesn't turn the radio back on and just sits, staring into the passenger's side door. Loretta doesn't know why he's looking that way, but she doesn't look away from her knees.

"Why are you still wearing that old thing?" he asks. He means her dress. They left in such a hurry, she's still got her blue-chiffon Ringmistress dress on.

"Don't know. I just like it."

"It's too small for you."

"I know."

"Damn. Look at those legs," he says. He's still looking her way. At her legs. "You must've got those from my side of the family. Your mother's side is all short and stubby."

Loretta doesn't want to talk about her legs.

"You shave them?" he asks.

Loretta doesn't want to talk about her legs.

"You do, don't you? With that cute little pink razor you got."

Loretta doesn't want to talk about her legs.

He reaches his hand over and rubs her knee. "Smooth, even in winter. Funny, you won't brush your hair but you'll stay smooth."

A horn beeps, short and impatient. Her father's eyes jerk from her knee to the rearview mirror. He sticks his middle finger up and moves the car up one space, then puts it in park. Loretta doesn't move.

"Your mother won't shave in winter, you know. Dumb bitch."

Loretta doesn't want to talk about her mother.

The person in front of them at the Drive-Thru only got a drink, so it's time to move up and pay. While her father is turned toward the girl in the window, Loretta yanks her dress down to cover her legs as much as possible. She's thankful her father doesn't allow her to use the seat belt because she knows how to unlock the door and roll out if she has to. She saw it in a movie. Or maybe a dream. She can't quite remember.

Her father says, "Gimme a bag of condiments while you're at it, okay?"

The girl in the window says, "Sure. You want straws again this time?"

"As many as you can gimme, sweetheart."

He's looking at the girl in the window the way he just looked at Loretta's knees. Loretta takes this opportunity to slide over toward the door so he can't reach her without leaning.

"And a shitload of napkins," he says to the girl in the window. She gets the bags ready and waits for him to pay, and he says, "I'm sorry, sweetheart. I'm trying to find my wallet. Wanna give those to me to get them off your hands?"

She hands him the Coke and the bag full of condiment loot first—ketchup, horseradish sauce, barbeque sauce, mustard, straws, and napkins—and he tosses it at Loretta, who places it in the back seat. He says to the girl working the Drive-Thru, "Call you later!" Then, before Loretta can turn back around, he plops the whole bag of hot food on her lap and takes off, wheels squealing and everything.

"Shit. I forgot salt," he says.

"We have some. I saw it when I was eating dinner."

"You don't tell anybody what you see in our house. It's our

private business. Nobody knows what I go through having to live with a crazy person. Damn shame she can't just die."

Loretta doesn't want to talk about her mother dying.

She thinks back to Holloway and how good he was at pulling that tiny train. He used to walk it in circles, backward, and even a figure eight once. What a performer. Always loved the spotlight.

Loretta doesn't like the spotlight.

"Can I eat this in the car?" she asks.

"Nothing to stop you."

She opens the meal on her lap and starts to eat. She tries to take bites slowly and chew enough, but it's been a week since she had good-tasting food and it's hard not to rush. The potato cakes are hot, and she burns her mouth a little with the first bite.

"Let me have one of those," her dad says.

Loretta wants to shove both potato cakes into her mouth at once so she doesn't have to give one away.

She hands him the one she already bit out of and he doesn't complain.

She eats the rest of the food in less than a minute in case he wants a bite out of her sandwich, too.

He drives too fast down the lane to the back lot, and pebbles hit the paint job. The car is fifteen years old already, so it's not like it matters, but he's the one who complains. By tomorrow it will be her mother's fault for the tiny scratches on the paint. By tomorrow it will be Loretta's fault for wearing that dress.

When she gets into her room, she opens the lunch box to make sure Gerald is still alive, and when she finds he is, she breathes a sigh of relief. Then she whispers, "Look at this one last time! I'm growing again." She peels off her sweaters and turns once to show off her dress and then she takes it off and puts it in a plastic shopping bag. She catches a glimpse of her naked body in her small jewelry box mirror and smiles. She closes the lid of the lunch box and lies on her bed. She has to do this so she won't die.

She gets dressed and grabs the bag with her dress in it, a can of lighter fluid that she keeps for the ring-of-fire act, and a box of matches. Climbs out her window. Walks to the far end of the lot. Lights the dress on fire. Watches it burn.

End scene. Curtain down. Audience applause.

CanIHelpYou?'s CallYouLater

Len says it's not worth calling the police on a Drive-Thru runner. Even if they catch them, all they do is bring them back to the store to pay and Len says it makes them angry.

"But they stole it," I say.

"Yes. And they'll be back for more," Len says.

Len is only here for an hour to check in on things, and he seems about as interested in this Drive-Thru robbery as I am in doing my homework. He goes back to the office and I'm left talking to the manager, Susan.

"The guy said he'd call me later," I say. "It was creepy."

"You know him?"

I run through my client list in my head. "No."

"You sure? Maybe he knows your parents."

"Definitely doesn't know my parents."

"He probably said it to distract you—you know, so he could take off like that without paying."

I can't explain the look the guy gave me when he said "Call you later," but it was the kind of thing you'd see on that government website for registered sex offenders.

I suddenly want to check his face, while it's still clear in my mind, against the sex offender database, but then the Drive-Thru bell sounds and I slip my headset back over my ears and say what I always say.

Three cars come one after the other and I feel jittery— more jittery than I should because that guy shook me. Each car arrives and I make them pay first. Always pay first. It's the primary rule of Drive-Thru. I wonder why I didn't think of this with the CallYouLater guy. I was looking at the girl in the passenger's seat. I couldn't see her face, but I saw how she sat, almost facing away from him, curling in on herself, shrinking.

That's what distracted me.

Now I really want to call the cops, but I know Len wouldn't listen to me and Susan would tell me that maybe the guy isn't kidnapping/trafficking girls and maybe my imagination is taking off from the runway that is my brain, but that's what the plane says and that's what the runway is for. *Something was wrong with that picture.* That's the name of my airport.

When I finally leave work, no word from Ian all day, I decide to skip texting him and just call him. My mother is always saying how my generation doesn't know how to use a phone properly.

"Dude," he says.

"Dude."

There's a weird silence. I'm not sure if it's me still distracted from CallYouLater guy or if something is wrong. Ever since our acid night/I started falling in love with him, Ian has been different.

"I skipped AP history today," he says finally.

"You love that class," I say.

"That research paper. My thesis statement was all over the place. All my sources were lame. I stopped caring."

I think about how I'm probably a bad influence on Ian. We should have never done that hit of acid. "I had a creep at the Drive-Thru tonight. It freaked me out."

"Creep how?"

"Stole food," I say. "Said he'd call me later."

"Ew," he says. "Do you know him?"

"I don't think so. He's older, you know? Had a girl in the car with him and she seemed scared. I didn't piece it together until a few minutes later. I feel like I just helped a girl get kidnapped or something."

"Probably not."

"How would you even know?"

I feel like he thinks I'm hysterical or something for thinking the most obvious thought in the world. He says, "Do you remember the car?"

"It's the guy who always asks me for straws. I know that much."

"Call the cops?" he asks.

"I don't know. Would they even care or believe me?" I say. "And what if I'm wrong?" *And what if they know me? What if they know how I really make money?*

"Then you tried—just in case. I mean, if you really think he was that creepy, then you should do something about it."

This is when my brain runway does its best work. The plane is in the queue, not taxiing yet. I consider the same guy has asked me for straws and condiments at least twice before tonight. I consider the fact that he must be local. I consider the fact that I didn't see the girl's face. No planes ever really take off from my airport.

"I won't be in tomorrow," Ian says. "They suspended me for a day."

"For skipping?"

"Mmm. My mom's freaking out."

"Dude, you're a genius. Can't you just come up with a thesis statement?"

I feel wrong talking about thesis statements while nearly calling the cops on a guy who's probably fine and isn't on the sex offender list. They teach us how to write a clear thesis statement long before they teach us how to deal with creepy-maybe-sex-offenders.

By the time my dad comes to pick me up, I'm scrolling through the sex offender registry on my phone browser. God, some of these people look like they climbed from the depths of Hell. I click the map view and as we drive home, I look around at how many there are. A lot of them just work around here. I knew a few worked at the battery factory because Mom rang her bell one day and we had a family meeting about it—*places to avoid: the mall and the battery factory*—but now I see a lot of them work at the bakery on Broad Street.

Makes me never want to eat another shoofly pie in my life.

THE FREAK LOVES
WHOOPIE PIES!

The Freak is warm. She misses winter and snow and big, fluffy coats. She closes her eyes.

The Freak is somewhere flat. Too flat. You-can-see-a-hundred-miles flat. You-can-see-your-neighbors flat. You-can-see-airplanes-descending-to-land flat. It's cold. If she was to guess, she'd say she was in Canada.

She closes her eyes and flickers.

Too hot. Palm trees. Flickers.

Top of a mountain and the wind is unbearable. Flickers.

A pebble beach in the rain. Green fields. This place is nice. There are sheep. The Freak loves sheep.

She searches her pocket for her lighter and flicks it and watches the flame. It blows out in less than a second, but it was real and that's what matters. There are no people on the pebble beach. She walks to the edge of the fenced-in field and she baas like a sheep. The sheep baa back at her. She is conversing with sheep. She decides to ask them where she should go next. She says, "Baa-baa-baaaa."

A medium-sized sheep approaches the fence. She looks pregnant or ready to sheer—The Freak wouldn't know because The Freak isn't a sheep expert or anything. The sheep says, "Go back to Pennsylvania. That kid with the shovel still needs your help."

The Freak says, "Okay. Thank you."

The sheep says, "Baa."

Pennsylvania. All The Freak knows about Pennsylvania is that her father hates it there. He grew up there, so this was a luxury—to hate where you're from. All The Freak knows about Pennsylvania is that artists in residence don't get paid much, because that's the job her mother was working on the night The Freak nearly got punched by Kelly Pointer.

The Freak walks to the water's edge. She's pretty sure she's in Ireland or Scotland or New Zealand or one of those places where the grass stays vibrant green all year and the sheep speak English.

She flickers. Tries to aim herself toward Pennsylvania like guided dreaming. She is surrounded by a herd of oryx. Their horns are the most amazing things she's ever seen—some two feet long. Pure spiral. She's fascinated. Fascinated until they start to run toward her with their heads down. Flickers.

The big church. The statue of Mary. A traffic light on a big intersection. The Freak spins slowly to take in her surroundings. She sees the row of houses where the shoveling boy lives.

She has the same coat on as the last time she was here, but it's warmer now. March sixteenth. Should be colder in Pennsylvania in mid-March.

The Freak walks. It's sunny and she follows the signs for a yard sale. She has ten dollars in her pocket. It's always there because she never spends it.

Six blocks later she's in a quieter part of town. Bigger houses, older trees, and people who tend their flower gardens. She sees the yard sale from down the block. People park and scan, leave their cars running, facing the wrong way on the wrong side of the road—people even park next to fire hydrants for a good deal.

The Freak walks to the unstable clothing rack that bends in the middle from the weight of the clothing no one is buying. She doesn't browse. She's here for a reason and she finds it because it's easy to find. She takes the dress to the woman who seems to be in charge and says, "How much?"

"Twenty."

"I have ten."

The woman dials her face left, then right as if she has channels. The Freak hopes the woman finds the channel where she'll take ten bucks. Not like it matters. She could just flicker out of there and pay nothing.

"Fifteen. It cost me more than a hundred."

"I have ten," The Freak says again, louder this time in case the woman didn't hear her right the first time.

The woman's face dials right and left again. A young woman interrupts. "How much for the play kitchen?"

"Forty," she says. She looks back at The Freak. Looks her up and down. "It's too small for you."

"It's not for me," The Freak answers. "Do I look like someone who wears sequins?"

"Fine," the woman says. She doesn't say the amount again. The Freak finally spends her ten dollars. Rolls up the dress and puts it into a grocery shopping bag the woman hands her. She walks south.

She has five miles to walk—she'd flicker if she could but she can't risk ending up in Montana or Namibia again. She takes her coat off and leaves it on an oil tank outside someone's house. She puts her free hand in her pocket and finds another ten-dollar bill. The Freak doesn't understand this. She stops at a mini market and buys a locally baked whoopie pie.

The whoopie pie is delicious.

She finally arrives at the place she needs to be—a small charity consignment shop in the city. She puts the dress on a hanger and puts it where it needs to be.

"You can't just leave things in here," the woman says.

The Freak pretends not to hear her and looks at herself in the wall mirror next to the racks of clothing. The Freak can barely see herself. It's either a trick of light or it's the side effect. She could be disappearing. She's not sure.

She goes outside and starts in a new direction. Toward the country. Toward the house in the woods—the house of Marla and Gottfried Hemmings.

Marla and Gottfried are well-known to The Freak.

The Freak is not well-known to Marla and Gottfried.

The Shoveler: Meet the Beach-Bum Grandson

When a ceiling fan falls, knocks over two gallons of water, and you're so busy cleaning up the water that it takes the client's beach-bum grandson to say, "What are you going to do about the paint?" while he points to an entire gallon of yellow wall paint spilled on the perfect oak floor to even notice that the paint fell, it always happens in slow motion.

I shouldn't judge the grandson—Malcolm—but he's not nice to Marla and he never showers and he's always talking about poverty. I'm not sure what he knows about poverty—in the two months I've been working in Marla and Gottfried's house, he's flown to Jamaica three times.

Malcolm is cool about the spilled paint, though. He jumps into action and that's good because I wouldn't have known where Marla keeps the shitty towels or the scrub brush. When he asked what I was going to do about the paint, he wasn't being a smartass; he was genuinely concerned about the paint. I was still beating myself up for not putting the tarp down yet, for maybe breaking the ceiling fan, for being allowed to breathe after making a mistake of this magnitude.

"Dude—if you wouldn't have noticed, it would have hit the rug. Thanks."

"It's cool. They're out for at least another hour. We can totally get this done before then," he says.

"I didn't think you were the kind to help," I say. But then I hear myself and I sound like an asshole. "I mean, I thought this wasn't something you'd do."

"If you want me to stop, I can," he says. He's got two paint-soaked towels in his hands and is maneuvering them into a black trash bag.

"Thanks. No. Don't stop. I meant something else. It didn't come out right."

"It's starting to dry at the edges," he says.

"It's latex. We can wash it once we get it all off the floor."

"I never thought Marla would go for yellow," Malcolm says. "She's not usually bold like this."

"It took me a while to convince her," I say. "Gottfried loves it, though."

"They're so weird," Malcolm says.

"Yeah."

"You have no idea what it's like having them as grand-parents," he says.

"Yeah."

"Seriously. It's hell," he says.

I don't want to explain my life to Malcolm. I don't want to explain that I wish I knew who my grandparents are. In fact, Malcolm's complaining enlarged my invisible family tree. I never really thought about the fact that I could have four living grandparents. Four people who might be wondering where I am. Four people who might give me Christmas presents or wish me a happy birthday.

I'm not sure what to say.

I concentrate on whether the rags I'm using are clear of color. I'm trying to see just how much more I have to wipe up before it seems as if I didn't make this huge mess. Malcolm is at the edges of where the puddle was and he's using a scrubbing pad to get the dried bits off. I'd say we're about five minutes from erasing this mistake from history.

"What do you want me to do with the can?" he asks.

Shit. The can. I look over and into it. It sat on its side for so long while I was busy cleaning the water spill that there isn't but an inch left in it. Nothing to salvage. "Close it up and put it with the others in the garage?" I say. "Shit. I guess I'm going to have to explain how a gallon of paint disappeared."

"They're not going to notice," Malcolm says.

"They notice everything," I argue. "You just said. It's hell."

"They're very happy with you so far. They can't stop talking about the great job you did upstairs," he says. "And they think you have great manners. Marla wishes you could replace me, I'm sure."

"Nah. They love you. They're just weird."

Malcolm looks abruptly heartbroken. He wipes the area down one more time and we walk around where the spill was. The floor looks shinier in that one area than the rest of the floor. We say, in unison, "We should mop the whole floor."

Malcolm puts his hand out to indicate that he's got this. He also points to the ceiling and nods as if to tell me to get back to the job I'm supposed to be doing. I wanted to get all the first-floor ceilings done this weekend, and now I just feel like driving home and going to bed.

Malcolm returns with a mop and a bucket. I ask, "What time do you think they'll be back?"

"Why?"

"I need a smoke."

He opens some app that allows him to see where Marla's phone is. "She's all the way over at the farmers' market. It's like an hour away. Plenty of time."

I go sit on the picnic table on Marla and Gottfried's back deck. I light a smoke and try to take a deep breath at the same time because, holy shit, I just spilled a gallon of paint on their floor and nearly ruined their rug and I may have broken their ceiling fan and I should have asked Malcolm for help when I was doing that but I didn't and I wonder why. All in one deep breath, I think that and a million other things. Only when I take a few more deep breaths do I see that my knees are yellow from the paint and my hands are covered and I realize there is no way to hide the whole stupid debacle from Marla when she comes in. She knows I'm doing ceilings today. All white. No yellow.

Malcolm comes outside. He sits down next to me and puts a cigarette in his mouth. Only it's not a cigarette.

"You look stressed," he says.

"I'm so fucked."

"Not really. I mean, Marla's a reasonable woman for the most part."

"I know this is gonna sound like I'm being a dick, but you should be happy you have them, you know. Not everybody has grandparents—let alone grandparents who would take a kid in. Like—you know. I mean, I don't know what's up with your parents or why you're here, but it's nice that you have a place to go."

None of that came out right.

Malcolm nods while inhaling from his not-cigarette. He offers it to me. I pass.

"That sounded like I'm a dick. But I hope you know what I mean."

He nods again, slowly, like he's either taking it in or trying to figure out what to say or both. But he doesn't say anything.

"I only have a mom," I say. "I don't even know who my dad *is*."

"My dad's dying of cancer," Malcolm finally says, still nodding.

"Oh."

"Yeah. It's fucked up."

"But he takes you to Jamaica like twice a month," I say.

"Beats him just dying here and it being the only thing I remember about him, I guess," Malcolm says. "I'd rather go to treatments with him, though. I miss my room and my stuff, and Marla's always trying to make me eat shit I don't like to eat."

"I've heard," I say.

"You should see what we eat in Jamaica. I'd eat anything, really. Except lamb. I hate lamb," he says. He stubs out the joint on the sole of his shoe and puts the half he didn't smoke in his wallet. "I'm gonna stay down there when he dies. I have friends and people who can take care of me and stuff."

"And a girl, I bet."

Malcolm nods. "And a girl."

"I think I'm just going to clean up and take off before they get home," I say. "I'm sorry about your dad. That must suck."

"I'll help you put the fan back up if you want."

"Nah. I still have to do that room. I'll put it in the garage and get the ceiling done tomorrow."

Malcolm goes inside first. I finish my cigarette, go inside, and move my supplies back into the garage. I think about how Malcolm has a plan and I wonder what my plan is. So far, my plan has been to follow Mom around everywhere. That's probably not normal.

On my drive home, I pass a lot of farmland. It's all dead now, soon ready for spring planting. I've always felt like I belong in those fields—not those specific ones, but just working outside or something, like I'm supposed to be a farmer. I don't even know how often to water a houseplant. This is probably the stupidest thought I had all day except for thinking I could take a ceiling fan down by myself.

Jake & Bill are coming for your daughters

The tuxedo shop is full of scary-looking guys. Bill Marks is getting married. No one ever would have guessed that this could happen, least of all Jake. Best man. He's trying to look happy, but tuxedoes aren't his thing. Never been to any event that required more than a T-shirt, jeans, and shitkicker boots.

Jake's been waiting years to go to a gathering. Not a wedding. A gathering—the kind Bill and the rest of his groomsmen go to. Bill said he had to wait until he was eighteen, but Jake knows there are guys there his age. He and Bill walk around with Bill's snake—school parking lot to school parking lot—and talk to the other boys like them. Boys like them. That's what Bill told him to look for since he got to middle school. *Look for other guys like us. Bring them to see the snake after school. The more, the better. We'll win this country back.*

Now Bill's picking out which tuxedo he thinks looks good on him. "Tails?" he says. Bill's two friends, both shaved to bald, shake their heads. *No. No tails. Guys like us don't wear tails.* Jake just shrugs. He'll wear what he has to.

"Don't look so sad, Jake," Bill says. "Didn't you know the best man always gets laid at the reception?"

Jake rolls his eyes. "Don't need to get laid."

Bald friend #1 says, "You getting enough with the high school girls?"

Bill says, "Let's just say Jake doesn't know the meaning of the word *no*."

Jake feels discomfort crawl up his legs. Sweat forming at the back of his neck. Bill's bragging on his girls when he hasn't had a girl since their trip to New Jersey and Bill knows it. And she didn't want to do it anyway. Pissed Jake off. He isn't responsible for what he does when he's pissed off. That's what Bill said.

"How about this?" Bill asks. "Real mobster shit, right?"

The bald friends nod. Jake nods. Whatever it takes to get out of the tuxedo store.

On the way home, Bill turns to Jake and says, "Ashley says I can't keep the snake. Will you take care of her for me?" He rolls through a stop sign and doesn't even notice.

"Ashley or the snake?"

Bill laughs. "I'm serious."

"On one condition," Jake says. Bill nods to hear it. "Before you get married and leave me in that house with those freaks we call parents, you take me to a gathering."

Bill looks thoughtful for a minute. Nods. Says, "Anything for my little brother." Then he runs a second stop sign. Two blocks later he rolls through a third stop sign with a cop right across the intersection. Bill waves. The cop waves back.

The roads are wet from spring rain. The mud from the new addition to their development covers everyone's cars. Jake and Bill's dad tried to get the construction company to shell out for neighborhood car washes at the last township meeting, but no one wanted to listen to him. Mr. Marks thinks he has power he doesn't have. That's what people say about him, anyway. Jake's heard it at school. *So what if he's the manager of some company?*

He's not anyone special. Jake isn't anyone special, either, and so Jake's not responsible for anything he does when he's pissed off. That's why he spends most of his days in the in-school suspension room.

Fact is, Jake can't see a future without Bill around. Bill's the closest thing he has to a father even though his father lives right there in that house with them. *Cuck.* That's what Bill calls their dad. *He's an immigrant-loving cuck.*

Jake rarely thinks about how their mother is half Mexican. She's more white than Mexican, but she speaks Spanish. Or she can. She doesn't because Bill told her that in America, we speak English. Had her pinned up against the kitchen wall and was about to beat her in the face with the toaster. She's never spoken a word of Spanish around them again.

Loretta Bleeds

The bites never heal because Loretta scratches at them every night. Her sheets are pockmarked with brown stains. Probably six months since her mother last washed them.

Act Two, Scene Whatever. It's a Saturday; two weeks to Easter. It's been more than two weeks since her dad took her to Arby's and stole food. Since then, she's eaten small freezer pizzas or stale cheese sandwiches. Three nights she didn't eat anything at all because no one told her to. The actors who play her parents have been working really hard on their fight scene. They replay it every night and the husband character is working on his improvisation. Sometimes she hears the sound effects—the slaps and kicks and breaking things. He's really coming along for a guy who only has nights to rehearse.

Even on Saturdays, he leaves for work at five in the morning, which gives her mother time to practice lines between rehearsals. Loretta thinks maybe she'll take her mother to the laundry room to wash sheets today. But when she goes into the living room, her mother isn't there. She's not in the kitchen area either. Loretta checks her parents' bedroom door and it's open a crack. She presses her body against it so she can walk in but something is blocking the door. She pushes harder and it doesn't budge.

"Mom?"

No answer.

"Mom?"

She pushes harder. Whatever's blocking the door isn't hard like furniture. It's soft. Loretta presses again. She hears a low moan.

"Mom? Wake up. Mom?"

Nothing. The door is only open about an inch. Loretta can't see in. She gets on the floor and wiggles her fingers in the crack that's open and tries to feel what's in the way. She feels hair.

"Mom?"

Nothing. No moan. Nothing.

Loretta sits in the hallway with her back against the door. She doesn't want to push too hard, but if her mother is what's blocking her entry, she knows she needs to get in. *Could be a pile of laundry. Could be a bag of trash. Could be my mother.*

This was not in the script.

She braces her legs on the opposite wall and presses her back into the door. No sound. A little movement. She rocks until the door is open a few more inches. And she finds what she knew she would find.

There's always a surreal moment before dialing 911. A moment when you think you should do something else. A moment when you think it's all a joke or a mistake or maybe you're just not seeing things right.

Loretta squeezes through the bedroom door and leans over her mother. She turns her on her side. Listens for breathing. Barely there. But there. Barely.

"Mom?" She shakes her. "Mom, wake up."

There's always a moment before calling 911 when you don't see anything but the foreground. You don't think to look for weapons or evidence of an intruder. You only see fleas jumping and Loretta marvels at how high they bounce and how she wishes she could catch a few and train them. Add them to her troupe. She thinks of Gerald and how he'll feel replaced and how low his self-esteem already is. *Poor little guy will never get out of his father's shadow.*

There's always a moment before calling 911 when you think you're the one in trouble. You think you're doing something wrong. Your life is wrong if you have to call 911. Your thinking must be faulty.

"Mom! MOM! I'm calling nine-one-one. If you're okay, show me so I don't have to call them."

No movement. Barely breathing. Fleas jumping. *Did one of them just flip? Do they think this is open audition?*

There's always a moment before you call 911 when you think this must be your fault. You overslept. You ditched school last Wednesday. You burned that blue dress and maybe when they come and look for evidence they'll find it in ashes, in the corner of the lot. Maybe they'll think you're the problem, not the mother barely breathing on the bedroom floor, not You-know-who.

You've heard them on TV. Those 911 calls. The callers are always so desperate and crazy. You don't want to be one of those. You want to be calm. You want to express your concern and not seem like you come from a place like this. A place where you know you have to call 911.

Loretta shakes her mother one last time and looks at her face. Pale. Bruised. Bitten. Drawn sad like a clown in the center ring, waiting to be cheered up by the next act.

Loretta knows her lines. She's practiced them. She dials the phone. "Hello?" she says. "Nine-one-one? We have an emergency."

Audience sits motionless. Loretta's improvisation has always been impressive.

Marla Still Believes Blood Is Sacred

Marla has a secret. She's had it since 1962 or 1970, depending on how you look at it. That's a long time to have a secret. It's a long story, and she never finds the time to tell it. It's a mix-up and a solution at the same time.

Fact: If Marla's mother hadn't done what she did in 1962, Marla wouldn't be alive right now and she would have never married Gottfried and they would have never had five beautiful babies and they would have never had such success in real estate and they wouldn't have this house and they wouldn't have the money they do.

Telling the secret wouldn't make those things go away, but it's too late to tell now and it's not like any of her children would understand. Things were different in 1962. Some things. Other things are the same. Any time Marla thinks about the secret she's vague like this because details are the problem. Details are always the problem.

Gottfried insisted on going all the way across town to the farmers' market and she doesn't like leaving the painter boy in the house by himself. But Gottfried wanders and squeezes grapefruits and asks vendors about which cut of pork is best, and he stops and samples the new peanut brittle on sale at the candy booth.

"We have to get home," she says.

"I'm just tasting this. It won't take that long."

"I mean we should leave now."

"Why leave? I wanted to get some fried chicken at that place." He points to the fried chicken stand. Marla's heart sinks. She thinks of her father and what he'd say about people who ate fried chicken.

"I don't want that boy in our house alone for too long."

"He's not alone. Malcolm's there."

Marla nods because when Gottfried has an idea about food, she knows she can't change his mind.

When he asks if she'd like fried chicken, she says no, and skips eating anything at all, which is dumb because she knows she's hungry and if she doesn't eat when she's hungry, she can get so dizzy that sometimes she faints.

She ignores her stomach and waits for Gottfried to finish.

"We have to go, okay? Now."

Gottfried looks at her, concerned. "Are you all right?"

"I'm fine."

"I wanted to get some of that milk I got last time. The nut stuff. I'll grab it and then we can go."

Marla breathes in and exhales slowly. The market spins. She feels warm. *Probably a hot flash*. Marla hasn't had a hot flash in years. She walks behind Gottfried to the booth where they sell cashew milk and her eyes try to focus, but trying just makes her more dizzy. She closes her eyes and hopes.

She doesn't hear Gottfried buying two pints of milk. She sees it through blurry eyes and she feels the counter under her elbow as she leans. But she can't hear.

I'm having a stroke. I can't make it to the car. I'm going to pass out. I'm going to die because Gottfried had to have his *soul* food. I feel like I'm melting in this coat. Too warm for a coat. I can't move my arm to unbutton it. I can't move my eyes. I can't see. I can't hear.

I'm going to die in the farmers' market surrounded by immigrants and Amish people. This is not where I wanted to die. I never told Gottfried about the blood.

He'll never know unless I tell him. He has no idea what he married.

Marla hears the clatter of the antique stand's jewelry rack. She feels earrings and necklaces fall on her. She reaches for anything to grab hold of, but nothing is there. She can't tell if she's on the floor or floating. She's dying. She knows that. She's dying with a secret that has swallowed her up.

Loretta Has Found a New Holloway

The ambulance cast isn't on set yet, so Loretta grabs a small cardboard jewelry box from her bedroom and starts to collect the fleas that are jumping over her mother's barely breathing body. She tries to find the one who does flips. She catches about five and puts the box lid on. Then she opens it to test the new talent. The flipper is there. He tries to escape with a somersault the minute she opens the box.

"This won't make Gerald very happy," she says, "but you're perfect. He'll see that. He'll know it's for the good of the show."

Sirens sound in the distance as Loretta puts the jewelry box in her backpack next to the circus lunch box. She knows how to do this. She's rehearsed the last scene of Act Two a hundred times. Even the unscripted parts. The unscripted parts are her favorites. Life is about going off script anyway.

Wardrobe has dressed her mother in a pair of flannel pajamas that don't match. Loretta looks around for a bathrobe and finds the worn fleece one her mother wears every day. She puts it around her mother's shoulders and grabs the new afghan Loretta gave her for Christmas and puts it overtop. As the sirens grow louder, she realizes that she should go to the bathroom now because she doesn't want to pee by accident in the ambulance.

The sirens still sound far enough away.

She stops in her room and takes care of the curse. She's breathy and flushed by the time she gets to the bathroom and pees. Sirens grow louder. She checks to make sure her pits don't smell and she puts on deodorant anyway. She uses her mother's so she'll smell like her. Goes back to her room for her two bags—one, a backpack with her circus equipment and the troupe; the other, a suitcase with everything she wants to keep from her room inside it.

Sirens stop—now it's just the sound of a truck barreling down the stone lane—and Loretta steps onto the porch of the wagon and waits. It's there she gets a new idea for a dress. Thin straps, and sequined—maybe red. Something about the color red is right for now. The powder blue was a child's life. Now she's a circus woman, not a circus girl. Things have changed. And if her mother doesn't live through the day, things will change more by nightfall.

The wagon feels like a stranger's house with strangers in it. No one ever comes in except their cast of three. And the fleas. And a few times, police or the landlord. Loretta sits in her mother's chair in front of the TV. The TV is off. She was told to sit here by the ambulance men who know the script better.

She doesn't hear what they're saying even though they're loud and are clearly saying things—just not to her. Soon, they have her mother on a stretcher and are maneuvering her down the steps of the wagon and sliding her into the back of the truck. Only when they look like they're leaving without her does Loretta speak.

"I'm coming with you," she says.

"Um—"

"I have to come with you," she says.

"You can ride up front," the guy says.

"No problem." Loretta walks slowly, taking each step in a measured, dramatic stride, lugging her two bags with her. She walks in front of the ambulance and they seem to be waiting for her, which is not an ambulance's job, waiting. The driver is mesmerized, though, as if Loretta were already wearing her red-sequined gown. She can see him saying something to her, but she can't hear over the roar of the crowd. Act Two is over. Act Three is going to be the best ever.

CanIHelpYou?: Kiss Me I'm Irish

"Welcome to Arby's. Happy Saint Patrick's Day! Want to try our limited-time Irish green Jamocha shake?"

No one ever says yes to the shake. The only green I'm selling today is between five and seven. Ten customers for me—five of them new since Jake Marks got another two quarter ounces off me last week. I don't trust that kid, but I'm five hundred bucks away from buying my own car.

We do what we do to get what we need.

And I need a car.

My mother seems to think I need an Easter dress. I've never understood this because we don't go to church on Easter. All we do is go to her mother's house and pose for stupid pictures and then eat ham and three kinds of potatoes.

I try Ian three times, but he's not answering his phone. I'm pretending I don't care but I do. When I see him in school he's nice and all, but he stays after for debate club and we don't walk home together anymore. This happened last year, too, so I try not to get paranoid.

It's not that, though.

He said this thing to me about two weeks ago, right after the CallYouLater guy. It was a day or two after, and I was still kind of obsessed.

Kidnapped girls. I can't get away from them.

He rolled his eyes at something I'd said. About maybe going into the police and talking to them about it.

"You're so white." That's what he said.

I've been thinking about it ever since. I stopped thinking about the maybe-kidnapped girl and started thinking about how white I am. So white. I am so white.

If you're best friends with the black kid, you don't have to notice you're white, you know? I never thought of myself as white when I was around Ian and I never thought of him as mixed race. He was just Ian. But we're not in fourth grade anymore.

Being one of five black kids in a high school of all white kids is not like fourth grade at all.

Being a black boy growing into a black man here in this white town is not like fourth grade at all.

I talked about going to talk to the police the same as I'd talk about going to Arby's for a Beef 'n Cheddar. So convenient.

There's another complication.

I'm definitely in love with him.

You think this is some typical white-girl thing. Being attracted to the black kid in school. Maybe you think it's part of my badassery, as if Ian were some symbol for me being cool, same as scoring you Percocet. That's how the other white kids treat him. The football players make friends with him during a group project and in the hallways they can say, "Hey, bruh! What's up?" and they never have to think about how white they are. They get to run stop signs, drink beer, and do all kinds of stupid shit and they never think about why they get away with it. I guess I do that, too. Maybe I'm just another white kid to Ian, now. But what Ian and I have—or had—was different. I can feel him kissing me on the couch in his living room as if it just happened.

Loretta, Act Three: Cold Open

"I just want to see her!" Loretta yells. "She's my mother!"

The actor playing the nurse behind the desk tells Loretta that she'll have to wait. She's said this eleven times already, and it's not even noon. She tells Loretta to go take a walk. Tells her she will take care of Loretta's suitcase. Tells her it will be a while. Tells her to not worry. Asks her if there's anyone else coming to take care of her.

"I take care of myself, thank you very much."

Loretta does a double take at the nurse. Makeup did a great job on the dark circles under her eyes. Then Loretta walks out the door of the emergency room. She gets to the sidewalk and opens her flea circus lunch box and asks the troupe which way she should turn. They can't agree, so she closes the lid again and goes right.

She doesn't come into the city very often. The sets are well built and realistic. Beautiful. There are restaurants here with food from other places. One is Greek. One is Thai. One is Moroccan. Loretta wishes she had enough money to try any of these but all she has in her pocket are four dollar bills and two packets of Arby's horseradish sauce. She walks past a few clothing stores for ladies like her teachers. A tattoo parlor. A lawyer's office. A music shop. A pet store with a sign that says REPTILES A SPECIALTY!

She comes to a thrift shop—mostly woven scarves and modest clothing in the window—but something tells her to go inside. There's a rack of prom dresses in the back. Or dressy dresses. Formal things with tulle and satin, a pair of matching bridesmaid dresses. Something sparkles at her. Red. Red sequins. And Loretta grabs at it like there are hundreds of shoppers when she's the only customer in the store.

She holds it up to her body and it's probably too big but that's better than too small. It's ankle length—no more bared knees—with a slit up the right side, but not too high up. The straps are spaghetti style but thicker—an inch maybe—and sturdy. She makes a joke in her head about lasagna straps when the actor playing the woman at the counter asks, "Can I help you with anything?"

"I want this dress."

Look at Loretta. Look at her unwashed hair and her dirty teeth and her bitten-up skin and her ears too big for her head. Look at her lunch box and her eyes that shine as if she were not the thing you see before you but the thing she sees in her mind. Ringmistress.

"It's a pretty dress," the woman says.

"I have to have it," Loretta says.

"God finds mysterious ways."

Loretta scowls. "Well, he can't just show up and buy me this dress." She walks toward the counter still holding it close to her chest. "I have three dollars."

The woman laughs. "Oh, sweetheart, that's got a price tag of thirty."

"I have three dollars," Loretta says.

The woman just gives her a pathetic smile, then purses her lips. "You're barely a size one if I was to guess. That's a ten, easily."

Loretta looks at her sideways. "You check dress size on every customer before you sell them things? This is the weirdest store ever."

They stand, staring at each other.

The woman finally buckles. "I'll take three dollars."

Loretta throws in one of the two Arby's sauce packets for good measure and doesn't even stay for a bag or a business card. She doesn't say thank you, either, because that bitch just took three of her last four dollars.

Loretta heads back toward the hospital with the dress wrapped around her neck, her face framed by red sequins.

When she walks through the emergency room doors, the first actor she sees is her father. The second actor she sees is a police officer. The third actor she sees is the nurse who told her she'd keep her suitcase safe.

This was in the script, so she's not surprised.

None of them see her, so she turns and walks back out the door and finds another entrance to a different part of the hospital. She asks an actor who's playing the role of security guard where the nearest bathroom is and goes inside and locks the door.

She slips her new dress over her T-shirt and lets it fall down over her hips and legs; the fabric is silky on her bare bottom and legs. She spins and trips over the extra at the lowest hem. She gathers the slack in the straps and says, "About four inches." That's how much she'd have to take off before she could wear it without tripping over it.

Five minutes later, Loretta is walking down the sidewalk again. She has her dress on over her clothes and the straps have two slipknots in them, like single-petal flowers on each shoulder.

When she arrives back in the emergency area of the hospital, the woman who was minding her suitcase isn't behind the counter anymore. A new actor plays the part now. Makeup must be practicing black circles today because this actor has them, too.

"Do you still have my suitcase?" Loretta asks.

"Are you Loretta?"

"Yes."

"Your mom wants to see you," she says. "Come on back."

As they walk through the hallway, the woman turns to her and says, "I love your dress."

"Thank you," Loretta says, and curtsies once in each direction, bowing her head so she doesn't get hit in the face with thrown roses.

The Shoveler: Marla Really Has a Thing for Easter

I don't really know what to say to Mom when we sit down to eat on Saturday night. I've changed so I'm no longer covered in my yellow mistake. I've showered the embarrassment off my skin and it's down in the sewers now.

I don't have much to say to Mom, really. Since the whole thing at school, we haven't talked a lot, and I'm so busy at Marla and Gottfried's house we never see each other.

"These mashed potatoes are different."

That's what I decide to say. *These mashed potatoes are different.*

"I added onions and cheese," she says. "Are you working every day this week again?"

I nod while chewing on my different mashed potatoes.

"You must be making a fortune," she said.

"They really have a thing for Easter," I say. "So I have to work until I get it done because I guess they decorate? Don't know. Easter is a big deal. That's all I know."

Mom stops eating and looks at me. I give her the why-are-you-looking-at-me-that-way face. "What's their last name?" she asks.

I shrug even though I know that Marla and Gottfried's last name is Hemmings. It makes me think about last names. Mom's and mine is Smith. Mom always says her name in a weird way, stressing the Smith part. *Amber SMITH.* That's how she says it.

I just say mine like normal people say their names.

"Weird that they're that into Easter," she says. "Do they have a big party or something?"

"They barely talk to me," I say. "I'm just the painter."

"You've been there most days for two months. You'd think they'd be nicer."

"They're nice. They just don't talk to me. I'm working," I say.

"Huh," she says. "I knew a family that made a big deal out of Easter when I was growing up. I always found it weird. Must be super religious, eh?"

"Not really."

"Huh."

"How's the car lot going? Did you sell anything this week?"

Mom shakes her head. "I just do the paperwork. I told you that already."

"Did you ask them about a cheap car for me?"

She shakes her head and chews. "Forgot," she manages, with a cheekful of mashed potato/onions/cheese.

"Maybe I can come over one day and talk to the guys. There's a car auction near here. I bet they could find me something cheap."

"I'll ask them on Monday," she says, but I know she won't ask them on Monday because she probably wants me around and not in my own car going to work or other places. I'm growing up. I'm all she has. And she can't shoplift me in the deep pockets of her spring coat.

Mike comes over at seven to apologize for missing dinner. I didn't even know he was invited.

"Small neighborhood emergency," he says. "My brother's sister-in-law has a sinkhole."

Mom seems unimpressed.

I say, "Is it big?" while trying to navigate Mike's family tree. It must be huge if he's helping his brother's sister-in-law. They all live near one another. Must be nice.

"Nearly swallowed her car," Mike says.

"What'd you do?" I ask.

"Blocked it off with cones and caution tape. City says they'll be out later this week. By that time, the whole street could go under!" Mike says.

Mom looks down at her phone and grunts.

He looks at me. "Wanna watch some baseball?"

Marla & Gottfried's Saturday Field Trip Overtime

Gottfried has always been practical. It's something Marla found attractive from day one. And so, when a crowd gathers—the antique seller, the cashew-milk seller, a few Mennonites who sell meat—Gottfried fans his wife's face and tells them to stand back.

He hands Marla's purse to the cashew-milk seller and says, "In her wallet. The change-purse part. Smelling salts."

A man says, "I'll call nine-one-one."

Gottfried levels an intense stare at the man and says, "Don't call nine-one-one." He holds the smelling salts under his wife's nose.

The cashew-milk lady hands back Marla's purse and asks, "She gonna be okay?"

"Yes," he answers, "she's always doing something dramatic." He laughs a little to put the woman at ease. She's very nice. She's the reason he tried the cashew milk in the first place. He doesn't really like the taste outside the chocolate flavor. It's her. She's the reason he's been insisting on trips to the farmers' market. She gives free samples of raw vegetable juice that sometimes burns Gottfried's eyes out. Nothing like that around when he was younger. Just regular juice. Orange, apple, the occasional cranberry. This woman sells juice that makes Gottfried's system really work again. He reckons it's the ginger or the turmeric. Either way, things work—things that haven't worked in years. Also, the cashew-milk woman is beautiful. She dyes her hair interesting colors. She wears low-cut tops and has tattoos.

"What in the world are you doing?" That's Marla saying that. She wakes up and finds her husband talking to the tattooed girl who sells the nut milk. She seems to be on the floor. There's gaudy jewelry all around her. Two young Mexican kids stand, wide-eyed, as if Marla's fainting were the most exciting thing they saw all day.

Gottfried helps her up slowly and apologizes to the antique seller, who is collecting the jewelry from the floor.

The Mennonites go back to their meat stand.

The cashew-milk lady goes back behind her counter.

Marla and Gottfried stand, feeling old, in the middle of the walkway. People have been avoiding that area, and Gottfried feels bad that he may be losing the cashew-milk lady some business.

He takes Marla's arm and walks toward the parking lot.

She wants to walk more slowly, but he hurries her. He feels a rush of embarrassment. Like the day with the robins. Like the time when he was ten and he broke his arm sledding. Marla asks, "I didn't V when I was out, did I? It smells like V." Gottfried doesn't answer.

Only when he gets to the car does he look at Marla's face. She seems like a little girl—suddenly simple as she climbs into her seat. Gottfried gets in his side and starts the car. Marla sighs and puts her head back on the headrest and says, "Oh!"

Gottfried sees her jolt in pain and puts his hand on the back of her head. There, he finds a lump the size of a plum. "Shit," he says. "That's not good, kiddo."

"It's probably nothing," she says.

"Doctor should see it. We're not twenty anymore."

Marla doesn't answer. Gottfried drives.

Gottfried swears at a car that cuts him off. "Marla? You okay?"

"I'm fine," Marla says. "Is that your phone ringing?"

Gottfried's ringtone is set to the song "Jingle Bells" all year long, and indeed, it's ringing but Gottfried doesn't answer it.

Marla sounds far away when she says, "I wish you'd change that damn ringer song. It's embarrassing."

Gottfried makes a right turn toward the hospital emergency room.

"The hospital!" Marla squeals. "What're you bringing me here for?"

"Just getting you checked out."

"I don't want to be near sick people," Marla says, sounding far away again.

Gottfried is worried.

"Sick people throw up," she says.

"Sick people cough on me," she says.

"Sick people die," she says. "Like Harry."

"Harry isn't dead," Gottfried says. "He's gonna be fine. Got our genes, didn't he?"

"When he comes back from that stupid island, I'm going to lay down the law about that boy." Marla can't remember the boy's name. *Some temporary memory issue. Getting old is weird.*

"Yep, got our genes. He'll be fine," Gottfried repeats to himself.

Malcolm Worries Sometimes

Dad isn't answering his phone, and I have a feeling he went to Jamaica without me. There's no other explanation for not seeing him on a weekend. Marla told me that he wasn't feeling well, but that just makes me worry.

Fact: Dad never says he's not feeling well.

Fact: Dad must be feeling like crap if he didn't want me around this weekend.

Fact: Maybe the treatments aren't working.

The painting kid left more than two hours ago. Marla and Gottfried were supposed to be home by now. It's past dinnertime. Marla is a stickler for dinnertime.

For the last hour I walked around the house turning lights on and off depending on what feels least scary. All the lights on feels least scary, so I kept them all on. I sent three emails to Eleanor and she didn't write back because she's probably walking the beach looking for tourists to sell her bracelets to. She has to go to the library to check her mail anyway. Or school. And it's not like I'm her first priority. I don't think I should be, I guess. But right now I need her.

I try to do the thing Dad's Ruth told me to do when I used to be nervous about flying. I breathe in peace and breathe out stress. In. Out. Peace. Stress. It doesn't work, not even with all the lights on.

I check the phone-finder app on my phone and see that my grandparents are at the hospital.

I call Dad again and he doesn't answer.

I call Gottfried and he doesn't answer either.

If I had anyone else to call, I'd call them. But I don't have anyone else to call. Being an only child is like being that guy in David Bowie's "Space Oddity." You're all by yourself, floating up in space and the world is beautiful, but the best you can do is sing into the blackness.

I mean, when times are dark, anyway.

Times are dark.

I don't know how to drive but Marla's BMW is in the garage and it's telling me to drive it. I mow Gottfried's lawn sometimes on his ride-on mower and that can't be too different from driving a car. Right?

I give them all a cutoff time.

Eight. At eight o'clock, I'll drive myself to the hospital to see what's going on.

If Dad thinks he's going to die without me there with him, he's wrong. If Dad thinks I want the college tuition in his will any time soon, he's wrong. I don't want to go to college; I don't even want my own shoes.

I can't make it to eight o'clock. The BMW is screaming at me. I've got the keys, and I click the remote start button. After a minute of carbon monoxide, I open the garage door. *Dude— you've just proven that you shouldn't be driving a car.*

Dad always told me that I'd never be perfect because no one is perfect. He told me I'd always make mistakes. He told me the key to life is making smarter and smarter mistakes. I can't tell if stealing Marla's BMW is a smarter mistake than my last mistake . . . which was probably smoking half a joint at the picnic table while I was talking to the painter kid. I don't usually smoke the stuff, but sometimes Dad's business cards don't do the trick. The cards are laced with THC and CBD—the perfect mix to cure cancer—but nothing like the high-grade shit he has stashed. Plus, eating paper gets old. Anyway, I'm not really stoned anymore. I'm sure I'll be fine.

The BMW has a very feisty accelerator compared to Gottfried's lawn mower. It's also a lot quieter, and that's good because I have to concentrate. Backing out of the garage is easy enough. The driveway, steep and curved, isn't so bad. The road out of the cul-de-sac is a straight run, and I stop at the stop sign like I've been doing this all my life. *Malcolm Hemmings, lifetime driver of many cars.*

The three back roads I have to take to get to the highway are twisty and I can't figure out how to keep my eye on the road and the speedometer at the same time. It was fine when I was alone on the first road, but the second road has presented me with a challenge—a car behind me driving so close I can barely see anything. I have no idea if I'm driving too slowly. I know I'm doing forty miles per hour, but there are no speed limit signs.

The BMW has a rearview mirror that adjusts automatically.

As I navigate the curves in the road trying to ignore the car behind me, I think about how cool it would be to have human-automatically-adjusting rearview mirrors. No. Check that. I think we already have automatically adjusting rearview mirrors. That's why life is so fucking easy for so many people.

Like, before they invented the flush toilet with the ballcock like we have now, we were either shitting in outhouse pits or, if you had a toilet, you had to flush it by pouring water into the bowl. Either way, you had to deal with your shit. You had to look at it. You had to figure out what to do with it. Now, we all just flush and pretend we never shit in the first place.

Most of the kids I know at school just want to get their license, get a car, and get out of this town. They don't even know where they're going or how much it'll cost—as long as it's away from here. That's a flush toilet.

Speed limit is forty-five. Just passed a sign. I hit the gas a little and then the brake. Forty-five on this road is too fast. The car behind me will have to be patient. *Deal with my shit, car behind me.*

Then the car makes a weird move—a swerve—and it catches my attention. There's no passing, but he passes me and when he races by, his engine makes a race-car noise. When he gets in front of me, I see he's got those under-car lights—his are blue—and they light up the road and make his car look like a spaceship. I imagine the mouths he could feed with the money he spent on under-car lights. *Malcolm Hemmings, bleeding heart.*

Eleanor has to sell twenty bracelets at three American dollars a day to live. Every day. But the fact is, she'd still be alive if she didn't. She'd just be hungrier.

Oncoming cars are not like mowing the lawn. Have I mentioned that?

By the time I get to the gas station right before the highway entrance, I feel like I've been driving for five years. I'm sweating and nervous. I know the speed limit on the highway is sixty-five. That just seems impossible.

THE FREAK LOVES ACCIDENTAL FRUIT!

The Freak likes watching the shoveling boy paint. She knew the paint would spill. She knew the beach-bum grandson would help. When the boys came outside to talk, she flickered.

Now she's in a farmer's field. To her right is a patch of dead weeds—killed with something called Roundup. She marvels at the kill rate. To her left is a field that's sprouting random potato plants. *Go Spuds!* They are random because these are abandoned potatoes from last year's crop. Volunteers. They make more potatoes without meaning to if you leave them alone.

Accidental fruit. Accidental fruit that makes more fruit. Accidental seeds. More marvelous than the kill rate of Roundup.

Fact: It will rain enough for these plants to grow.

Fact: No one needs to do anything to help these plants thrive.

Fact: Sometimes accidental seeds are stronger because no one gives a shit about them.

Fact: The crop from a volunteer plant tastes just as good.

Loretta's audience sits in the orchestra seats. The Freak looks at them and says, "Potatoes are one thing. People are another. You can't abandon people and think they're going to be fine. People need things. Probably love most of all."

She closes her eyes. Disappears.

CanIHelpYou?'s Boxing Glove

I haven't sold one green milkshake all day. But I just made two hundred bucks selling weed to mostly strangers. Jake Marks has weird friends. At least three of them wouldn't be allowed to park in the high school parking lot.

The speaker beeps.

"Welcome to Arby's Drive-Thru. Can I help you?"

"Gimme a number two meal with a Coke."

God, sometimes I wish there was one of those big boxing gloves rigged into the speaker so I could press a button and punch people in the face.

"Eight fifty-four. Second window."

"What?"

"Eight fifty-four. Second window," I repeat.

"Weren't you trained to be nice to customers?"

I am pressing the boxing glove button. I am punching this person in the face a hundred times. I don't know what to say. I'm tired of being a doormat. I say, "Second window."

I have never spit on anyone's food. Never. I've never done anything remotely tempting like that, even though I've had opportunities. Suddenly, I'm looking around the Drive-Thru for anything to put on this guy's order.

I look under the register and there's glass cleaner. *Too obvious.* On the tiled floor, jammed in between the stainless-steel counter leg and the plastic wall protector is a lump of mop dirt—the kind that looks like a miniature dead mouse—part

209

mop fiber, hair, dirt, and the gray goo that probably used to be grease. Len has the place wired with two cameras in case cashiers steal money. I make it look like I'm picking up a dropped napkin. I drop the napkin first, then bend down to pick it up and grab the mop blob and put it next to the register. Then, as I'm bagging the sandwich, I open the wrapper while it's still inside the to-go bag and stick the blob into the roast beef sandwich and rewrap it. It feels equally wrong and right. *If the boxing glove was real, I wouldn't have to do this.*

I take my time filling the Coke. I think about what I've done. I consider sabotaging my own sabotage—dropping the sandwich on the floor and asking for a new one. I decide Gimme people deserve what they get.

I don't want to hold their hands through life anymore. I don't want to help them with the real problems that await. I don't want to help them understand that a simple please or thank-you goes a long way. I want them to fall into impossible love with their best friend. I want them to be kidnapped from a mall. Live in a tunnel.

"Eight fifty-four," I say when I open the window. I don't make eye contact even though I can feel his stare.

He hands me a ten-dollar bill.

I get his change and hand it back to him along with the Coke, and then I hand him the bag.

"Have a nice day," I say, and close the window.

I want to text Ian and tell him what just happened but I also want to pretend what happened didn't happen. Just like being in love with Ian. That can't happen. Nothing in my life can happen.

I feel like I'm getting a manicure in Wichita. Twenty-four hours a day.

I turn to Susan, my manager. "I don't feel well."

She doesn't say anything.

In the bathroom I'm in the tunnel. The stall walls are gray, like my submarine. A cockroach skitters by and says hello. I reply, "Hello." It stops and adjusts its eyeglasses and says, "You know you can't really be in love with your best friend."

I want to kill it, but I don't. It's probably not even there in real life. It's just my brain fucking with me. The tunnel. There are rules. The rules are: nobody helps you in here. No one can give you answers. No one can give you a hug. Other people come and go, but you can't see any of them. Makes you want to get out as soon as you can, but once you get out, you only want to go back in again. It's comfortable because it's what you're used to. The truth lives here. Underground.

"Do you have any spare toilet paper?" someone in the stall next to me asks.

The bathroom was empty when I got here.

"Hello?" she says. "This stall is out. I could really use a little if you have some."

I take a bunch of toilet paper and hand it under the stall wall.

"Where did you come from?"

"I don't know," she says. "I was in a field a minute ago and now I'm trying to find the boy with the shovel. I think."

"You sound as confused as I am."

"Just trying to find the right time to do the right things. It's hard to know."

211

"Yeah." I don't tell her that there's no right time to fall in love with your best friend.

"You're right," she says. "There's no right time for that."

I don't say anything because this has to be a hallucination, just like the bug with the glasses.

"Not so. I'm real. So was the bug. It was a cockroach."

I must be going crazy.

"You're not going crazy. Believe me. You should see what I have to deal with in a day."

"Who *are* you?" I ask.

"I'm The Freak. Who're you?"

"CanIHelpYou?, I guess."

"You're not really in love with him," she says. "You just have a bond is all. It's normal. Girls our age just want to find one guy who isn't out for pussy or a blow job."

"Um."

"Too harsh?" she asks.

"Don't know. Could be accurate. Not sure," I say. I remember her name from the night Ian and I tripped in the park. Hard to forget a name like that. "Is that what the shoveler guy wants from you?"

She blows her nose and I wonder if she's crying. Can't hear it in her voice, but it sounds like the kind of snot that only happens when you cry. "I don't know what he wants from me. I just showed up one night to help him and he thought I was the meaning of life or some shit."

"Oh."

"I'm hungry. Any chance you can give me some food when we get out of here?"

I think about what I just did. How I put mop dirt on a sandwich. Crossed the line. "Sure. What kind do you like?"

"The kind with the cheese on it. The gooey cheddar from the can."

"You want fries with that?"

"Potato cakes if you have some."

That'll be a pain. We usually make those fresh. But I say, "Okay."

We meet at the sinks and look at each other through the reflection in the mirrors. She was totally crying in the stall—her eyeliner is a mess. "You're pretty," I say.

She laughs. "Don't go falling in love with me, now, too."

Jake & Bill pick up Bill's check

Jake and Bill Marks pull into the parking lot of the bakery. Saturday half shift, so there are plenty of spaces. Usually Bill tells Jake to stay in the car, but this time he says, "You coming?"

If Jake knew how to use the word *prelude* in a sentence, he'd describe this invitation as a prelude to a gathering. Bill doesn't usually keep his promises, so Jake appreciates this.

Jake's only met two guys who work with Bill. Seemed nice enough. Bill's always talking about his best buddy, a guy named Jeff—"short for Jefferson Davis, motherfucker!"—who's worked there for, like, ten years and showed Bill the ropes when he started working there two months ago. Jeff can't be in the wedding party because he'll be out of town or something. Jake's never met him, but he hates him because Jake's supposed to be Bill's best buddy. Jake knows Jeff's working today because Bill talks a lot about Jeff's bright yellow short-bed pickup truck and the truck is parked diagonally in the corner of the lot across four spots. It has an Iron Cross decal on the cab's tinted back window and a small symbol on his license plate holder that says he donates to the Fraternal Order of Police.

"What's up, fuckers?" Bill says, high-pitched and loud when he walks in, so everyone in the place can hear him, even with the exhaust fan whirring.

Jake's stomach twitches. *How many guys here know?*

A bunch of guys grunt back at Bill and keep working. Jeff stops what he's doing and approaches with his hand out.

They shake hands arm-wrestling style, and Jeff doesn't take his eyes off Jake.

He knows.

"Hey," Jake says.

"Been looking forward to meeting you, son," Jeff says, and Jake doesn't like it because Jeff is only five years older and he's acting like he's some old man.

Jake knows what Jeff's done. Jake knows Jefferson D. Kirwin is on the registry. He knows Jeff brags—*more where that came from. Only got caught on two.*

Jake hasn't been caught on one yet, and the minute Jeff calls him *son* he's sure there won't be a second. Wishes he could go back in time and undo the first. Bill knowing was one thing, but this is different.

Marla & Gottfried Can't Believe Their Luck

Marla and Gottfried Hemmings have more than ten million dollars in the bank. As they sit in the emergency room waiting area, Gottfried looks at the other people waiting there, wondering how much they have in the bank. He doubts anyone there has what he has. Even his own brother doesn't have what he has—what with having to secretly support the Mexican girl from shipping and the daughter they had on top of his own family all those years—John was too busy to learn about how to sell off his share of the farm. Missed the boom, spent the money, ended up living on a single acre in some development last time Gottfried knew.

He's not sure what to think about his luck. He worked hard, sure, but no harder than people who dig ditches all day. His father used to tell him that if he didn't do well in school, he'd end up a ditchdigger. Now we have machines that do that and more people without jobs.

Gottfried tries to pick out the people without jobs from the waiting room selection. The mom in fleece pajama pants and ripped-up sneakers with two kids under four. *Definitely.* The man clutching his arm in his gym clothes. *Probably loaded.* The girl who looks like she's in college in shoes too expensive for her age. *Unemployed and spoiled.* An African American father sits quietly with his two boys, one of whom has a bandage over his eye. Gottfried can't get a read on the man. He's dressed in a short-sleeved plaid button-down shirt and a pair of khakis. *Probably a teacher.*

When Marla is called to be seen, Gottfried helps her walk to the triage area and smiles at the teacher man and his sons. He even winks at the littler one—probably five years old—and makes a funny face. The kid makes a funny face back, and Gottfried feels good about that.

Triage is a series of rapid-fire questions from a seemingly exhausted and unfazed nurse. *What happened? How long ago? Are you on blood thinners of any kind? Are you dizzy? How's your vision?*

"It felt like a sort of panic attack," Marla says.

Gottfried feels shame, then. It could be the fact that Marla whispered it or the fact that it's been their secret for nearly fifty years—Marla's panic attacks. Their family doctor said it was just the stress of raising so many kids. Gave her some pills. Usually she's fine. But sometimes she wasn't fine.

"Why didn't you tell me?" he asks.

The nurse and Marla look at him as if he were having a different conversation than they are. The nurse is fitting a hard plastic neck collar onto Marla.

"I could have gotten you one of your pills," Gottfried says.

Marla can't turn her head to face him, so she stares at the ceiling and says, "You were so busy eating your fried chicken."

Marla has to get a CAT scan and the nurse puts them in a room with a curtain and says she'll be back to let them know how soon she can go up to radiology.

Gottfried doesn't know what to say, so he sits quietly and looks at a poster about diabetes. He lasts about a minute. Never could sit still.

"I'm going to go find a bathroom," he says.

Marla just raises her hand in a wave.

Gottfried really doesn't have to go to the bathroom, but he asks a staff member where it is anyway so Marla can hear him. He walks in that direction, but then takes a rogue right turn toward what looks like a way outside. He wants fresh air.

And then he sees the most remarkable thing. A girl—a tall and skinny teenage girl—walking around in a red-sequined gown over her clothes. *She's a bit old for dress-up. Maybe she has mental problems.*

The girl seems to be doing some sort of dance with herself. Gottfried feels joy from the girl. Joy he hasn't felt in decades. Joy Marla wouldn't allow. Or he wouldn't allow. He's not sure which. As he watches the girl twirl, he isn't sure who to blame for what happened to him and his wife. He wishes he were a teenager again and that he could twirl and play dress-up. He wonders why he thinks this isn't allowed for men his age. *They'd call me demented and lock me up in a home.*

Growing up ruins everything.

Loretta's Flea Check

"I'm going to need to see your ankles," the nurse says. They haven't been back to see Loretta's mother yet. They've stopped in some sort of business office smaller than the living room in their wagon. The sign on the door says EDUCATION.

Loretta stops spinning in the hallway and puts her lunch box down on a swivel chair and yanks up her red-sequined gown, then tugs on the leg of her jeans to show her ankles. Her socks are gray from wear and washing. Loretta thinks: *This is just another audition. My ankles will get the part, for sure.*

The nurse composes herself. "How long have you had these bites? Would you mind if I put something on them? Are they itchy?"

Loretta thinks. "They itch a little. Not bad, though."

"Your mom has some bites, too."

"Yeah."

"You have pets at home?"

"No. No pets." Loretta feels bad saying that. But no one understands that fleas can be pets. Can be friends. Can be talented performers. Can be world famous.

"When did they start?" the nurse asks.

"When did who start?"

"The bites."

Loretta doesn't remember a day without bites. "About two months ago," she lies. She turns the page in her script and it's blank. So's the next one. And the next. And the next.

Loretta's mother hugs her for more than a minute. Loretta notices that her mother has a bruised face—it's a weird bruise, though. It's one big bruise and not the smaller kinds that blend into one another like usual.

"Where's Dad?" Loretta asks.

Before her mother can answer, the nurse says, "He's not going to be back. You two have all the time in the world." The nurse pulls up a chair that looks sterile and yet comfortable and puts it next to the bed and then she leaves.

Loretta's mother doesn't say anything for a while, and Loretta feels the curse inside of her. Two curses, really. It's been a day since she had the fleas out for exercise and food. And it's only been two hours since she, you know. She notes the private bathroom in the room and figures she can take care of both inside it.

"Your dad isn't going to come back," Loretta's mother says. "Not to here and not to anywhere."

"Okay."

"We're going to go live somewhere else."

Loretta doesn't understand somewhere else. She's lived in the wagon on the lot her whole life. "Somewhere like where?"

"Not sure yet."

"Can we still live in the wagon?"

Loretta's mother starts to cry a little. "No. No wagon."

"Can I still go to my school?" Loretta doesn't know why she asks this. She saw it once in an article about parents divorcing and the questions kids ask. This is a normal question. Loretta isn't normal, so she figures she should at least seem it while her mother is crying.

"I'm not sure," her mother answers. "We have a lot of options."

"That sounds promising," Loretta says.

And her mother smiles.

The audience is waiting for the big moment, but there isn't one. Loretta just sits there, the machines attached to her mom beeping, and an occasional flea jumping up from the bed.

Eventually Loretta asks, "So what happened?"

"I can't even tell you."

"You can tell me anything," Loretta says.

"I—I don't even know you." Her mother sobs this out and takes a few deep breaths.

"I'm Loretta. Ringmistress of the best circus you'll ever see. I'm also skilled in the basics of ninth-grade education—grammar, biology, geometry."

"Ringmistress?"

Loretta stands up and shows off her new dress. "Isn't it perfect?"

"It is, I guess. I can shorten those straps for you."

Loretta's confusion shows on her face. She looks at the IV unit and wonders what the hospital was giving her mother to make her able to sew. Loretta wants some, too.

Her mother asks, "When was the last time you took a bath?"

"A bath or a shower?"

"Either."

"I took a shower three days ago. Or four. Something like that," Loretta says.

"The bathrooms here have those walk-in bathtubs."

"Are you staying awhile?" Loretta asks.

"Seems so."

"Am I staying with you?"

"This is no place for a kid," her mother says.

"But if I'm not staying in the wagon and I'm not staying here, then—"

"Be patient. We're working it out."

"No foster parents. Right? You're not going to put me in with strangers."

"No foster parents. Promise."

Loretta pulls her chair so close to the bed that she can rest her head on her mother's chest. "So what happened?"

"I—last thing I remember was not being able to breathe. Something tight around my neck. I really don't know."

"Is Dad with the police?"

"Yes."

Loretta takes a few seconds to answer. "Good," she says.

The audience relaxes its shoulders.

A light knock sounds from the doorway. An older man pokes his head into the room. Loretta recognizes him somehow and can't figure out how. The audience knows him only from holidays and birthday parties back when Loretta was young.

Malcolm Discovers Sixty-Five Miles per Hour

Sixty-five miles per hour is a death wish. I seriously don't know how anyone does this without having a mental breakdown. I've almost turned around twice but you can't turn around on a highway and only now that I'm driving do I realize I don't know the roads around my town as well as I thought I did.

As a kid it was all about landmarks. The sign for the sheepskin store meant we were going camping. The road with the falling rocks sign and the river to the right meant we were going to the pool. Mostly, I counted mile markers.

Everything is different once you're driving. Mile markers? I don't think I've seen one on this road. Can't read billboards. Have to keep my eyes on my lane.

Growing up must ruin everything.

By the time I'm doing sixty-five for more than four minutes, I make a promise to myself. *I'm moving to Negril, going off the grid, and I'm never getting a car.*

The GPS voice on my phone tells me to take the next exit. It's a giant loop exit so I slow down before I get to the off-ramp and a car slides in behind me and lays on his horn so hard I go numb and my sinuses clear from the surprise. I pull onto the ramp's shoulder and let him pass me. It was a her, actually. She seemed really angry for no reason.

Everybody rushing. *Breathe in peace, breathe out stress.*

Everybody complaining. *Breathe in peace, breathe out stress.*

Everybody dying. Everybody around me dying and me not allowed to feel a thing about it like I'm some kid who still counts mile markers. *Breathe in peace, breathe out stress.* Fuck breathing. Fuck peace. My family is dying and it's the weirdest feeling in the world because I was already alone. What's this, then? Ultra alone? Super alone? Mega alone?

If I was a superhero, my name would be Lonerman. My superpower would be the Existentialism—a ray I could shoot out of my hand that renders people powerless to face anything but their own personal pointlessness in an absurd world.

Lonerman pulls back onto the road when he's sure no one else is entering the exit ramp. He gets to the stop sign. He follows directions all the way to the hospital. He parks in the parking garage and gets out of his grandmother's car. He is alone in the world and not alone in the world at the same time. The responsibility on his shoulders is so heavy he can't breathe in peace or breathe out stress. His diaphragm is crushed with the weight of knowing that if his father is dead, then he will be the only one left.

That's a nice daydream and everything, but I can't bring myself to pull out onto the road again.

I look around the dashboard and find the hazard lights and press the button. I can see the rhythmic pulsing of the lights and the BMW feels like it's breathing. I turn up the heat even though it's not cold outside. I'm cold inside. That's my problem. Lonerman has always been cold inside. Even when he's on Negril's seven-mile white sand beach. Even when he's kissing Eleanor.

I feel something familiar. Something like I ate bad shrimp. Something like I swallowed the weight of the world.

I am digesting Dad's cancer, and my system is rejecting it. I try to open the driver's side door, but I'm locked in by BMW engineers. I can't see the buttons on the armrest. Saliva starts flowing. I swallow.

Lonerman swallows it down. Swallows everything down. Lonerman has been swallowing everything for fifteen years like a wave hit and he's bouncing around under the surf trying to find a way up. Salt water and pineapple. That's what it tastes like—swallowing everything. Salt water and old fish. Salt water and force-fed lamb chops.

I lean into the passenger's seat and it all comes up in heaves. I have just vomited on Marla's BMW leather seats.

The other stuff comes out of my mouth—the pineapple and the old fish and lamb chops. The salt water comes out of my eyes, though. Steady and streaming like tropical rain that doesn't stop for days.

The car stinks and I turn the heat off. I find the window buttons, and I roll them all down. I close my eyes so I don't see the flashing hazard lights, and even with my eyes pinched so tightly, the tears keep coming. I reach in the back seat for Marla's tissue box and she only has four left. I use one to wipe my mouth and chin. I use another to wipe my eyes and blow my nose. I turn on the interior lights and I look at the puddle of vomit and know that two tissues won't make a difference.

I take off my sweatshirt and clean up as much of the vomit as I can and then I toss the sweatshirt out the window. I know there's a car wash near here. The kind with the rainbow soap bubbles. I want to go to the hospital, but I know leaving vomit to dry in an emetephobe's car is like leaving a million spiders in an arachnophobe's bed.

The tears stop. I can breathe again. It still stinks. I ask my GPS to direct me to the rainbow car wash, and it's only three miles from the exit ramp.

I think I just puked out the last of my childhood because I feel like a man now.

The Shoveler: Mike Needs a Hand

It's an old World Series again—I think Mike said 2005. A lot of action, but to be honest, I'm getting sick of baseball.

Mike pauses the game. "You good?"

"Yeah."

"You gonna share those Fritos?"

"Sure." I toss him the bag.

"You're not bored, are you?" he asks.

"Nah."

"When I was your age, I was doing way cooler things on a Saturday night," he says.

"This is fun," I say. "But I gotta pee."

"I have guacamole," Mike says. "And salsa and shit."

"Cool," I say, on my way up the stairs to the bathroom. Last week it was pita chips and hummus. The week before it was white queso dip heated in the microwave.

I don't bother turning on the bathroom light. I just aim and pee and hum a little because I do that sometimes.

Shake. Shake again. Turn around/zip up combo and someone is in the bathtub.

I scream.

I see it's an old woman. Her legs are dangling over the side of the tub.

I reach for the light switch.

"You okay up there?" Mike yells.

"Come here! Your mom!"

Mike's mom is staring at me as if she's staring at a TV. No expression. She's naked but doesn't seem to know it. She refuses to answer Mike when he comes upstairs to help her back to her room.

"Mom. Do you know who I am?"

". . ."

"Can you hear me?"

". . ."

"Mom! Look at me!" he says.

She keeps staring into an invisible TV. Mike tries to get her to wrap her arms around his neck so he can pick her up. Her arms fall back to her sides in the tub. Dead weight. She's not going anywhere. He leans over her and says, "Ma, can you help us? Can you help us get you back to your bed? I have Oreos!"

She moves her arm—ratchets it back and swings.

"Be nice!" he says. Then he turns to me. "I need a hand, dude. Grab her under her shoulder and on the count of three, lift, okay?"

I have no idea what I'm doing. I've never touched anyone's naked mother before. She's little. Looks like she might weigh a hundred pounds. But she's not helping us at all. She just lets us pull her out of there like a doll. Mike adjusts her in his arms as if she were a bride being walked over the threshold and coos into her hair. "Jesus, Ma. You scared the shit out of us. You can't go wandering like that. I worry about you."

He tells me he's got it from here and to wait in the living room.

He comes down ten minutes later.

"Sorry about that."

"No problem," I say. "Is she okay?"

"I got her dressed."

228

He goes into the kitchen and comes back with a plate of Oreos. "Only thing she'll eat now. Doctor says it's better than nothing." He goes up the steps and comes back down.

"Sorry about that," he says again.

"Really. No problem. Call me any time you need help."

"Thanks."

I don't know what to say.

He says, "I can't get her into a home yet. Waiting lists. Too expensive. Not everywhere takes people with dementia."

"Gotcha."

Mike turns on the baseball game again. I can hear the pellet hopper release another load into the stove. I look at him, and he seems different now. I can't tell if it's his expression or the fact that he doesn't get another beer once his is empty. I realize it's probably time for me to go but I don't want to go too soon after that because he'll think he has something to be sorry for. I wait through a whole inning.

"I'm beat," I say. "Gonna head home."

"See you tomorrow," he says. "Aw, shit! I forgot the guacamole!"

"It's cool, man. Save it for tomorrow."

He nods and I feel like an adult.

I think what happened in the bathroom made us closer friends. If nothing else, now we've both probably seen each other's mothers naked.

Gottfried's New Secret

Gottfried follows the girl in the red-sequined dress. She walks with the confidence of an actress on her way to accept an award. But really they're both in the emergency room and she's going back to where she belongs, he assumes. She seems to know her way around, and when she slips into room 12-C, he slows down and listens.

The rooms in this wing of the emergency room are different from the place where he left Marla. They're bigger for one thing, and they have sliding doors, not just curtains.

"That's weird," he says to himself. "I have ten million dollars and I get a curtain. These people must be loaded."

"Can I help you, sir?" A woman in green scrubs comes out of room 12-C stands next to Gottfried and repeats herself. "Can I help you, sir?"

"Just taking a walk," Gottfried says.

"Are you lost?"

"I'm old, yes, but I'm not lost, no," Gottfried says. *Why does everybody think old people are lost?* "My wife's getting a scan," he says. "I'm just waiting for her to get back."

The woman in scrubs seems satisfied with Gottfried's answer, and she walks to a cart with a computer on it and starts typing. Gottfried's mind is racing because he knows the girl in the sequined dress. He knows but he can't catch the memory. He's racing up behind the frontrunner—like in his old track-and-field days. He's kicking it in for the last hundred yards until he finds the image and matches it to the information already stored in his brain.

He stands up and goes to the nurse's cart and looks at the screen, and he reads the name of the patient in 12-C. The nurse feels him there, but by the time she does, he's already seen it.

He only needs to read the first two letters of the last name and he catches the frontrunner in his memory and wins his own race. And then the robins are there, frolicking in the middle of the road in 1965, and he's sadder than he's ever been.

Gottfried the runner has always been running. Running from his family home. Running from the farm fields. Running from Marla. Running from his five kids who were too loud and unruly for him to handle because he was making money and needed to do that in a quiet place. Gottfried is running toward the bank. He's depositing money. He's investing intelligently. He is going to be a rich man one day and that will make him happy one day.

My children are a reflection of me. Marla always meant this in a bad way. If Harry got suspended from school, she'd say he was making the family look bad. When their youngest girl got knocked up at eighteen, Marla cut her off, kicked her out, and said the family didn't need a scandal. If one of the kids got sick and stayed out of school for more than three days, she would lament how it looks bad to be out of school—even if the kid had the mumps—how it looks like their parents aren't responsible enough to keep them well. But that's not what Gottfried feels sitting on a hard, plastic bench in the ER. *My children are a reflection of me and one of them is here, probably beaten up again—her daughter so used to it that she twirls around in the hallways dressed in red sequins. Another one is dying of cancer and is so buried in medical bills he can barely afford rent and he can't afford to feed his own kid.*

And I have ten million dollars in the bank.

Gottfried stands and smiles. He exhales. He inhales. He holds back tears—a dam ten million dollars high—and walks to the door of 12-C. He knocks and pokes his head through the opening in the sliding door.

In the bed lies his daughter—who was a very good baby. Always slept well and did what he said. Got good grades. Played the flute in the marching band. His Melissa. *Miss Missy, he called her, and she would giggle.*

Her face looks dirty with bruising—as if copier toner had exploded in close range. Her smile is pained and confused.

"Dad?" she asks, squinting through swollen eyes.

"Missy?" he says.

She looks at him, perplexed. "How did you know I was in here?" she asks.

"I didn't."

The girl in the sequined dress is having a race of her own, Gottfried suspects. He can see the look of slight familiarity in her eyes, but she's trying to catch the memory of who he is. Now that she's closer, Gottfried sees she wears worn sneakers of poverty and her wrists are covered in sores. The dress is a cover, the same as his bank statements.

"Oh, Dad," the woman in the bed says. "I'm so sorry!" She starts to sob and Gottfried doesn't know what to do.

"Pop-Pop!" the girl says, and before he can go and comfort his Melissa, he has to catch his granddaughter in his arms and hug her. She hugs like a baby robin eats. Desperate and determined.

As Gottfried hugs his favorite granddaughter and hears his daughter crying, his mind only gives him one image. The robins. Always the robins.

Always the robins.

Malcolm Experiences the Benefits of American Consumerism

There are all sorts of cool things to buy at the car wash. They have these weird vending machines with window cleaner wipes and dashboard wipes and all sorts of other disposable stuff. Air fresheners. Tire polish, whatever that is.

I try the wet vac, leather seat wipes, an air freshener, and the car still smells like puke. Finally, five minutes with a steam cleaner does the trick, and by the time I'm driving into the hospital parking garage, I feel like the BMW is my car. I know parts of it that Marla doesn't know. Bet she has no idea, for example, that she has twelve cents under the passenger's seat. And I don't think she ever noticed the back seat USB charger before.

I look at my phone and walk so the blue, blinking dots on our phones get closer and closer together. Into the emergency room.

"Can I help you find something?" someone asks.

I smile. "I'm looking for my father. And my grandparents."

"Name?"

"Malcolm." She looks at me. I look at her. "Oh. Sorry. I mean Harry Hemmings—that's my dad—and Marla and Gottfried Hemmings. That's my grandparents."

"And you're Malcolm?"

"Yep. Hemmings with two *m*s." That's how Gottfried always said it at the pharmacy when he picked up his prescriptions.

"Let me go have a look," she says. "Have a seat."

Only once I'm in the waiting area chair do I realize that I'll have to explain how I got here. Why I got here. *Malcolm, why did you get here?* If they would have answered their phones or Dad would have, I wouldn't be here at all. *I'm here because my dad could be dead. And I didn't want to miss that. No kid wants to miss their parent dying. Or at least I don't.*

It takes about three minutes before she's back. "Your grandma is up getting a scan. Nothing to worry about. Can't find your grandfather at the moment. He may just be using the restroom or something. When I see him, I'll tell him you're here."

"Can't I wait in the room?" I ask.

"Sorry. Not yet."

I get back to the waiting room and I open my phone and text Dad. There are already ten texts from me to him in the last four hours, still unanswered. I add this one. Hey, Dad. I thought you were dying in the hospital so I stole Marla's car to get here and see you one last time. But now I know you're not here. Something's wrong with Marla, but I don't know what. And you're a shitty dad for not calling me or texting me back yet. All I do is care about you and all you do is ignore how much I care. I know you were raised that way, but it doesn't mean you have to be the same way. Please call me when you get this.

CanIHelpYou? Is Not Going to the Mall

The Freak is standing at the counter like a regular customer. Her tears have dried and her eyeliner looks okay.

"Here you go," I say, as I hand her the bag of free food.

"Thanks," she says. "Good luck with your best friend." She blinks her eyes slowly, and she then completely vanishes. Gone. I'm hoping the same thing happens to the security video footage of me giving away free food.

I just made that up to sound like I'm cool with her disappearing like that, but really I'm standing here wondering what the hell is my life? Did a human being just vanish in front of me?

I check my phone before Dad picks me up, and there's a text from Ian. I'd be lying if I said my chest didn't hiccup when I saw it. Party at Paul's tonight. You going?

Party at Paul-the-lacrosse-player's house. Bound to be a great place to make cash. I know I'm welcome. I'm a superstar. I show up and everyone knows the party's just starting.

I text Ian back. I'll meet you there.

Dad listens to talk radio for the six-block drive, and the only thing he says to me is that I smell like grease. No shit.

When I walk in the door, my mother says we're going to buy me an Easter dress. "I'm not going to the mall," I say.

"You'll be with me," she says. "We'll stick together."

"I don't need a new dress. I never wear dresses. I just want to be comfortable."

"But it's Easter."

"You say that like it means something," I say.

"It means something to my family," she says. "So we dress up. Tradition."

Tradition, my ass. What do we have here that's tradition? Only the bell. And the words. And the ridiculous excuse that rappers say it all the time so why can't she?

I walk up the steps toward my room. "I'm not going to the mall," I say.

"Fine," she says. "Wear a bath towel for all I care."

I close my door and look through my clothes. I change three times. This never happens to me. I'm CanIHelpYou? and no one cares what I wear, as long as the right shit's in my pockets. I think about putting makeup on. I think about wearing a hat. A hat. What's wrong with me? I AM CANIHELPYOU? AND I DON'T NEED TO WEAR A FUCKING HAT.

I look at my mirror. School pictures of Ian. Seven of them. I slipped them around the edge of the mirror every year when I got a new one. Every time I rearrange my room and change my posters, I think about rearranging those pictures or replacing them with other ones. But I left them up. I like to think I left them up because Ian's been my best friend for so long. I like to think it's because I've always been a little in love with him. Really, I left them up because I knew my mother hates that my best friend is black.

Even in two-dimensional form, I'm using him.

I'm halfway to Paul-the-lacrosse-player's house via the alleys when my phone rings. I answer it because it's not my mother.

It's Len. From work. He tells me that a guy came in after I left. Showed him what was in his sandwich. Told him I was rude. Said if Len didn't fire me, he'd sue.

"So I'm fired?"

"Oh yeah," Len says.

". . ."

I have a freeze frame right here. I don't care. So I hang up.

Jake & Bill are thunder and lightning

Bill's ear is bleeding, and he's holding it with his left hand while he reaches out toward Jake with his right. Jake's eye is swollen shut and already turning black. The storm that is the Marks brothers is tumbling from the living room into the kitchen.

"Ruaagh!" Bill says.

"Guaaah!" Jake says.

Jake is younger, more sober, faster. He dodges Bill's charge and looks for the first thing he can pick up. A coffeepot. Threatens an approaching Bill with it, but the older brother can't stop. He's aimed for Jake's midsection like a linebacker in for a sack. So close Jake can't avoid him, and he brings the coffeepot down on whatever he can reach and the glass breaks over Bill's back. More blood. More groans and garbled words.

Bill stops and tries to feel his back. Jake sees it's bleeding. Nothing major. Nice stain on Bill's T-shirt; Jake almost envies it.

Jake calls temporary truce. "Gotta piss," he says.

Bill holds up his hand in agreement. "Me too."

Jake says, "I'll use the upstairs." This not only gives him the advantage of hearing Bill's thunder if he decides to charge the bathroom door, but it also gives him a few minutes.

He doesn't want to be fighting his brother. Sometimes Bill's just impossible. Got angry because his check from the bakery was missing a hundred bucks and the boss wouldn't pick up his phone. Nothing to do with Jake, but Jake takes it because he can't make the drive to New Jersey go away and

Bill's got him by the balls. Always will. Stupid. It's all so stupid.

Jake's been thinking, though. Thinking about how to deal with it when it happens. Because it *will* happen. Jake'll say Bill was the one who buried her. Jake'll say he was only fifteen. Jake'll say that his brother was always violent.

He looks directly into the bathroom mirror with his one unswollen eye. Pulls out his phone from the front pocket of his jeans. Snaps a picture.

WATCH THE FREAK EAT ROAST BEEF JOY!

The Freak is happy with a lukewarm roast beef sandwich. It doesn't take much to be happy. Food, somewhere to sleep, a good friend, maybe, though she doesn't have any. Love doesn't matter. Money doesn't matter. Success doesn't matter because does it really last? Maybe as long as an order of potato cakes. What's success anyway? Family probably matters, but The Freak wouldn't know.

The Freak isn't angry anymore at anything or anyone. Everything is unfolding as it should be.

Malcolm has stolen his grandmother's car.

Loretta has found her red-sequined dress.

CanIHelpYou? has been fired from her job.

The boy with the shovel is still lost, but until he figures out that accidental fruit grows just fine there isn't a thing The Freak can do about that.

Easter is in two weeks and The Freak has decided never to go home again. Hasn't she always been a missing person? Missing a bra, missing tampons, missing parents who care less about her than they do their own bickering—and calling that love, like when they send her a birthday ecard.

The Freak just turned eighteen last week. No one noticed because she was flickering between Borneo and Idaho, and she no longer has a device on which to receive email, so her parents' ecard is lost in the ether somewhere if they sent one.

Borneo was nice, though. The rain forest there is 140 million years old—one of the oldest in the world—and The Freak thought it was a pretty cool place to land on her eighteenth birthday. It beat having a party and getting presents that she doesn't need.

The Freak has transcended Stuff.

The Freak only has room for Experiences.

Once The Freak met a boy who lived in a car. Once she met a girl who sold her body for drugs. Once she met a girl who was so ordinary she hated herself. Once she met a deer in head-lights. Once she met a man on a boat who didn't know how to swim. Once she met a baker who ran out of flour. Once she met a famous singer who had twenty million dollars but still cut the highest part of her thighs with a razor blade because the pain had to escape somehow.

The Freak knows the deal.

The Freak does what she can. She puts newspapers in mail-boxes. She delivers food to cars with boys sleeping inside. She delivers flour and teaches swimming lessons. She puts the right dress on the right rack at the right time. She is the Easter Bunny. Magical. Impossible to believe.

The Freak loves Easter because of the chocolate, not because of the Bible. She thinks Jesus probably lived and probably hung out with lepers and prostitutes and cared for the poor. But you can't just be alive again. She's tried. She's tried so hard. But nothing allows her to be alive again. She's atoms. She's the Consciousness. She's here to help, but not to interfere.

Except the boy with the shovel.

She can't stop herself.

PART THREE: OUR CAST IN A STRAINER

Malcolm's Phone Finally Rings

Dad says he's sorry right away. It's nearly eleven. Last flight from the island tonight. I can hear the echo of the arrivals exit at the airport and the taxis going by.

"I'm so sorry, kid. I didn't mean to worry you."

I'm outside Marla's hospital room, and Gottfried is wandering again. He keeps having to pee and says it's because he drank tea today, but I've never seen Gottfried drink tea, not before tonight or tonight. "Marla's in the hospital, but she's okay."

"What happened?"

I walk down the hall so Marla can't hear me. "She fell at the farmers' market. Has a concussion. She'll be fine."

"Did you really steal her car?"

"Yep."

"Are you okay?"

"Yep."

"Where's the car now?"

"In the hospital garage."

"Do they know?"

"No."

He laughs. I love his laugh. There are times in first class when I can see him talking to his new stranger-friends, and I watch him and wait for that laugh. Always comes. He never disappoints.

"I'll come get you. We can get the car home before she notices."

"You don't have to do that," I say.

"I'll be there in about an hour, okay?"

"Okay."

"I'm sorry again, kid. I hate that you worry."

I'm about to say a bunch of smart shit about how I'd worry no matter what. Telling me I'm not allowed to worry doesn't mean I don't worry. It makes me worry more, really. But I see Gottfried walking around up the hall with this skinny girl in a red-sequined dress and I'm confused and I'm too busy watching to say anything.

"Eleanor wanted me to tell you she misses you," he says. My gut drops.

"How'd you find out?"

"She told me. Honest, smart, and works her ass off. You could do worse."

"That's not actually a compliment, you know. The you-could-do-worse part. Okay?"

"I didn't mean it that way."

"We'll talk when you get here," I say. "I can't live with Marla anymore. It's not that she's a bad person," I whisper. "It's just the antithesis of everything you ever taught me—living here. They're not good for me."

"Well, I—"

"Just think about it on your way. Talk to the driver about it. He's a people person. He's great at stuff like this."

Dad's still in his hat and sunglasses when he gets to Marla's room. He kisses her on the head and says, "You need to stop doing that trapeze act, Ma."

She shakes her head.

Gottfried gives Dad a hug and says, "You stink, kid."

I can see Dad's hackles go up and then smooth back down. Gottfried always wanted a different son, I guess. And Dad does stink. He doesn't use Jamaican tap water unless he has to. *That's what the sea's for!*

I could really use a sea bath right about now.

Right when I think this, tears well up in my eyes. My chest heaves a bit, and I look down so no one can see. *What's wrong with you?*

It's not Eleanor or Dad or Marla or anyone. It's not school or the entitled kids I have to navigate every day—the ones who complain about how their Internet is slow or their phone has a crack in the screen. It's the beach. The sand. The people. The fish. The pelicans. The sunset. I found a place I belong.

Most people I know are lost—never found a place they belong. I'm fifteen and I already found mine. Except I don't really belong there. I'm Lonerman. I don't belong anywhere.

Dad's made some excuse—I didn't catch it. He motions for me to get up.

"We're gonna take off. If you need anything, call me, okay?"

Marla says, "What about his backpack and clothes at our place?"

"We'll drop by and get them," Dad says. He looks at Gottfried, who somehow knows what's going on. Man language. I'm learning it. I was born with it. I try not to use it, but sometimes it comes in handy. Especially when you're doing something you shouldn't be doing and getting away with it . . . like stealing a car or whatever.

I feel so white right now, I can't stand myself.

~~~

Dad drives Marla's BMW back to the house. We don't say much to each other because he wants to test the car's speakers. Harman Kardon. Marla always gets the best even if she doesn't use it.

The airport driver follows us in his black Town Car, and once I get my stuff from inside the house, we get into the Town Car and go back down the driveway.

"You know I stole her car when I was in high school," Dad says. "Crashed it, though. Into a parked car. Lied. Got away with it. I was totally stoned."

The driver laughs. All of us white, all of us lucky we get away with things. I still can't shake the feelings I was having in the hospital. Overwhelming sadness, really. At having to be here. At having to be in this family, where a father tells his dying son that he smells bad.

I start to cry and Dad does something he hasn't done in a long time. He hugs me. Pulls me across the back seat and puts me in his arms and he squeezes me. No pats on the back, no chatter in my ear. He just hugs and lets me cry on his lap even though he has no idea why I'm crying.

When I can finally talk, I say, "I need to get out of here. Now. Tomorrow. I need the beach."

"Okay," Dad says. "I can get us on the first flight tomorrow morning."

"You don't have treatments this week?"

"Nope."

I sit up. "Why?"

Dad sighs. "Nothing more they can do for me."

I look at him in the highway light.

"And I want my fucking hair back." The driver laughs at

this. "If I'm gonna die, I want to do it with hair, you know?"

"You do have great hair," I say.

I stay in his arms, and it feels like the world is both ending and beginning. "I can't go back there. I can't live with them anymore."

"You can't be wiping my ass a few months down the road, either," he says.

"I'm not leaving you. You're stuck with me. This is what happens when you have a kid, Dad. You can't just push me out of your life now."

He's quiet and I look at him and he's crying, too.

The driver keeps driving. Dad keeps crying. I hug him and he sobs into my chest. It's as if we'd just switched places. Except it's not. I think this is what families are supposed to do.

Marla & Gottfried Run
Off at the Mouth

Gottfried can't shake the feeling of seeing Missy in her hospital bed. Marla keeps complaining about how fast he's driving. Gottfried isn't driving more than sixty, but Marla doesn't care.

"Why'd he have to bring Harry in like that? Why'd he have to come at all?" Marla asks.

"Malcolm?" Gottfried knows she's talking about Malcolm.

"Of course Malcolm. Who else would I be talking about? Harry coming all the way here in the middle of the night. So stupid."

Gottfried sighs. "We have a lot to talk about tonight."

"I'm tired."

"You can't go to sleep for more than an hour or two at a time. Doctor's orders."

"I'm fine. It's just a bump. That kid thinks he runs the world, you know. Got it from you. All you boys think the same."

"Settle down," Gottfried says. "The kid has a lot going on. Not his fault."

Gottfried doesn't want to talk to Marla about Malcolm because he's afraid he might tell her that Malcolm stole her car. If he was to be honest, he's pretty proud the kid did it and managed to get all the way to the hospital.

"I saw Loretta," Gottfried says.

Marla doesn't really hear what Gottfried says. She hears the words, but they seem like nonsense. "It's late," she says. "You need sleep."

"True. But maybe you didn't hear me. I saw Loretta tonight," he says. "In the hospital. With Missy."

Marla sighs. "What kind of kids did I even raise?" She sighs again. "Let me guess: Loretta's bites got infected, and Missy was too stupid to just take her to a regular doctor."

Gottfried sighs.

"What?" she says. "Just tell me."

"Why do you have to be so mean about Missy? Girl can't help that she married a bad guy. Can't help that she's broke."

"She's not broke, she's poor. Remember how she looked last time we saw her?"

"Exactly. And what did we do to help?" Mating with purpose, Gottfried thinks, looks different from this.

Marla grunts. Gottfried feels something he hasn't felt in a long time. Anger. He feels anger.

Marla and Gottfried argue through the night. Gottfried insists that their children hate them because of Marla's meanness. Marla insists their children hate them because Gottfried was never home when they were growing up. They can't come to an agreement, and eventually Marla opts for the silent treatment. Gottfried keeps talking. Yelling. By himself. At himself.

Everything Gottfried ever did washes over him like poison. Regrets are something he could deal with, but every day he's racking up new ones.

At 5:33 Sunday morning, Gottfried yells, "Don't need a degree in psychology to know that, Marla! Kids with shitty parents eventually figure it out!"

The Shoveler: Wrong Words

This morning when I went out for a smoke, I found one of those *Merchandiser* newspapers in the mailbox again. Inside there was an ad—circled in purple highlighter—for a decent Nissan right around the block; and I call the number and the guy says to come see him at two.

So I do. And I leave my shovel at home.

"I don't even know how to buy a car," I say to the guy.

"Have a look at her. She's a good machine. Just had her serviced and she runs great." He smiles a lot and I try to look at the car as if I know what I'm doing. He says, "That ding in the door is from some dumb bitch and her shopping cart." I nod. He says, "And the paint up front is just wear from the sun."

"How many miles?" I know the answer, but I ask anyway.

"One thirty. These cars go a long time, too."

I wish I had Mike with me. I realize I *should* have Mike with me. I say, "Do you mind if I have a friend come and have a look, too? He's good with motors and stuff."

"Be my guest," he says.

I nod and dial Mike's number.

"Yeah?" he answers.

"I need a hand with something. You got ten minutes?" I want to ask him how his mom is, but it seems weird. She's been there all this time and I never asked before.

"Sure. Your place?"

"Yeah. I'll meet you there in five minutes."

I tell the guy I'll be back in ten minutes and walk home. Mike meets me out front and I tell him the deal—that I want to buy a car and I have the cash for it but I don't actually know how to buy a car. *This is what fathers are for.*

He rolls up the sleeves on his flannel shirt and says, "You like the car, though?"

"Yeah. Seems good. Great deal. The guy just wants to get rid of it. New tires. Just inspected and serviced. One thirty on the clock." *One thirty on the clock?* I don't even know where that came from.

"How much is he asking?"

"Twenty-five hundred. Only damage is from some dumb—um—there's a little dent in the door."

Mike laughs. "Twenty-five hundred? I got this."

While we walk over, I feel like throwing up. I can't believe I almost said *dumb bitch.* Mom taught me better.

When we get to the house where the old guy lives, Mike says, "This is Roy's place. Oh, hell."

When Roy comes out, he and Mike shoot the shit for a minute or two. I pretend I know how to look at a car engine after popping the hood and propping it up. Looks clean. Yep. That's all I got. *I probably should have brought the shovel.*

"You're not gonna screw my neighbor on this car, Roy. He trusts me and I trust you so we're gonna find the right number here. Because twenty-five is high for this thing. You know it. I know it. He knows it."

"Blue book has it at twenty-seven," the old guy says.

"Bullshit," Mike says. "Kid—you got your phone on you?" I hand Mike my phone. He hands it back and says, "Look up the

Kelley Blue Book." I open the browser and type it in, and the site opens and I start putting the details in. Blue, 2004, 130,000 miles, good condition.

"What's our zip code again?"

Roy and Mike say it simultaneously. I enter it.

"Got the number?" Mike says. I nod. He walks over to me and has a look. It says $2,300 is about right for a private seller. Mike says to Roy, "Buddy, eighteen hundred is where we'll meet you."

Roy doesn't look impressed. I look at the time on my phone. "I have to go soon. Work calls," I say. Gottfried sent a text last night and said I couldn't come over until after four.

Mike winks at me and I'm not sure why.

Roy says, "Come on. Two. Two grand."

Mike sticks his head under the hood and touches the parts in there like he's done it three million times before. And he probably has. He says, "New starter?"

Roy says, "Six months ago."

"Alternator?"

"Been a while."

"Battery? Roy, this one looks older than me."

Roy looks at his hands. "Probably needs a new one after this winter."

Mike nods. "Nineteen."

This is the most mannish shit I've ever experienced. I'm used to my mother pulling pork loins out of her pants and cosmetics out of her socks.

"You paying cash or check, son?"

Even though I knew *son* was a term people say when you're not their son, I wasn't comfortable with this when it happened the first time or any time since. Son is something I am, but I don't know whose I am, and when it happens, even that time it was the nice old man at the grocery store in Omaha, I can't say anything because my throat closes up and refuses to work. I could barely breathe that first time.

When Mike said it to me, he seemed to be saying it in that way where he knew something I didn't. I have always felt out of the loop. The one who will be the last one to know. I was born with this disease. It makes me think too much.

Am I the only one who feels like this all the time? Like someone is keeping the most important information from me? Like I'm stupid not by choice but by bad luck?

Son. Don't call me son. Son. You're not my father.

"Kid?"

I'm dizzy and holding on to the taillight of the Nissan.

"You okay?"

I nod. "Fine."

Roy says, "You just went blue, boy."

"I'm fine. It's just hot in the sun."

"Daydreaming about driving away and never coming back, I bet," Mike says. "Oh, to feel that again, eh, Roy?"

"I took off the day I turned eighteen. Drove all the way to Florida," Roy says.

I am hyperaware that everyone on the planet has an escape plan except me. I guess my first plan is to find out who my father is. It's like there's an escape-plan door but he's blocking it.

"Eighteen fifty cash?" Mike says.

Roy looks disgruntled. I say, "Sounds good."

Mike looks at me. "Test drive?"

I shake my head. "I'm late for work."

"Take it to work," Roy says. "Bring it back later if you don't want it."

I look at Mike. I don't think this is how test-driving a car works. "Sounds good. Get to work, kid. I'm gonna have a beer with Roy on the stoop."

Roy says he has to get the title and it's inside. I'm left standing there with Mike, who just called me *son*. I take off my hoodie and put it on the passenger's seat.

Mike takes off his flannel shirt, and all he's wearing underneath is a sleeveless T-shirt. Roy comes out and hands me the title and tells me we can sign it over tomorrow if the test drive works out. He puts his hand out for me to shake. Mike smiles, and the wrinkles around his eyes do that thing I bet women love. They make his eyes twinkle extra hard or something. Mike's a good-looking guy. And even though his arms are winter white, they're toned and look like man arms.

He has a tattoo on his left deltoid. I never thought about that over winter. You never know what's under all those layers, same as I didn't much wonder about what was under the snow. I want to see what it is and I guess it's some baseball thing. He comes over to me once I get into the car and leans in. "Drive safe, okay? Not too fast. It's not technically your car yet, right?"

I see the tattoo.

I read the words, sketched in a banner above a symbol I don't know. It's an eagle or another kind of bird. The words, though. The words are wrong.

The words are wrong.

Mike gave me my shovel. He brought me warm home runs in a blizzard. He helps Mom with money sometimes. He taught me that controlling my brain made the rest easy.

100% WHITE POWER.

The words are wrong.

The whole time I'm putting the undercoat on the living room walls, I think about Mike's tattoo. I lay the paint on thicker so I can't see it, but it's still there because I'm painting the wall, not Mike's arm.

Gottfried and Marla aren't really talking to each other. It's not just them being weird—something's actually wrong. Gottfried explained that Marla was in the hospital last night. That she fell and got a nasty bump. But still, something else is going on. It's so vibey in here I paint twice as fast. I'm an expert now. This is my last room.

Marla says, "OH MY GOD! That's not the color I picked!"

"It's an undercoat, Mrs. Hemmings. I promise by tomorrow night, your color will be here and you'll love it."

I realize now that I know them, that I should have never talked them into a color. Should have just let her paint it pastel-blue-beige again.

But the whole time she talks and I explain and Gottfried helps, I can only see Mike's arm in my head.

100% WHITE POWER.

Wrong words.

Wrong words.

Wrong words.

Jake & Bill no longer share an address

Jake Marks gives a fuck. This is new. This is not what he expected after going to the bakery with Bill. This is not what he expected after their millionth fistfight. He's not sure what to do about this feeling.

Bill moved out over the weekend, and their mother is making breakfast for their dad and Jake. Jake's face is still bruised and cut from the thunderstorm that was his brother on Saturday night. Jake says, "I love you, Mom," and she turns green.

"What did you do?" she says.

Jake holds his hands out.

"What's got into you?" Mr. Marks asks.

"Damn. I can't say something nice?"

When the home phone rings, Jake jumps. His parents notice. It's a telemarketer on the phone, and Mrs. Marks says something in Spanish to her. Swearing, Jake guesses from her tone.

"I wish I'd have learned Spanish from you," he says.

Jake's parents stare at him.

"I'm serious," he says. "It's good to know Spanish these days." He heard that from his guidance counselor a year ago. Not like Jake was ever going to take Spanish.

Jake eats his breakfast and goes upstairs to get ready for school. Stops on the steps and listens to his parents talking: . . . *Probably has something to do with Bill moving out . . . Can't wait until*

we're on the other side of that damn wedding . . . Nice to see him hap-
pier, though . . .

Jake hadn't recognized that. She's right. He's happier. Happier now that Bill has a best buddy named Jeff and a fiancée named Ashley. Happier now that Bill has a job, even though Bill gets off early enough to still come after school to recruit with the snake. Jake has a new plan for that. He doesn't want to recruit anyone for anything. He's going to sneak out the gym doors and walk home by himself. He's looking forward to the exercise.

Loretta's Lamb Symphony in V-Flat

Act Three, Monday, new set, three new cast members, no script. Big house, eternally seventy-two degrees. Lots of rugs and deep shag carpet, always vacuumed. Mom-Mom and Pop-Pop and a cousin cast member Loretta never met before who isn't here at the moment.

Her dressing room is freshly painted a calming pastel yellow. Every room on set is pastel—a basket of Easter eggs. Her suitcase is still backstage because the nurses wanted to make sure the fleas were fleas and not bedbugs or anything else. Before Loretta ever left the hospital, the nurses had her showered and in a change of clean clothing. The only piece of clothing she was allowed to bring into the house was her new sequined dress because Loretta wouldn't let anyone at the hospital take it—not even her pop-pop. It's in the dryer on high heat . . . for two hours now. She hopes the sequins aren't melting.

She told her grandparents she needed a nap, but she hasn't slept at all. Just touching the spot. Over and over again. Because she can. A nurse talked to Loretta last night about self-care. This is self-care. A nurse talked to Loretta last night about staying safe. This is staying safe. The nurse talked to her last night about being happier now. But Loretta has always been happy since she found the spot. It's a natural way of things. Find spot. Be happier.

It's soon dinnertime, and Loretta sits at the made table and puts her napkin on her lap. Her pop-pop keeps smiling at her. It's four o'clock in the afternoon.

"You sure eat dinner early," Loretta says. "We don't usually get around to it in our house until the reruns are over."

Her pop-pop nods and says, "And what time is that?"

"About nine, I guess."

"And what do you eat, usually?" the voice comes from behind the kitchen counter. It's Mom-Mom, but her face is half in the oven checking on a casserole dish.

Loretta says, "Sandwiches."

For a whole minute after that, no one says anything. Loretta fidgets with the packet of horseradish sauce in her pocket. Her grandparents bring food to the table. In the casserole dish, something Mom-Mom calls *Au Gratin*, and a large bowl of buttered peas. And a plate of roasted meat, Loretta isn't sure which kind.

"Do you remember Malcolm?" Pop-Pop asks.

Loretta shakes her head.

"He's your cousin? Your mom's brother's boy."

Loretta shakes her head again.

Pop-Pop says, "Well, he lives here during the week most weeks. In the room next to yours. You'll like him."

Loretta is slowly chewing her first mouthful of food. This is no sandwich. The meat tastes weird, though, so she pulls out her packet of Arby's horseradish sauce and rips the corner open with her teeth. She squirts it on the meat, and only when she feels their stares, she looks up.

"It's good sauce."

"I'm sure it is," Pop-Pop says.

"Is Mom gonna move in here, too? Like—we're all going to live here together?"

This question makes Mom-Mom's face twist up.

"We'll figure it out when she gets home," Pop-Pop says.

"I won't have to see my dad again, right?"

"No."

"Good."

Pop-Pop nods his head. "Yes. Good."

Loretta looks down and eats her food. Eats too fast—not used to being unrushed between scenes. Her plate is clean in five minutes while her grandparents seem to chew everything a hundred times.

"Ya want seconds?" Pop-Pop asks.

"Yes, please," Loretta says, and she hands him her plate.

Two servings later, Loretta needs to lie down. Twenty minutes after that, Loretta needs to use the bathroom. Two minutes after that, Loretta is throwing up all the food she ate. Not used to rich foods like lamb or the Gruyere cheese, she can't help it. But her mom-mom is furious all the same.

The audience thinks the old woman is cruel, and she turns to them and says, "Don't judge me! I took her in! I gave her the yellow room! I bought her new clothing and will dry-clean that awful dress. But, goddamn it, I can't love anyone who Vs in my house. Not ever. Not ever again."

The audience yells an amalgam of "You never loved her!" or "You're selfish!" and "You're crazy!" or "Stop making people eat lamb!"

She turns away from them, disgusted.

Sits on the back porch step and hugs her knees.

Says, "This isn't going to work at all."

The audience boos and throws anything they have handy—breath mints, loose change, an umbrella.

Upstairs, Pop-Pop puts Loretta to bed and gives her a kiss on the forehead. Loretta is so happy, she can hear violins playing in her head. Her pop-pop says, "Don't worry—Mom-Mom will be fine. She's just a little weird about throw-up."

"Tell her I'm sorry."

"Nothing to be sorry about."

"I'm used to sandwiches."

"I know."

"I miss Mom," she says.

"She'll be here in a few days."

"I'm tired," she says.

He gets up and walks to the door. "Get some sleep," he says. "That medicine should keep everything down now."

"Night," Loretta says. Lights fade. Stage crew rolls the bed from center stage to off left.

CanIHelpYou?: a Girl More like Him

Ian and I went to Paul-the-lacrosse-player's party Saturday night but I only stayed for an hour. Sold goods. Counted money. Stopped in the bathroom where three girls were snorting coke out of their pinky nails, and they said, "Hey, you want some?" It sounded like *HEYYOUWANTSOME??????*

People on coke are awful.

I rolled them a joint for their comedown. They said, glassy-eyed, "You're the best!" That's me. The best. Whatever.

Ian wanted to stay because he was with a girl. A girl more like him. A girl named Jennifer who looked totally in love-at-first-sight with him. I should be happy for him because Ian hasn't ever really had a girlfriend. I'm not. I should be happy for him because he found a girl who understands what it's like to be Ian in Whitesville, USA. I'm not.

Got fired from my job and lost my best friend in the span of two hours.

Sunday was different. No work. No one waking me up early. No Easter dress shopping with my mother. When I rolled over and looked at my phone it was two o'clock. I felt tired and hungover, but mostly happy for the sleep. And the texts—thirteen old clients suddenly needed me.

No texts from Ian.

I spent my day at the local coffee shop, pretending to do homework on the free Wi-Fi, and meeting a lot of "friends." What

I was really doing on the Wi-Fi was looking at college entry requirements, trying to find one that would accept my 1.84 GPA.

You think I deserve this. You think I wasted my life already. You think I'm bound to end up being a nobody, but really I can do things aside from working a Drive-Thru and my weed scale. I like psychology. I liked my sculpture class last year in school so much I got an A in it. I like learning about other cultures.

It's as if seeing Ian with this girl made me see what I'm doing to myself. He's already done his college visits and he's been working on his application essay all year even though we won't apply until fall. The debate team came in third in the state. Ian will have his pick of places to go. His pick of scholarships. His pick of girls.

I don't understand why I'm like this. In love with Ian or thinking I should fall in love with anyone, ever. I'm seventeen years old. Maybe all girls think this way—that our entire focus should be on getting a guy to fall in love with us. Maybe we're all in a tunnel that way. And maybe we're all walking around heartbroken because we just want to be loved in a way that isn't even possible. Because, let's face it—boys aren't taught the same things. They aren't taught to be prince charming or even nice, for the most part.

Maybe this is why I should never get a manicure in Wichita. Maybe that's the point. Maybe the point is: there are times and places to do things and times and places not to do things. Maybe high school isn't where we should fall in love. Maybe Wichita isn't the best place to get a manicure.

I feel lost without my job at the Drive-Thru. I feel lost without Ian. I feel lost pretty much all the time now that I had a whole day to think about it. Just like the tunnel. But, for some reason, being lost underground isn't half as scary as being lost up here in the sun.

"So, are you and Jennifer going out—like out-out?" I ask Ian at lunch on Monday.

"She's amazing."

"And gorgeous."

"Smart. Funny. And her parents already like me, so that's good." This is an obvious jab at my mother. At least for me.

"Wear a fucking condom," I say.

"Stop."

"I'm serious. Your mother will kill you if you knock up some girl before college."

Ian's laugh is infectious, and I laugh, too. Nothing is funny, because we know what's about to happen, but we laugh. As he walks out of the cafeteria, I make a plan to steal my mom's bell and bury it. Or burn it. Or smash it with a hammer.

The Shoveler: Last Room

Marla left a message on my phone while I was sleeping. She's panicked about the undercoat in the living room and how it looks purple, not red . . . which is why it's called an undercoat but I don't feel like explaining it again.

I think at the end of the call, Gottfried pulled the phone away from her. I could hear jostling. I'm glad they have each other to pick at. They have yet to notice the missing can of yellow paint that I spilled on their dining room floor.

I don't call her back because I'll talk to her when I get there tonight and my mind is on other things.

Today in school two kids beat on each other so bad that there wasn't just blood on the floor, but teeth. I nearly shoveled the teeth up but then I stopped myself. I had to leave. Just walked out. I have things to do. Pay Roy for the car, set up car insurance, return my shovel to Mike-wrong-words, and then get to Marla and Gottfried's to roll the final coat on the walls.

I stop at Roy's house and give him $1,850 cash, and he gives me the Nissan's signed title. I don't stick around for conversation. I walk to Mike's side porch, where his snow shovels are lined up, and I place my shovel at the end of the row. I whisper goodbye because it's my friend and I'll miss it. Or maybe because Mike's my friend and I'll miss him.

I've been trying to picture Mike sitting around talking shit about white power. I watched him pick his naked mother out of a bathtub. He's always talking about party snacks. To me, until yesterday, that was Mike. Now I know he's wasting his life on bullshit. I still don't even know what to say about it. It's just bullshit.

I'm so excited to get this job done I get the first coat of red on the living room in two hours. I don't even take a dinner break. Once I get the second coat on and look around, I feel prouder than I have in a long time. I stand next to Gottfried looking pleased.

He looks pleased, too.

"Where's Malcolm?" I ask, because Gottfried likes that we get along even though he's never seen us get along.

"We have another guest, now. She's sleeping upstairs."

I don't pretend to understand this, and I close up the paint can.

"Is she sick?" I ask. I've been here since five and haven't seen her.

"Who?"

"Your new guest."

"A little. We gave her the day off school. Maybe tomorrow, too. She sleeps a lot," Gottfried says. "My favorite granddaughter. Don't tell the others," he jokes.

"You're nice to open your house to people," I say.

I'm not sure why, but when I say that, Gottfried looks sad.

"I hate to sound ungrateful," Marla says, "but I'm not sure about that color."

"Go put ice on your head," Gottfried snaps.

She stomps to the kitchen and gets an ice pack and then goes into the bedroom to lie down.

Gottfried follows me to the garage where I clean the

brushes and rollers. He doesn't say much. Just stands there looking around.

"I don't understand why they paint garages white," he says.

I grunt and keep cleaning brushes.

"I think it would look better in gray," he says. "What do you think?"

I'm so tired. Tired of painting. Tired of this house and these people even though there isn't anything I can pinpoint that makes them bad people. I'm sure they're fine people. I'm pretty sure they forgot my name months ago, so it's not like I've been part of the family or anything.

"Gray would look nice," I say.

"You have a new car," he says.

"Yeah. Got it yesterday."

"How much did it set you back?"

"Like two grand. Good deal." I turn the water off in the sink and take my tin of clean brushes toward the back door in the garage. I walk out to the barrier of the forest and I shake the water out like I always do, but when I turn around Gottfried is standing right there.

"What are you doing for Easter?"

"Probably sleeping late and enjoying a weekend off," I say.

He laughs. "Man, do I miss sleeping late."

"Yeah. I hear old people can't really do that anymore."

"Lots of things old people can't do, son."

There it is again.

"You okay?" Gottfried asks. I notice I've stopped shaking the brushes out.

"Yeah. I'm good."

"You interested in more work? We can probably get that garage done in two days if we work together."

"Let me think about it."

"Must be lonely moving so much and not having a family," he says.

"I have friends." This is a lie. I have Mike. And the words inked on his arm are wrong. He's not my friend. He's Mom's friend. Or maybe a lot of other things I don't want to think about right now.

"You must be missing a lot of parties working here every weekend," he says. He gets this look in his eye like he remembers raucous parties.

I leave the clean paintbrushes by the garage sink and wash my hands. Gottfried hands me a towel to dry off. "I'll be back tomorrow for a few touch-ups, then we're done, right?"

"Come inside with me for a minute," he says. "I have something for you."

When we walk in, a girl is standing in the mudroom. She's wearing a red-sequined dress and she's beautiful, but probably too skinny for her own good.

Gottfried says, "I thought you were heading to bed."

"Hi!" she says, ignoring Gottfried completely.

"Hey," I answer.

"Loretta, this is our painter, um . . . uh."

Gottfried totally doesn't know my name.

"I'm the shoveler," I say and I put my hand out so she can shake it.

"I'm the Ringmistress!" she says. She's smiling like crazy. She's simple but not dumb. She's a puppy with a chew toy.

Gottfried looks at both of us like he's just witnessed some sort of miracle.

And I think he may have.

Gottfried reaches into his pocket and then transfers what he has into my sweatshirt pocket. It feels like a plastic Easter egg. I pop it open while it's still in my pocket and there's cash inside.

"Are you staying for a while?" the Ringmistress asks.

"Have to get home."

"He'll be back tomorrow," Gottfried says. "Around four?" he asks.

"Sounds about right," I say.

The Ringmistress throws herself at me and hugs me. It's not sexy in any way. It's like she's never hugged anyone before. I hug her back and she whispers in my ear, "Thank you. Thank you so much."

She's the meaning of life.

She is. Look at her.

> What's wrong with me? Every time I see a girl I weigh her in my mind like flour. Like she's a commodity. Like she's here to give me some answer. The answer I'm looking for is: Son, you are marriable. You are father-able. You are spend-a-life-time-able. I met this girl four minutes ago and I'm already wondering what our babies would look like. This makes no sense.

The guys I've known would cut her up like The Freak said the first night I met her—ass, chest, legs, face, hair. They'd notice her big front teeth and how she doesn't wear makeup. They'd laugh at the bites on her arms—when I want to apply salve to them. Boys are fucked up, man. Whether you're a typical one who talks about girls like they're here only to suck your dick, or whether you're me, looking for a soul mate, you're weird. I'm weird. This is all weird.

Malcolm's Strainer

Two years ago Dad and I were walking down the street on our way back from eating at Nino's. He had a turkey club and I had a grilled cheese kid's meal, which sounds like I'm seven years old but it's my favorite. At the time I was fourteen. In eighth grade and hating every minute of it. He was still working—a graphic designer with about twenty accounts.

He had hair back then, and he'd style it every morning to make it look like he'd just woken up. Women loved this but he never noticed. Since Mom died when I was so little, he always said he was married to fatherhood. Not married to me, because that would be creepy, but married to fatherhood.

"You're driving me crazy with your grades," he said.

"Eighth grade sucks," I said.

"All of it sucks, but you have to get good grades. Or at least try." He side-hugged me, and even though I was fouteen and he was forty-one, it didn't make me feel like a little kid. We were close.

"I'll try harder," I said. "But it's all stupid. Like. American History is bullshit. Andrew Jackson for three whole days? And no mention of the Removal Act."

Dad cringed. "Same when I went to school. Wish I could have raised you in a place where the history books don't lie, but pretty much all history books lie."

"Yeah," I said. Dad always encouraged me to be skeptical of shit in school, was the one who put the "Question Authority" sticker on my binder in fifth grade.

"So, I have some news," he said.

"Okay."

I genuinely thought he was going to tell me that we were moving to Europe. This wasn't something I made up in my head. He'd been talking about it and he had three new clients there and it was on subject, right? Surely Europe didn't lie as much in their history books.

"Well, I, uh. I don't quite know how to tell you this so I'll just say it."

I suddenly didn't think he was going to tell me we were moving to Europe. I looked over at him and his face looked like rain.

"The doctor told me I have cancer," he said. "It's not great news, I know, but it can be treated."

" . . ."

"I have to start treatments ASAP and I'm sure I'll be fine a year from now." I must have been quiet because he said, "Are you okay?"

"What kind of cancer?"

"Pancreatic."

Pancreas. That was the one kind of cancer I knew about. Kills you fast. Killed Violet Numeyer's aunt the year before.

"That's bad," I said.

"The doctor is hopeful."

"The doctor is paid to be hopeful."

"I'm hopeful."

"Are you sure? Like, did you get all the tests already or is this, like, just the first test?"

Dad pulled me in for a side-hug again. "We've done all the tests we need to do."

"Why didn't you tell me?" Stupid question. He just told me.

"We had to make sure first."

"You can't die," I said.

"I won't die," he said.

"Pancreas is bad. I'm not stupid."

"We caught it early."

See, that was the lie. They didn't catch it early. They just caught it when they caught it. Dad wasn't one to get regular checkups because he's self-employed and his health insurance sucks. No way he'd go to a doctor if something wasn't already wrong.

I don't remember ninth grade at all. Nothing stands out, really. I couldn't tell you the classes I took. I don't even remember my schedule and it was only last year. I could tell you I nearly failed three classes, but teachers had mercy on me because Dad got balder and whiter and skinnier and we moved from our house into the apartment. I went on free lunch. I went on free everything.

Dad was still cool and he still sat at his drawing table and made logos and drew sketches. He worked on his computer all day and all night. Got new clients. Expanded. One time he said, "If I knew cancer would get me more work, I'd have gotten it years ago."

That's how we get through things. Laughing. Joking. Sarcasm.

But Dad didn't seem as married to fatherhood as he'd been before. He was disconnecting and maybe I was, too. Makes sense.

I helped him shave his head. I shaved mine, too, in solidarity.

We ate a lot of grilled cheese sandwiches—but not at Nino's. We were on an impossible budget that started with a minus sign.

That's what ninth grade was for me. A blur of free lunch,

275

no hair, and minus signs. We sold furniture. We sold old video games. We sold anything we didn't need. We embraced a life without stuff. It can get addictive—downsizing. I sold almost everything I owned, and we only kept the couch and our beds and one comfy chair.

That was the chair I was sitting in when, a year after our first cancer conversation, Dad said, "So now that you're done with ninth grade, I think you should move schools."

"That's stupid," I said.

"Hear me out."

I nodded.

"I can't do this anymore," he said. He cried a little when he said it, too. "I can't keep trying to work and beat cancer and pay all these fucking bills."

"Um."

He sighed. "I talked to my mom this weekend. She said she'd be happy to have you move in."

"With her and Gottfried?"

"Yeah."

"Why?"

"I'm not able to be a good dad anymore, Malcolm. You must already know this."

"Fuck that!" I sat up in the chair. "No. No way I'm living with those two. I haven't even seen them in like two years. You know how they are. I mean, you're the one who told me about how they are."

Dad did that thing where he moved his hands like I should tone it down. I only wanted to get louder.

"No!" I said. "I'm not going to calm down. Look. You

wanted a chance to be a great dad and you *are* a great dad. The whole reason you wanted to be a great dad is because your dad sucked. You told me all this. Why would you want me to live with your sucky dad?"

"I can't provide for you anymore. It's—I don't know. It makes sense from where we sit."

"No way. I'm not leaving you. And anyway, if you die then I don't get to spend time with you before you die? No Bruce Lee movies? No impromptu Bob Marley dance parties in the living room?"

He had tears on his face now. They escaped and raced down his cheeks. "Malcolm. Stop. Look. I'm exhausted. I can't even feed you anymore."

"I love fucking grilled cheese sandwiches. I love cereal. I'm easy to feed," I said. "And who'll be here for you when you feel like shit? To make you eat?"

He stopped and wiped his face and blew his nose. I felt like I was in eighth-grade history all over again learning about how Andrew Jackson was such a great guy. The room was spinning with stupid ideas.

I said, "You managed to beat this so far. You managed to beat this. So now, if you die, you'll just die alone and with client work piled up on the coffee table? I mean, if we still had a coffee table. We just became new people, Dad. Remember when you said that? About how we shed our mountains of bullshit? About how stuff didn't matter—about how we'd start going cool places and doing cool things because we don't have anything to lose?"

"Jamaica."

I was in such a rage I didn't hear him. "You said all these people were working so they could afford more shit in their lives and you weren't going to be a part of it anymore. You said we'd be minimalists. You said all that mattered was *human connection*. And you're moving me in with your *parents*? The only thing minimal in their lives is human connection. I don't think they ever talked to me beyond a hello and small talk. Fuck. Please tell me you haven't already made this decision without asking me first."

"I—"

"Because that's how you told me about cancer, too, and I'm tired of being the last one to know about something this big," I said. "Hold on. Did you say Jamaica?"

That was the trade-off.

Dad can work from anywhere. He chose Jamaica because he had friends there. Mostly Ruth, who he used to go out with in college, but she has a lot of friends—one of whom owns a hotel on the cliffs in Negril.

Our first stay was a month long. We didn't talk about Marla and Gottfried for the whole time. I met Eleanor during the second week. I bought three bracelets from her and asked her to tie them around my wrist.

"All of them?" she asked.

"Yeah."

She giggled.

"Do you want to come and have dinner with us tonight?" I asked. "It's just me and my dad and sometimes Ruth. Over on the cliffs."

"I have to get home," she said. "Make dinner, you know. And I have to study."

"It's summer."

She tied another bracelet around my wrist. "I'm taking a class. Next year I sit my exams."

"I just want to see you again," I said.

"I'm here every day. You can find me."

"Okay," I said.

And every day I bought one more bracelet and asked her to tie it on my wrist. Every day we talked more and I learned that Eleanor wants to become a politician. "Women need to have more power here," she said. "We can't get ahead if there's no one to represent us in our own country." She told me how she'd never date a boy because he'd only get in the way. "Imagine! Me with some American boy and trying to represent the women of Jamaica! No, mon."

By the time I left after our month, my left arm was almost to my elbow with bracelets. I'd convinced Eleanor to kiss me only once, but we both liked it.

"Don't worry," I said. "I won't get in the way of your bid for prime minister."

"Good."

"I just like you a lot."

"Good."

"Maybe I can be on your cabinet or something."

"Minister of bracelets," she said, pointing to my left forearm.

We laughed and didn't kiss again. She had no idea I'd be back. I had no idea I'd be back. Neither of us had any idea that Dad was there on a mission. A new mission to beat cancer— not his personal cancer, but capital-C Cancer. No pharmaceutical bills. No hospital bills. He was sure he'd found a cure, except he was too late to save himself.

This was how he got the idea for the business.

That's what we would call it. The business.

Except he didn't buy or sell anything. Ruth had a friend who had a kind heart, enough money, and fields up in the mountains. You know the kind of fields. Dad did whatever he did to make it into an easy-to-transport product. Stationery, brochures, business cards—all of which looked totally normal in a graphic designer's luggage.

"If I sell it, I'd be as bad as the drug companies. You can't sell life. You can't buy life. You can make life and offer it to anyone who needs it. That's the only way to do this shit. First come, first served, and free."

Dad was so excited by the business that I couldn't talk to him about how it made me feel.

Secondary. That's how it made me feel.

He was more worried about being as bad as a pharmaceutical company than he was about being as bad as his own crappy father. Fact is, I've never felt as alone as I've felt in the last two years. I couldn't complain because people dying of cancer have it worse than me. I couldn't explain because I sounded like I was whining.

Funny thing was, all those squares he'd meet on planes and in airports—every one of them knew someone dying of cancer. Didn't matter that they wouldn't smoke a joint if you lit it for them. What mattered was they didn't want to watch their loved ones suffer.

And outside of my grandparents, I can't say I've ever met anyone who wanted to watch their loved ones suffer.

CanIHelpYou?'s Strainer

I've had a credit card since I was twelve. In my own name. I keep it in my wallet for emergencies, but I've yet to have an emergency that requires spending my parents' money. They disgust me. You're rolling your eyes because I'm so typical. *What a spoiled brat. I'd have killed for a credit card! For parents who cared that much!* Thing is, I'm just a flower bed. Christmas decorations. I'm an Audi coupe. A new linen suit. Pair of Jimmy Choos. A fresh coat of white paint on the garage out back in case anyone looks. I'm not a person. I'm a check box. You need to understand, this isn't a childhood. This is a diorama. It's a fucked-up diorama and I can't get out of the shoebox.

I didn't need the Arby's job. I don't need any job. The thing about my mom is, she's trying to be the opposite of her mom, and her mom wouldn't loan her a quarter for the pay phone. Grubby. That's what Mom says. She says her parents are grubby.

I don't think that word means what she thinks it means, but it fits.

We're the only ones who show up to Easter dinners anymore. I haven't seen my cousins in years, and I never even met two of them. Last time I saw Malcolm he said I was just a brat, which was a bummer because I always liked him. He was, like, ten and I was twelve and I guess I looked like a brat. It's why I liked the Arby's uniform. The day I brought it home Mom was mortified.

"At least you can buy your own khakis," she said. "We'll go out later. Maybe some shorter ones. Oh! With loafers!"

"I don't need loafers."

She looked at me in that way. Exasperated that I didn't want loafers. "You're just like my mother," she said.

"Did she work at Arby's, too?"

"Stop being coy."

"Maybe *you're* just like your mother," I said.

I hadn't tried this before and I found it effective. My mother can be a fucking nightmare on most days, but don't ever tell her she's like her mother. Even my father wandered into the room to watch what would unfold.

Good word, *unfold*. Because that's what she did. Like one of those magical origami shapes—one minute a crane with moving wings, then next a crumbled blob of paper that looked like it went through the washing machine.

"DON'T YOU EVER SAY THAT TO ME AGAIN," she said. Her jaw was clenched—teeth together—and yet she managed to yell it. "You don't know anything about my parents! Do you even know what they're like?"

"They seem okay to me," I said. It was a lie. They don't seem okay to me, but I liked watching the origami unfold.

"Give me your credit card," she said to me, hand out. She got up. She walked over and I swear I thought she was going to hit me but she didn't. She just kept her hand out for the card.

"It's in my wallet."

"Go get it."

"I don't even use it," I said.

"Go get it."

When I brought it to her, she already had a pair of scissors ready. And she cut it up over the kitchen trash can with a strange sort of smile on her face.

I mustn't have looked as upset as she wanted me to look. "You did this! You did this!" she said.

Dad looked like he wanted to put his hands on her shoulders to help her calm down but he stayed two paces behind her.

"From now on, you live on twenty bucks a week. And anything you make in that uniform. No help from us."

"Fine," I said.

"Won't be so fine when you figure out how much you cost."

Sorry, but that's totally something her mother would say.

It turns out I did just fine on just my Arby's money. I used to cash out their twenty into quarters and put them in the parking meters on Main Street on my walk home from school just to do something good with it.

Mom cried on my lap one night about two months later. Told me how sorry she was. Gave me a replacement credit card. Said, "I don't understand why you don't love me."

She wanted an answer. She had hold of my elbows, her head in my lap, her tears soaking through my greasy-smelling khakis. "Why?" she asked again. So I figured I'd try.

"I wish you weren't so racist," I said.

It was like watching origami fold itself. She went from this heap on my lap into a massive origami rhinoceros. "I'm not racist!"

"Mom. You're totally racist."

She stuttered over words until she found one. "You're too young to understand the world."

"Do you remember my ninth birthday party?" I ask.

"What? God." She sighs. "What did I do wrong?"

"What?"

"What did I do wrong at your ninth birthday party?"

I looked at her. She was an origami swan. She was an Audi coupe. She was a pair of Jimmy Choos. She was perfect now, and no longer a sobbing mess in my lap. Ready to fight. You've been there. I know you have. You've been in that place where one minute you're miserable about who you are, and the next minute, you're your own defense lawyer ready to dazzle the jury with bullshit.

"Go on. Tell me what I did that was so wrong at your ninth birth-day party. Was it the gifts? The money you got? The savings bonds?"

"You didn't do anything wrong."

"So why'd you bring it up?"

I couldn't do it. I wasn't going to win. "I don't need the credit card," I said. I left it on the coffee table next to her stupid bell.

The stupid bell—her mother bought it down south. The handle painted black with a blackface set of white eyes, two dots for a nose, and a wide-open red mouth. The bottom of the handle and bell part covered in a big house-slave gingham dress with an apron on the very top of the handle above the caricature face, a red handkerchief tied up, you know the kind, from the old maple syrup bottles. How she could deny being racist while in the same room with that bell is beyond me.

"What was SO WRONG with your life when you were nine?"

She was a screaming swan on the couch. I was a flying crane on my way up the steps. I left her question in the living room where I couldn't answer it.

But my life changed in that roller rink, and she'd never understand because she was, despite all her efforts, just like her mother. If there was a pill—some kind of healthy bacteria pill—that cured racist nightmare people, I'd use the credit card to buy enough to treat the both of them. Instead I used it three weeks later for a cash withdrawal to buy my first half pound.

You think I'm an idiot. Putting myself at risk like this but you know what? My clients are nicer to me than my own mother. She can't love. She can't connect. She has so much stuff that it blocks her reach.

You can think what you want.

You can look at our Audi coupe and think we're lucky.

You can marvel at our flower beds and smell our lilac shrubs.

But you can't envy what it's really like to live like this. Trust me. This is not the kind of thing you say *gimme* to.

Malcolm Isn't Going to Be a Plumber

I'm starting to realize that my love for Eleanor isn't really love. I mean, I love her and she's beautiful and she's so smart and she wants to be Jamaica's first female prime minister. I love all of that. I love her bracelets and her ankles and her eyes. I love her jokes. I love how she's got all these plans but still has that relaxed Jamaican no-problem attitude. But for all that love, I'm really just looking for a way out of where I am. She deserves better. She's a human, not a door.

This week she brings her big sister, Judy, with her everywhere. I like Judy, but she makes me feel inferior—more inferior than usual. Could be because she's twenty. Could be because she's already married and has a kid. A life. Here in paradise.

"You staying longer than a few days this time?" Judy asks.

"I think we go back Friday," I say. "Longer than usual."

"You're lucky you get to travel so much!"

I look at Eleanor. "Does she know what's going on?"

Eleanor nods.

I look back at Judy. "He's not getting better."

"I know," she says. "I'm sorry."

Eleanor reaches out for my hand and holds it. I want to tell Judy about my plan to live here and be a beach bum and help out in any way I can, but I don't. It's laughable, really. All of a sudden, it's just laughable.

"Whatchya going to do when he dies?" Judy asks.

I take a few breaths. No one has ever asked me this before.

People usually tell me what I'm going to do when he dies. "I don't know. I want to move here. Never leave."

"You'd move from America to *here*?"

"Yeah."

Eleanor says, "He's not like the tourists, Judy. I keep telling you that."

"Whatchya going to do here, though? You fish? You build? What skills do you have, you know?"

"Haven't thought of that yet," I say. "I could take over my dad's business, maybe." It just came to me. I don't mean it.

"You could always learn a trade," Eleanor says. "Judy's husband is a plumber."

Judy smiles with pride.

"I don't know," I say again. I'm not going to be a plumber, no matter how much I love the flush toilet.

I want an older sister like Judy. I want someone to challenge my dumb ideas and tell me to shut up when I sound stupid.

I excuse myself while we approach the resorts and I run into the water. Negril beach is shallow for a long time before you get to a place you can really dive in. I run to it until my quads burn and then dive. I open my eyes underwater and let the salt rinse them. I love the stinging feeling. Clears my sinuses. Clears my ears. Clears my head.

I picture Dad's memorial service and who's really going to be there, you know? Me. Me and who? Marla and Gottfried. And maybe my nightmare aunt. Dad doesn't talk to his other siblings. Told me two of them disappeared from the family decades ago. What a waste.

If I had a brother, I'd call him every other day. If I had a sister, I'd call her on the days I didn't call my brother. Just for the connection. Watching Eleanor and Judy—even when Judy tells Eleanor that she's doing everything wrong—makes me see how alone I'm about to be. Eleanor knows how to tell Judy to hush up and leave her alone. Probably knows how to hug her and help her when she cries, too.

I'll never have that.

I love Eleanor because I'm alone in the world. And that's no reason to love anyone. I need someone my age to share the burden. It's such a big burden and no one over thirty can seem to see that I walk around with it every single day. So concerned with my grades or my eating lamb chops to stop and really think about what it's like to have the only living human I'm connected to dying, right in front of me.

You wonder why I'm so uptight about entitled white culture? It's not just that I live here half the time and see real poverty. It's not just the snack baskets in first class. It's because entitled white culture encourages those inside it to never look outside their own fucking worlds. We blow everything off because we're so concerned with looking good we can't just feel. My own fucking grandparents can't stop for a minute and understand what I'm going through.

You can't fill that hole with a fucking lamb chop.

THE FREAK LOVES SWIMMING NAKED AND AUTHENIC JERK CHICKEN!

The Freak has been naked for months, wrapped in her burrito of dirt. Flickering takes her so many places, but none of them is comfortable. Until now. She's so buoyant. The water is so warm. She's thankful her first swimming-flicker is to here, wherever this is. The water is crystal. The beach is uncrowded. There's a boy here—about fifteen feet away. He's floating on his back and grimacing into the sun. The Freak can feel sadness from him.

"Excuse me," she says.

The boy doesn't hear.

"Hey. Pardon me? Can you hear me?"

His ears are underwater, so The Freak splashes a bit and walks closer. His eyes open and he stands in the water.

"Sorry I'm naked," The Freak says. "I just got here."

"Oh."

"You're sad," she says, once she gets a good look at his eyes.

"You would be, too."

The Freak walks into deeper water so her nakedness isn't so obvious to the people on the beach.

"I'll be your sister," she says.

The boy gives her a look she's used to by now.

"Don't ask how I know," she says. "Just trust me."

"Okay."

The boy doesn't know what to say. So he says, "I'm Malcolm," and he stretches his hand out.

The Freak doesn't shake hands. She's a hugger. So she hugs him and she knows it's awkward because she's naked, but everyone is essentially naked so she hopes he doesn't mind.

He hugs her for longer than she expected. He's sobbing. She says it will all be okay.

"Not okay," he says.

"It will be. I promise."

"It's too much."

"It's too much for now. But one day it won't be, okay?"

He breaks the hug and steps back. Scans the beach for someone, and then turns back to The Freak. But she's gone.

The boy doesn't know what to do with his grief. A minute ago, he had a sister. A minute ago, he had someone with which to share the burden. Family—even though it was just a naked stranger. Now, he's alone again.

The Freak didn't flicker. She swam to shore. She wrapped herself in a resort towel and followed the smell of jerk chicken. Two girls stop her and ask if she'd like to buy a bracelet.

"I don't have any money," she says. "But I'm hungry."

The two girls take her to the jerk shack and get her a paper plate of jerk and rice and peas. She sits on the sand and eats like she hasn't eaten in days.

"Where are you staying?" one girl asks.

"Nowhere," The Freak answers.

"Where did you come from?" the other girl asks.

"Nowhere," The Freak answers.

"How do you know Malcolm?"

"The boy in the water?" She pulls a chicken bone from her mouth. "He needs a sister."

The girls give each other that look only sisters can give. The Freak knows these looks. She sees them on siblings wherever she goes. Even animal siblings communicate like this.

She can't stop herself from thinking that maybe if she had a sister, someone would have found her by now. She would be at peace. A sister is a special thing. Magical. More magical than flickering. More magical than sand. More magical than sea.

She writes a note to Malcolm on the back of her jerk-stained paper plate.

Rancocas, NJ. 39.992372, -74.844528.

Come find your sister.

Loretta, Act Three: with Pop-Pop

Loretta has never had a real audience before. You were always here in her mind's eye. In her imagination, you were eating cotton candy and peanuts. You were being entertained by clowns who made shapes out of balloons.

Loretta's been working on her balloon shapes for years in real life. It's her favorite act. Her finale—but she's never tested it on anyone else. She's gotten good at balloon genitals. In Loretta's circus, this makes sense. She has the curse and it's nothing to be ashamed about. Everyone does it. Unless they don't, and if they don't, Loretta worries about them. She's had issues getting the clitoris just right inside the balloon-folds of the labia minora and majora. Penis and testicles are much easier. Of course.

She has no idea how her pop-pop will react to her balloon shapes, so she decides to take the risk and introduce him to the troupe first. Marla is taking her usual midday nap, and Loretta has the week off school. It's Monday. Her mother will be at the house tomorrow. Gottfried will help her mother move her possessions from the wagon. The police have already been arranged just in case. Loretta's father is on the lam. Just like him—running away from the consequences. Just like him to control everything even though he can't control himself.

Intermission is over. Audience jostles in their seats and people try to open their snacks quietly.

Loretta twirls in her red sequins and says, "Come on! Come

on! Best show on Earth! Six acts! Clowns! Fun for the kids and grown-ups alike! Only five dollars!"

Loretta's pop-pop says, "Five dollars?"

"Yep. Five."

He waits for Loretta to start the show but she won't until he hands the money over. He has to go find his wallet and comes back with a ten-dollar bill.

"Do you have change?" he asks.

Loretta cocks her head to the side. "Does it look like I have change?"

"I guess not."

"I'll give you credit for tomorrow's matinee."

Her pop-pop shrugs. "Seems fair."

Loretta retrieves her lunch box and the tiny ring. She opens the sides of the ring and assembles Gerald's train. Only four cars. Poor thing, that's all he can handle.

She has the troupe harnessed already and puts on the show. Her pop-pop looks a mix of enthralled and mortified.

"Are those real fleas?"

Loretta answers, "I'm no shyster. This is the greatest god-damned flea circus in the country."

"Oh," he says.

The audience stares at the back of his head. They send messages. *Shut up, old man. Don't say what you're thinking.*

Doesn't work.

Gottfried scratches his ankle and says, "I don't think a pretty girl like you should be playing with fleas."

Loretta rolls her eyes and says, "Keep your weird ideas to yourself."

The Shoveler: Last Day

It's Tuesday and Mom says she wants me to stay home from school. Says she misses me. Says she wants to talk. Says she wants a test drive in my car because she wants to see if it's better than her car. "Maybe we can trade," she says. She can't help it. She is who she is. But she catches herself now, a minute later, and adds, "You really worked your ass off for this. I'm so proud." She hands me the keys. "You drive *me* somewhere."

"I don't have anywhere to drive, really," I say.

"I do."

"Then you should drive," I say, and I hand the keys back to her.

We drive through town, toward the mountain with the bizarre pagoda on it. She knows the streets in the city—she's taking lefts and rights like she's lived here before. It's not like anywhere else we ever moved. She usually gets lost.

We land in a suburb about ten minutes from the city.

"See that? I went to preschool there," she says.

I nod. It's a church with an addition tacked on to the side.

"There used to be a great drive-in ice cream place here. And that used to be a gas station where guys would actually pump your gas for you," she says, pointing across the road at what looks like a high-end apartment complex for urban professionals. "It's a sleeper town now," she says. "They drive all the way to Philadelphia every day for work. Two hours of traffic each way. I couldn't do that. Could you?"

"Nah," I say.

She takes a right onto a road that becomes deceptively twisty.

"You know your way around," I say.

She says, "I learned how to drive on this road. On all these roads."

We've lived here for nearly three months and she's only telling me this now.

I don't say anything—not because I'm mad, but because what is there to say? She had a home. A place she grew up. Has roads she knows.

"You okay?" she asks.

"Yeah."

"You're quiet."

"Not sure what to say."

"You see all this?" she says, gesturing to her left and then to her right. "This was ours once. Or supposed to be."

"Town houses?" I ask. Because that's what's here—town houses.

"Potatoes," she says. "Six hundred acres of potatoes."

I can't imagine it. After the town houses, there's a development that looks like an Easter display—Marla's taste in interior paint. Pastel siding on cube houses.

"All this. Everything here—both sides of the road. For another mile, too."

"So." I stop here because since she's never told me anything about our family, I feel stupid guessing. But I do it anyway. "You grew up on a farm?"

She turns on the radio and shakes her head. "Almost. I *almost* grew up on a farm. Almost."

Nope. I'm not guessing anymore. I'm patient. Surprisingly patient for a kid who's been waiting on this conversation for sixteen years.

Mom knows the radio stations. She finds classic rock. She seems angry.

I'm not angry.

I was so angry for so long but now I just keep looking out my car window and trying to unsee the houses and aboveground swimming pools and road signs and those flags they put up when they install an invisible dog fence and imagine six hundred acres of potatoes. Isn't working.

"My elementary school was back there," she points. I can see the brick building. "They renovated it. Too small for all these new kids."

"You just went to one?" I ask. "Like just one elementary school?"

"Yep."

I try to calculate how many elementary schools I've gone to.

"Kindergarten to sixth grade," she says.

"So your school was surrounded by your own farm?"

"Almost."

"You keep saying that," I say.

"It's a long story."

"You already started it," I say.

Mom sighs. She takes a left and pulls into a small parking area next to a white clapboard chapel across from her elementary school. "Look at it. It's the size of a fuckin' high school." She looks at me. Looks back out into the almost-farm-life she did/didn't have, and adds, "I want to show you more."

We drive down a road with older houses on it. When we get to the end there's a traffic light and Mom stops. "That Rite Aid? Used to be a diner." She points directly across the road at a law office. "That's where the owner's family lived—right across the

street from their diner. God. Great grilled cheese sandwiches."
Across the intersection is a huge shopping plaza—the usual big-
box stores, supermarkets, and fast-food chains. "That was a mom-
and-pop gas station and a motel. Great little guest pool. Had a hot
tub. We rented it for our senior party. My friend Jen worked as the
lifeguard." She gets that faraway look people get when they have
memories from their past, so this is new to me. Up until today
Mom didn't have any past. "Great party."

"You rented it?"

"A bunch of us. We all had summer jobs."

"So you grew up here all the way to graduation?" I ask. I'm
trying not to feel the tunnel closing around me but it's there. I
can't deny it.

"I didn't graduate," she says, turning right and doing the
full circle again—the right off the main highway, the twisting
road, the town houses, the Easter egg development, the school,
the chapel. I stay quiet for the whole circle and try to visual-
ize the whole place as potatoes. I'm not even sure what potato
plants look like.

"You didn't graduate because of me, right?"

"Not because of you, no. That's *almost* true, but not true."

"A lot of almosts today."

"This is the land of almost, I guess," she says. "Always was."

"So where'd the potatoes go?" I ask.

"We owned most of this land since the late 1700s. Crazy,
right? We were famous for potatoes. Shipped them all over the
country. And my dad just sold it." She snaps her fingers. "One
minute we had a two-hundred-year-old family history and family business. The next minute, we were just normal people living

in the same house with no family. My dad's whole side stopped talking to us," she said. "I was the last born—a few years after they sold the farm. My grandparents probably didn't even know I existed."

"Wow," I say, but I don't point out that we have this in common.

"I don't think my dad knew how bad it would mess things up," she says. "Or maybe he did. But it messed us up."

"Is your house still here?" I ask.

She nods. "And I don't plan on driving anywhere near it," she says and I realize only now that there's a good chance her parents still live here. My grandparents. My family. I suddenly feel shoplifted. I'm a pork loin. I'm a tube of lip gloss.

She drives over a bridge that spans a river then pulls into a fire company parking lot. She sits there quietly and if I was to guess, I'd say she might cry.

"So you have brothers and sisters?"

"Yeah. A few," she says.

"Wow."

"Yeah. Wow." Mom seems as surprised by her own information as I am. "I haven't talked to any of them since I was eighteen."

"You ran away?"

"Not quite," she says.

"Does Mike know them?" I say. "I mean, does he see them or your family or whatever?" At the mere mention of Mike, I shudder. Wrong words. Wrong words. Wrong words.

"Not anymore, no. I don't know."

I think about whether to bring this up or not but she seems open enough and I feel I should take advantage of it. "Did you know Mike had a tattoo? On his shoulder?"

"Oh god," she says.

"So you know it, then," I say. "I haven't been able to figure it out since I saw it."

"Nothing to figure out," she says. "Stupid tattoo says it all, right?"

"This is why you can't go out with Mike," I say.

"That and other things. He's a friend. Just because I'm older doesn't mean every guy I meet I want to marry, you know. Just because he's nice or whatever. Anyway, it's conflicting. He's into that shit and I'm not."

"I don't think I can hang out with him anymore, you know?" I stay quiet for a while. "I mean, I like him. He's nice. We have fun, I guess. But I can't be friends with a guy who thinks like that."

"I know," Mom says.

"But you're still friends with him."

"I know," she says. "He got me the apartment. I never really thought about having to live next door or getting closer—like dragging you into it."

"I still don't get it. How can he be so cool and be like that?"

"You'd be surprised who's like that. They're all over the place."

"Huh."

"Welcome to my hometown," she says. "That's how things are. It's just normal for these people to think the way they do. Runs in the family, usually."

"Like potatoes."

"Like potatoes," she says.

I look around while she drives us home and we don't say much. Then I say, "So, are you here to see your brothers and sisters or what?"

"I don't know."

"What's your old business?"

"I don't know anymore. I just felt like I should come home. If this is what home is. I can't tell."

"You seem to know your way around," I say. "And you have memories here."

"True."

"Must be home, then."

"I guess."

Mom doesn't sound convinced but she doesn't know what it's like to grow up any other way.

"About Mike," she says. "I can't be friends with him anymore, either. I don't know why it took me so long."

"It's not like he was born with that tattoo. How were you supposed to know?"

"I knew. It was just something I chose to ignore, I guess. I don't know."

"Next time we move, I'm not making friends with anyone until summer when I can see their tattoos," I say. I'm trying to make a joke, but Mom just nods as if I were serious. As if she's already thinking of the next move. As if she's already packing.

When we get back to the apartment I tell her I have to leave for work and she nods at me from behind her phone—which I imagine is showing her new apartments in a new state. We always said we'd try New England one day.

Mike is out front with his head under the hood of his car. I try to make it to my car without him seeing me.

"Hey! How's it running?" he says.

"Great! Late for work!"

"Come over for a beer later!" he says.

"Maybe!" I say. I feel stupid. *Maybe? More like never.* I drive to Marla and Gottfried's house thinking of the hundred other things I wished I could say.

"Where's Malcolm?" I ask.

"Don't ask," Marla answers.

Gottfried holds his arms out like he's an airplane. From this I gather Malcolm has flown back to Jamaica.

I look at Loretta, who is staring at me and smiling. I say, "So, you're going to live here, now, right?"

She nods.

"You're in great hands," I say. I feel so stupid.

"My parents always said they were assholes, but I figure I'll give them a try," she says. Marla and Gottfried are sitting right here. They don't know what to say. Or maybe they don't say anything because they already knew this.

I just nod and say, "A few touch-ups and I'm done!" I turn to Gottfried. "Do you want to inspect the work one last time?"

"He inspects everything all the time." Marla says. "He's like a spy."

Marla hasn't been the same since she fell.

CanIHelpYou?'s Doorbell Rings

Ian shows up at my front door after school on Tuesday. My mother is home, and half of me wants to let him in and sit on the couch with him. The other half—the half that took down all his school pictures from around my mirror except this year's—knows I can't use Ian to get back at my mother. I open the door and say, "We can't talk here."

Ian says, "Let's go for a drive," and holds up a set of keys. Car keys. I tiptoe out the front door, run to the driveway, and walk around it. It's the perfect car—blue Volvo with a sunroof. I try to be happy for him. I'm not. I try not to covet my best friend's car. I do anyway. I ask all the dumb questions: *Where did you get it? When? How much did it cost?* I don't even hear his answers over my jealousy. We get in the car, and Ian starts it up and puts it in reverse. He backs up a few feet and then puts it in park again.

"You don't have anything on you, do you?"

"Nope. I'm clean. Not even an Advil," I say.

He puts it back into reverse and glides slowly out of the driveway.

He says, "So, I got a job at Lakeside. In the office, helping with scheduling and stuff." Lakeside is a rehabilitation center—kinda like a nursing home. Jennifer works there, I bet.

"You quit Weis?"

"No more shopping for dumbass white people who can't make up their minds," he says.

"Hallelujah!" I say. "Good riddance to them."

I lean toward the stereo to turn it up and see how good the speakers are, but Ian says, "No. We have to talk."

"Oh."

He drives for a minute, but doesn't say anything.

Then, "I'm gonna pull in up here." He pulls into a parking space near the park. I think we're going to get out, but he doesn't unclip his seat belt.

"You've been a good friend," Ian starts.

"Okay."

"I mean it. We've always been tight. You know that, right?"

"Of course," I say, but I've been doubting myself for weeks now.

"We're not in fourth grade anymore, though."

I don't know what to say. I love the guy. But I know what he's going to say.

He says, "I know we laughed about that text. You know?" He looks nervous. "The one that night back when we were . . . back in February?"

"I know the one." *We both laughed, right?*

"I know we laughed. And I know you don't think that way. But it hurt."

"I know—"

"You don't," he interrupts. "And that's the thing." He takes a deep breath and massages his temples. A bell is tolling for me. This is work. He's doing work now. For me. He's looking for small words so I will begin to understand something too big for me to know.

He says, "You know what happens, right? When someone like your mother decides that her daughter hanging out with someone like me is a bad look for the family?"

I nod, but I'm not really hearing. Not yet.

"I can't be that," he continues. "I just can't do that anymore."

He's my best friend. Right? He's been inside my tunnel. He's heard the echo. He knows what billboards are under my giant owl's wings. I don't have anyone else.

"You know I wasn't laughing because I thought it was funny, though, right?" I say.

"But do you know why I laughed? Because you *needed* me to laugh with you," he says.

I feel horrible. I should feel horrible.

I think back to that night on his couch. I strip the LSD from it and I try to put myself in Ian's shoes. *My fucking mother.* I strip the kisses from it and try to put myself in Ian's shoes. *My fucking mother.* I try to feel what he felt when he read that text but I can't. I have no idea. I don't even know what to say.

I say, "Fuck."

He says, "I know this whole thing is unfair to you."

"No. I get it. I really do." I say this but I'm really trying to figure out what I can do differently to make this not happen. *My fucking mother.*

"All those years we couldn't hang out at your house made me feel things I shouldn't feel. All that sneaking around because of who I am," he says. "And I am who I am."

"A best friend is the one person you shouldn't have to feel that way around. Not when you're stuck in a town like this," I say.

"Something like that."

I sit and realize that maybe I became a sneaky weed-dealing girl not because I needed a car, not because I needed the weed, but because I'd started out as a sneaky girl in fourth grade because of my mother. So the rest of the sneaky bullshit just fell into place.

"I'll miss hearing about complaining shoppers," I say.

"And I'll miss hearing about gimme-gimme Drive-Thru customers."

"Maybe you can text me when people complain about scheduling physical therapy now," I say but Ian's head is already shaking.

"No," he says.

"I just wish we could . . ." I leave it there. I want Ian to have a nice life. I want him to go to college and live through every unnecessary traffic stop. I just want him to be okay. I say, "Truth be told, I was falling for you anyway. This is probably for the best."

"Impossible," he says. "I'm not even your type."

"How wrong you are."

Ian looks perplexed now. He came here to break off our best-friendship and only now realized that he might be breaking my heart. Except he's not. He's Ian. I held on to his penis once because it was there. We kissed because we were on drugs. We pressed flowers because we were in fifth grade. We went roller-skating because it was my birthday. It's the becauses that matter. Which is what's making this so hard. Because I'm not a racist nightmare. Because it's my mother's fucking bell, not mine.

Ian starts the car again, and we head toward my house. A car follows him close for a few blocks, and Ian stops completely at four yield signs before the guy peels off. Ian parks on the street a few doors down from my house and I get out of the car. He waves. I wave. When he pulls out from the curb, he checks all directions because he's careful. When he drives up the street, I imagine him never looking back. He deserves that. Took some balls to do what he just did. Makes me realize how everything he ever does will require balls like that. Not just because of people like my mother, either. We're all a little like that. We never stop to think about it. But we all are.

Marla & Gottfried's Easter Dinner, Take Two

84 Days since the Snowstorm—April 1, 2018

Marla is hiding plastic neon-colored Easter eggs in the front flower bed. Gottfried is hacking at a patch of onion grass with a trowel four feet behind her. He stops to watch two spring robins chirp from a limb.

"Do you think these are too hidden?" Marla asks.

Gottfried goes back to his onion grass. "They'll find 'em."

"That's not what I asked."

"They always find 'em."

Gottfried looks back at the robins. He thinks of his five grandchildren. Four now. Only four left and he's only ever met three. They say outliving your children is the hardest thing but Gottfried isn't sure. *What if they're still living but they don't want to talk to you?* Gottfried wants to scream, but he doesn't know who to scream at. It's got to be someone else's fault, these missing grandchildren, this collection of grown children who never come around. His son Matt hasn't talked to them since the day he called to tell them about what happened.

Gottfried knows that he's opened his phone contact list at least fifty times since and stared at Matt's number but never pressed the call button. What do you say to your kid when he's in a situation like that? When you're not close to begin with? *Sorry about your missing daughter?*

"I'm going to the side, now," Marla says. She adjusts her gardening apron and watches Gottfried looking at the robins. "You'll have to get the ham on soon."

"Ham," Gottfried says. "Gotcha."

Marla shakes her head. She wonders sometimes whether Gottfried ever really loved her. She knows she got colder over the years, but these are the most important times. He drove her to the hospital two weeks ago when she fell. He's there if she needs a foot rub. That's about it. Always seems inside his own head.

Gottfried pictures five robins.

When Matt called, he didn't have any news. Missing is all there is. The kid is missing. Her birthday was a few weeks ago. Gottfried always remembers it. He didn't send a card this year. He wouldn't know where to send it. Missing. Worse than dead— Marla said that once. Gottfried's imagination runs away with him sometimes and he doesn't like what it shows him. Poor girl. She could be anywhere. Or, she could have run away. That's what the police said. That's what Gottfried likes to believe. *She ran off with some boy. They're probably having fun in Las Vegas or something.* But it doesn't stop him from crying sometimes.

Gottfried never believed in the resurrection. Marla's insistence on the perfect Easter egg hunt since the kids were little annoyed him. Her obsession with it now that there were grandchildren was infuriating, especially considering their grandchildren were mostly grown—teenagers. Especially considering one of them is missing and the three he knows may not show up. In his anger, Gottfried finally finds the word he's been searching for since the night he and Marla got home from the hospital. *Complicit.* That's the word. It was his thumbs that couldn't dial Matt's number. His mouth that told Marla about giving money to Missy ten years ago. It was his brain that made all those decisions.

She says, "And don't forget to peel the potatoes!"

He throws the lumps of onion grass into the woods that surround the house.

He goes inside and washes his hands.

He puts the ham in the roaster.

He empties a five-pound bag of potatoes in the sink and retrieves the peeler from the drawer. As he slices the skin off inch by inch, he thinks of his family again and cries.

Jake & Bill can bring the snake out now

84 Days since the Snowstorm—April 1, 2018

Jake Marks and his older brother, Bill, walk through the high school parking lot because Bill told Jake to meet him there. Bill took his snake with him when he moved out, cracked two sides of the big tank when he shoved it into the back seat of the car, but now he's trying to give the snake to Jake. "I can't believe you're not gonna take care of her," Bill says. Jake doesn't care. He doesn't want the fucking snake. Fuck the snake. Fuck Bill. Fuck Ashley-the-fiancée, too. Just seeing the snake wrapped around Bill's neck today annoys him.

Jake feels like he's going to puke. He's about to tell everyone about everything. He thinks: *Resurrection, motherfuckers.* He wishes he would have figured out Bill's scam earlier, but he was just a kid and Bill gave no fucks. Bill never gave any fucks. Now Jake gives no fucks about Bill.

Six years between them, and Bill is a man now, about to get married—about to go to prison if Jake has anything to do with it. Jake's just a kid. Tenth grade for the second time. Plans to act it now, too.

Today Bill is bringing his fiancée, Ashley, to Easter dinner at Jake's house.

Today Jake is telling his parents what they did.

Today changes everything.

The Shoveler: Easter in a Sinkhole

When I was little, no matter what apartment we lived in, no matter what state or whether Mom had a job or not, she always hid eggs for me on Easter. She'd hard-boil them in secret, color them in secret, so I never knew where the eggs came from. We never went to church and I never understood the significance of eggs. I just accepted that one day per year, I'd get to look for brightly dyed eggs. In the apartment. Never outside. Our hunts were always in our apartments.

This morning, she wakes me up with a loud knock on my door.

"It's time to hunt!"

I'm sixteen. Haven't hunted for Easter eggs since I lived in Florida—which was the time we lost one of the eggs and it stank up Mom's bedroom closet.

She comes in and I can't get out of bed thanks to my morning boner, so I just lie there on my side. "Give me a minute," I say.

"The Easter Bunny is waiting."

"He'll have to wait a bit longer," I say. "I need to get dressed."

I think Mom realizes then that I'm not nine anymore. The look on her face is funny. Not mortified, not embarrassed. I can't tell what it is.

"Okay, dude. Do your thing."

Fact: There isn't a guy on Earth who'd jerk off after getting verbal encouragement from his mother.

I arrive downstairs to an empty Easter basket and clear instructions.

"There are eleven. Go!"

She usually put great thought into where she'd hide the eggs, but this year they seem to be sitting around out in the open. I see four of them just from where I'm standing. I gather them up and find six more inside of five minutes.

But there's one missing. I can't find it anywhere. She sits on the couch, smiling, with her arms crossed. "Wanna play hot and cold?"

"Not yet. I can find it." I'm on my knees, looking under the chair. I'm on my tiptoes, looking on top of the fridge. I'm standing on a chair looking above the kitchen cabinets. I'm in the bathroom, rummaging through her makeup drawer. No egg.

"It's not in my room," she says as I take the stairs by twos.

"Is it in my room?" I ask, but she doesn't answer.

I look through my bags of clothing, my bed, my closet, which is really just a place we keep the old five-gallon paint buckets Mike loaned us for the leaks. No egg.

"Hot or cold?" she asks again when I get back downstairs.

"Sure."

"Cold."

I move around the entire downstairs. She keeps saying *cold*.

"So it's not in the house?"

She smiles.

I try to figure out why she has that look on her face. I already bought my own car so it's not like she can surprise me with that. Oh. My car.

We go downstairs and outside and she says, "Warmer."

I walk toward the sidewalk and my car. "Colder," she says.

I walk to her car. "Colder." I walk to the side of the house. "Warmer." Toward the shed. "Colder." Toward Mike's house. "Warmer." Toward Mike's back door. "Colder." Toward Mike's brother's sister-in-law's house through the backyard. "Warmer."

I stop and look at Mom, and she seems elated about something. I point toward the caution tape that Mike put there the night his mother fell in the bathtub. "Warmer." I walk to the edge of the sinkhole, next to a cone. "A lot warmer."

"It's in the hole?" I ask.

Stop the film. Press pause. Why would a kid's mother hide an egg in a sinkhole? She may have shoplifted meat all these years but she's not psycho. There is no reason I can think of that this would make sense.

THE FREAK HAS MADE IT
TO THE OTHER SIDE!

The Freak knows there are a lot of dead bodies underground. Seems obvious, but it's not. People don't think about that when they're making funeral plans. They don't think about how many bodies their loved one's body will meet down here. The Freak thinks: *Most people don't know about the tunnels or how many people use them. Living people, I mean. Living people who aren't really living.*

The Freak knows you are aboveground. The Freak knows she is belowground. There's more to it than just "passing on" the way funeral directors say it. There's more to it than a heart that stops beating. Some people's hearts are never quite right. It takes more than blood and muscle and tissue and a brain that works.

Bodies are machines and machines need love.

Without it, the heart can never figure out what it's doing here. Millions of people are walking around aboveground, but really they're down here in the tunnels. The Freak sees them all the time. They never know what to do when she smiles at them. They think she's mocking them, but really she's just trying to make them more comfortable.

Light pours into the tunnel ahead. This is not how tunnels work. Underground everything is supposed to be dark. You don't need to be The Freak to figure this out. Everyone knows.

She walks slowly toward the light. And once she gets close enough she sees something bright green.

"It's an egg," she says to herself.

The Freak goes to it and looks up to see the sky. Yellow caution tape moves in the spring wind around the hole she's in. Funny. A minute ago she was in a tunnel on her way somewhere, but now she's in a hole. Holes are different. Everyone is always trying to get out of them.

She picks up the egg and puts it in her pocket.

She looks up to the sky and says, "Thank you."

She turns back toward the tunnel, now sky-blinded, knowing she would do anything to live again on the other side of the sod. But you can't change things like this. Easter eggs want you to believe you can, but you can't.

Malcolm Holds Hands

Dad needs help to the car.

A driver has come to pick us up. Dad told me to dress in something classy and I decided not to. I'm not here to impress Marla and Gottfried. They're not here to impress me.

Dad's hat blows off in a breeze and I chase it.

By the time we get to Marla and Gottfried's house, there's already one car in the driveway.

"Shit," Dad says. "My fucking sister's here."

"Isn't that why we came?" I ask.

"No." He shakes his head. "I don't know. I guess, maybe."

"We'll get through it," I say. I reach over and hold his hand.

I go around to his side of the car and open the door for him. He climbs out and reaches for my hand again. We walk to the front door, which is awfully formal considering I've lived here most of the school year.

He says, "Ring the bell."

"Seriously?"

He nods. I ring the bell. Marla opens the door in her kitchen apron. "I didn't think you were coming!" she says.

Dad says, "As if you didn't make enough ham for half the county."

She doesn't know what to say to that, so she just hugs him. The look on her face isn't something I can explain. She's not letting it hit her yet, but it's pretty hard to ignore when your forty-two-year-old son weighs the same as he did when he was in middle school.

"Harry!" someone says from inside. It's her. My aunt Jean.

"Jean," he says in the way you'd expect—sarcastic and dry. He's got the upper hand here. I'm pretty sure pancreatic cancer isn't going to take any shit from Jean today.

They hug. She says, "Holy shit. You need to eat!"

"Nice to see you, too, Jean. You've really wrinkled up since I saw you last. Congratulations."

"What do you want to drink?" Gottfried says to all of us.

"Where's Katie?" Jean asks. Then she yells. "KATIE?!"

"Can I help you?"

"Where are you?"

"I'm right here," Katie says. She's under the table, reading a book. "Malcolm?" She crawls out and gives me a hug. Then we disappear as quickly as we can toward the sliding door to the deck.

"You can't go outside!" Marla says. "Egg hunt isn't until one!"

"Marla, you need to calm down," I say.

"Don't call me Marla."

"Okay," I say. And then I open the door anyway and go outside with Katie. I don't think I've seen her in maybe five years. Last time we were little enough that we still cared about drawing shit in sidewalk chalk and wore church clothes. This time, we're both dressed in teenage stoner chic.

"This sucks so hard," Katie says.

"So, so hard," I say.

"At least you're here, though. The last few years it was just us and listening to my mom and Marla talk made me want to hang myself." I must look worried because she says, "Not literally."

"Oh. Good."

"How are you?"

"I'm okay."

"Your dad," she says. "I'm sorry."

"Yeah."

"Mom says you've been in Jamaica a lot. Something about Harry being crazy on weed and dragging you there."

I shake my head.

"She's such an asshole, isn't she?" Katie says. "But hey, your tan is pretty serious."

"Gee, thanks."

"Want to burn one?" she asks, producing a joint from inside her bra.

"Maybe after the ham."

She puts the joint back in her bra. "Did you see Loretta yet?"

"Loretta's here?"

"They went out to buy flowers or something. They'll be back."

"Holy shit. This Easter is hopping."

"Punny."

Both of us stare into the woods and I know what I'm thinking and I think Katie's thinking it, too. Three of us. Me, Katie, and Loretta. That's who's left. I half think about telling Katie about the girl I met last week. The note on the paper plate. 39.992372, -74.844528.

"Do you have a car?" I ask.

"Not yet. Saving. Almost there."

"You're, like, rich."

Katie says, "I won't take their money."

"Fuck. I would."

Loretta, Act Three: Balloons for Easter

Loretta's pop-pop didn't tell Loretta's mom-mom what she made out of balloons during the matinee last week, so in her Easter basket are four balloon animal kits. Her pop-pop didn't recognize the female genitalia balloon at all during the matinee. The audience laughed at that. Since then, she's decided to do the penis and testicles first, because he recognized those right away. Of course.

Her mother's face bruise has faded and she's in a different mood now. Happier, but more tired. Living with her pop-pop and mom-mom isn't always easy. Loretta is still getting used to the food and her mother can't seem to sleep at night.

No one has found her father yet, but they're looking.

This morning Loretta woke up to her first Easter basket and she ate three marshmallow chicks before her mom-mom said, "Save that for later! When your cousins get here."

Loretta doesn't really remember her cousins. She's excited to meet them. She put on her red dress first thing, and her mother asked her to wear the stiff flowered dress her mom-mom bought her instead.

The audience grumbled. Loretta looked out into the bright lights and asked, "Do you really think this suits me? Looks like something Mom-Mom would wear."

"Don't do it!" the audience yelled.

"You do you!" they screamed.

"Burn it!" someone yelled, and then the audience turned on him.

Loretta put the dress on and thankfully it was too big. Right size, but didn't take into account that Loretta is only ninety-five pounds.

"We have to go out and buy flowers," her mother said to her.

"For what?" Loretta asked.

"Tradition! I used to always bring my mother flowers on Easter."

"Do I have to come with?"

"Yes."

"I like you better without Dad," Loretta said.

At the flower stall, Loretta's mother can't seem to function. She's always a solid performer on set, but location work isn't her strong suit. She needs Loretta to help her pick the right plants and to make the right calculations. She drives okay, Loretta notes, but she can't seem to figure out how much money to give the man.

And the man keeps flirting with her.

Loretta says, "He'd better back off."

"He's sweet!" her mother says.

"He's creepy. Trust me," Loretta says.

Loretta is afraid for her mother. She refuses to live with another man in the house again. Except her pop-pop, who seems to love her more than he loves anything.

The audience interrupts her thoughts.

"No!"

"You don't know the whole story!"

"What?" she asks. "He's a nice old man!"

"Talk to your cousins," the audience answers.

"I will," Loretta says. She turns to her mother. "Get the hyacinths. They smell so nice."

Her mother picks up two pots of hyacinths.

"And those. Whatever they are." Loretta points to tulips.

"They're tulips," her mother says.

"Really?"

"You don't know what tulips look like?" Loretta shrugs it off like it's no big deal, but her mother starts to form tears in her eyes. "You should know what tulips look like at your age."

"Who cares? Let's get back."

Loretta helps her mother figure out how much money to give the creepy flower guy. He tries to flirt one more time, but Loretta puts her hand out like the choreographer taught her. "Save it for the next lady, okay, buddy?"

CanIHelpYou?'s Name Is Katie

You think that's a nice little preppy name, right?

Katie doesn't sound like the name of your dealer, but it is. I only care that you pay me in exact change now that I don't have access to a cash register.

I've upped my prices to make it easier for you.

I was hating Easter until Malcolm showed up. We always got along, even though our parents don't. I always felt bad for him because his mom died so young. Okay, sometimes I felt envious. But his mom was probably cool, and mine owns a souvenir slave bell. I'm sure you can understand.

Anyway, now his dad is dying, too. After a bit of small talk, I don't know what to say, so I say stupid shit because it's all I got.

"What are you going to do? You know. I mean. Where will you live?"

Malcolm gives me a look like he's fifty. He probably is fifty in his head. I'm just an idiot. "I thought I was gonna move down to Jamaica, but I'm not old enough and it's probably a stupid idea."

"That'd be some pretty big culture shock," I say. "I'd feel like a phony down there, you know?"

"Yeah. I have friends and stuff but I'm still a white kid from here."

"Can't get away from it," I say. "Best I can do is get away from my mother."

"You okay?" Malcolm says.

"Rough week. Lost my job and my best friend," I say. "Well, kinda. He didn't die or anything."

"You mean Ian? What happened?" Malcolm was at my roller-skating party.

"Long story. Like I said, the best I can do is get away from my mother." I say this but my brain is still scheming to figure out what I could have done differently. I want to talk to Malcolm about it, but nothing either of us says will change the way the world works. Malcolm looks so sad. "So I guess when it happens you're going to live with Marla and Gottfried," I say.

"Do you have any idea what it's like to live with them?"

I shake my head. "I can't imagine."

He shakes his head and looks out into the forest. "So what's with Loretta? How'd she get here?"

I say, "Missy and Loretta were in the hospital and the cops arrested You-know-who. Then they moved in here."

"You-know-who used to beat them up, right? That's what my dad says. We don't talk about it much."

"Nearly killed her this time. He's gone now. Jumped bail."

"Shit. He's a psycho," Malcolm says.

"Yeah."

"Our family is so fucked up," he says. "So many missing pieces."

My mom has talked to me about her youngest sister a few times. Usually as a cautionary tale. Whenever I seemed too interested in boys, she'd tell me that she'd do the same thing her mother did if I got pregnant. Kick me out. Leave me to suffer. The usual Biblical shit. "I know, right?" I say. "I can't wait to get out of here."

"Thing is," he says, "we can run around the planet a hundred times and we're still who we are."

Malcolm is definitely fifty.

The Shoveler: Shoveler's Surprise

After breakfast, Mom tells me to take a shower and put on some nice clothes.

"Why?"

"We're taking another drive," she says.

"I have to take a shower?"

"You have time. No big deal."

I never ask her why she hid the last egg in Mike's brother's sister-in-law's sinkhole. I think she thought it was funny, but she doesn't realize it's not funny at all.

Mom wants to take my car, and I tell her that if we're taking my car, I'm driving.

"That's fine."

"Where are we going?"

"I'll give you directions as you go. Don't worry."

Ten minutes later, we're on the highway and Mom tells me to take the exit, so I do and I say, "Why'd you hide the egg in the sinkhole?"

"I don't know," she says. "It's something you'll never forget. I wanted you to remember this day, I guess."

I nod.

"Up here on the right there's a weird store. Take the left there."

I'm on a familiar road and I don't understand until I look around and realize this is the road to Marla and Gottfried's house.

She's taking me to Marla and Gottfried's to embarrass me because I didn't
tell her who they were. Shit. It's Easter.
She knows they do a big party on Easter.
Shit. This is like my seventh-grade talent show. She said, "I didn't know you
had talent for anything," and I asked her
not to come and she promised and then
she came. And she sat in the front row.

I choked. Was supposed
to be a comedy act but
I just kept saying the
lines and staring at her
and when she didn't
smile or laugh, then
no one else did, either.

"Where're we going?" I ask.

"To a party," she says. "Take this next left."

"Who lives here? And why didn't you tell me?"

"Old business," she says.

Marla and Gottfried's house is about a mile from here. Next left.
If she tells me to go left I'm going to pull the car over. Or something.

"Take this next left. Watch out. It sneaks up on you."

". . ."

I can't say anything. I can't pull the car over, either. I take the left.

"You're being mysterious," I finally manage to say. "First,
you hide an Easter egg in a sinkhole. Now, we're going somewhere weird. You're freaking me out."

"Sorry," she says. "Don't worry. No matter what happens
today, I'll be more freaked out than you are. Keep that in mind."

325

Marla's Pineapple Stuffing

Everybody loves Marla's pineapple stuffing . . . except for Marla. She makes it anyway because that's what she does. She is the original CanIHelpYou? She is the original Malcolm. She is the original Ringmistress. She is the original Freak.

When you water a potato plant, the liquid seeps into the soil. Helps the spud grow underground. The leaves may love seeing the sun, but the tubers need the dark. They seem so different—so unrelated—but when the blight hits and the whole plant goes, then you know everything was related.

Marla's been thinking about blight. She's been thinking about her bad luck. She's baked her bad luck into the pineapple stuffing and she's about to feed it to three generations of her family. She doesn't want to. She didn't mean to. She can't stop thinking about things she doesn't have.

Marla Hemmings has shoes for every occasion and always polished clean. Fourteen jackets. Dresses she's never had the opportunity to wear because Gottfried doesn't take her anywhere. She has investment accounts worth millions. The BMW. The best food processor on the market. But Easter, as much as she pitches it as her favorite holiday, is the one day she dreads every year because she has to see these people she made—people who don't really love her. Or people she doesn't really love. She can't figure out which came first.

It's only one o'clock. Time for the egg hunt. But Missy hasn't come back with Loretta yet. Marla isn't quite sure where they went or why, but she's sure Missy will foul up her schedule.

The ham will be ready in an hour. The potatoes—three kinds—will be ready at the same time. She has her microwave bags ready with peas and green beans. Her hands are shaking. She's made this dinner fifty times before, but she's nervous.

Marla Hemmings has her secret.

Like all secrets, it feels bigger than it is.

Like all secrets, it breeds shame.

In 1962, Marla needed three units of blood. She was in Arkansas because her dad was helping to set up a factory there. She was twelve. She'd been hit by a car and her mother rushed her to the hospital. Ruptured spleen. She'd be fine after surgery. No problem. All the staff were nice—Marla remembers the tapioca pudding they gave her once she came out of recovery.

She didn't know the secret until she was twenty years old. Fourth of July picnic, beer was flowing. Stories were flowing. Her mother was chattering away, enjoying her spotlight.

> "I never told Marla this one," she said. "That time in Arkansas when she had to go to the hospital? Show 'em your scar, Marla!" Marla showed them her side. "So they were out of blood," her mother said. "Did you know they used to separate it down there? Fools. They'd only give white people white blood and they'd give black people black blood. That doesn't sound right even now when I say it, does it?" She laughed. Marla's aunts and uncles laughed. "Well, either way, they had her blood type, but the nurse told me they couldn't use it because it was what they called *negroid blood*. I said, 'Hell yes you can use it!' and lucky for me and Marla it was a Yankee nurse."

327

Marla's aunts and uncles had a mixed reaction to this. Marla could feel it. Some of them felt uncomfortable with her automatically. Some of them hugged her and said things like "We were so worried when we heard what happened!" or "So glad you pulled through!" Marla couldn't meet eyes with any of them. Especially her mother. Then her uncle Bill said, "So does this mean you're gonna sit on your ass and collect welfare now?" She went inside and threw up in her mother's kitchen sink.

This is her mother's pineapple stuffing recipe. Uncle Bill loved it. Uncle Bill still made comments to her every time he saw her. Called her *half blood*. She tried to talk to her mother about it—asked, "Why didn't you tell me this in private?" Her mother just told her to relax. "Bill's just kidding."

Every picnic from then on, Marla avoided. Moved away. Married Gottfried. Had her five perfect babies. More secrets. The doctor prescribed pills. And more pills. That's just how they did things then.

Truth is, Easter is the only holiday that doesn't make her want to throw up. Except this year.

Marla takes off her apron so she'll look good in the pictures Gottfried takes on his phone camera. She goes to the bathroom and checks herself in the mirror. She hears Missy and Loretta come in the back door and meets them. Missy's arms are full of hyacinths and tulips, but Marla doesn't have time for flowers.

She walks into the living room with three plastic grocery bags and says, "We're all here! Kids, get ready! Your pop-pop and I hid twenty eggs for each of you!"

The only one who looks the least bit excited about this is Loretta, who's wearing that awful red-sequined thing again.

THE FREAK IS LURKING IN THE TREES!

The Freak watches as three teenagers scour the property for plastic neon Easter eggs. There's a pink one at her feet, and she picks it up and opens it. A Hershey's mini chocolate bar. Not her favorite, but she eats it anyway.

The Freak notes that the parents of these teenagers are all sitting inside the house. Marla Hemmings is standing on the back deck. Gottfried is running around taking pictures with his smartphone. The teenagers stick together and help one another find the eggs. Twenty each. The boy's eggs are blue. The taller girl's eggs are yellow. The skinny girl in the red dress got pink. The Freak feels bad for eating her chocolate, but she puts the now-empty egg into her pocket.

"You all should split up and make it a race!" Gottfried says.

The teens ignore him.

The Freak is missing, but really she's not. The parents inside the house would tell you that this is what made their family a broken mess, but it isn't. The Freak knows this family was a broken mess before she ever went missing.

"You guys don't know how to have any fun!" Gottfried yells into the woods. "The whole idea is to be the first one who finds all the eggs! Not to help each other!"

The teens ignore him.

The Shoveler's Mother Is Hyperventilating

Mom is taking a lot of deep breaths. I've decided that whatever's going on here is going to happen whether I want it to or not.

I'm guessing that I'm about to meet my father.

I'm guessing that this is going to be ugly.

I'm guessing that Mike's 100% WHITE POWER tattoo isn't the worst thing in the world because Mom never hyperventilated about that. But she is now.

"Do you want me to stop?" I ask. "You can catch your breath or whatever."

"You know where we're going, right?"

"Not really."

"You never figured it out?" she asks.

"My father," I say. "You moved back here so I could meet my father."

"Um," Mom says.

"I'm scared to meet him," I say. "What if he doesn't care or, like, hates me or something?"

"Pull over."

I pull over. Mom faces me.

"You're not going to meet your father," Mom says. "We can talk about it later if you want but right now isn't about your father. Okay? I know it must be a drag to not know. I'm sorry we haven't talked before now. I know it must be hard."

"You really don't know," I say.

"I'm taking you to dinner," she says. "That's all."

"Where?"

"It's just up the road. Old friends of mine. Something like that."

"Then why were you hyperventilating?"

"Just drive up here and take the right onto that little road with the newer houses."

"The cul-de-sac?"

"Yeah."

I sigh. It's Marla and Gottfried's cul-de-sac. "This isn't funny."

"I never said it was."

"Please don't embarrass me. I'll give you more of what I earned painting. Whatever it is, I'll give it to you."

"What are you even talking about?" Mom says. "I don't want your money! How could I embarrass you?" She starts breathing deeply. "I mean, more than shoplifting and the shit I've already done?" She points to the house. "Go up that driveway. Park. And get ready to meet your grandparents."

I get up the driveway. I say, "Marla and Gottfried are my grandparents?"

Mom looks more confused than I am.

When I park, I see Malcolm walking around with the girl from the park and another girl. They're all holding grocery bags. Gottfried is following them and smiling. Until he sees my car.

Until he sees that it's not just me in the car.

Gottfried's Robins Give Good Advice

Gottfried can't figure out why the painter kid is at the house. He searches his memory to find the invitation to Easter, but he can't find it. *Shit. If I invited the kid and didn't tell Marla, she'll kill me.*

Then a woman gets out of the car. *Probably the kid's mother.* She says, "Hi, Dad!"

The painter kid is still in the car. He's doing something on his phone. Malcolm comes over to say hi, and the kids all gather up around the car while Gottfried stares at the woman.

"Dad? You okay?" she asks.

"Amber?" Gottfried is struck by a giant emotion. He can't name it. He can't even feel it, it's so big. The robins appear, dying in slow motion, and Gottfried hears one of them talk to him. The robin says, "Hug her, for fuck's sake."

Gottfried is thankful for the robins.

He hugs Amber and then holds her at arm's length to inspect how she's grown.

"Holy shit, kid. You grew into a knockout."

"Probably not appropriate, Dad."

"Who cares? It's the truth," he says. "How long has it been? And how do you know the painter?"

"The painter is my son. Your grandson. His name is David."

"David!" Gottfried says, finger pointing to the sky as if that was where the name had been hiding all along.

"And It's been about sixteen years since I saw you," she says.

"You'd just graduated high school," Gottfried says.

"Yeah. Almost right, Dad."

Gottfried stands there and can't move. The painter kid gets out of his car, and Amber—his lost Amber—walks toward the front door of the house. Gottfried follows. "Come in. Come in. Your mother's gonna be so happy to see you."

"Ya think?" Amber says.

"What?"

"She's the one who kicked me out," she says.

"Water under the bridge," Gottfried says.

Amber rolls her eyes. "For you, maybe."

Jake & Bill are forensically evident

Jake and Bill are in Jake's bedroom. The whole house smells like a ham dinner. Bill says, "You can't just tell them everything." He looks genuinely scared, and it pleases Jake to see it.

Jake hasn't had any whiskey in two weeks. Got the shakes the first night but he's fine now. Bill doesn't scare him anymore. Jake's fucks have definitely shifted.

"You don't think they're going to find us all over that girl? Or her all over your car?" Jake says. "You're gonna have to figure out what you're saying. I know what I'm saying."

"You tell them, I'll kill you."

Bill walks down the stairs, out of the house, gets into his car, and squeals out of the driveway.

Fiancée Ashley stands, mid-setting-the-dinner-table, forks in hand, looking clueless. Jake wonders if Bill forgot she was there. Probably did. Bill's no good at remembering things like that. Never remembered to feed the snake, either.

Jake thinks back to a day when he was about ten. Fourth grade. Bill stuck Jake's hand in the toaster and tried to toast it. Twelve. Sixth grade. Bill stuck a toothpick up Jake's penis. The night of Bill's eighteenth birthday about four weeks after the toothpick, Bill did it to him. The thing he does. The thing he told Jake to do to the girl.

Jake is ready to come clean. In every way. Back on St. Patrick's Day, he stole his dad's credit card so he could pay for online video counseling and he told the counselor the truth. Not of the girl. Of Bill. Of shame. Of parents who didn't know what to do with a boy like that. Of Bill's friends and their gatherings and the smell of gasoline-soaked pine. Of the toothpick. Of the whiskey he'd been drinking. Of Jeff-as in-Jefferson-Davis-at-work.

Jake's feeling a lot better about things.

Even if he has to go to prison.

Even if he has to tell the truth about everything.

Truth isn't so bad once you look at it. It's like throwing up after drinking a whole fifth of bourbon. It's a purging that makes you feel better, not worse.

Easter Conversation on the Deck

Four teenagers sit around a picnic table, eating from a shared pile of Easter candy they've emptied from fifty-nine plastic neon-colored eggs.

MALCOLM. So, you're our cousin?

THE SHOVELER. Seems so.

MALCOLM. My dad says your mom was the funniest of all of them.

CANIHELPYOU?. Wouldn't be hard to be the funniest in this family.

MALCOLM. True.

CANIHELPYOU?. My mom said your mom was a slut. Sorry. She says stuff like that all the time.

THE SHOVELER. Bummer.

CANIHELPYOU?. She's a horrible person.

LORETTA. I never knew you existed! My mom never talks about her family.

CANIHELPYOU?. You don't remember Easter egg hunting when you were little? We have pictures of it. You were there.

LORETTA. We don't have pictures. I don't remember. I kinda remembered Pop-Pop when I saw him at first. I think we have a picture of him around. Or we did. I don't know.

MALCOLM. Loretta lives here now. And I guess I do, too. Maybe permanently, soon.

(*Loretta looks confused.*)

CANIHELPYOU?, *to Loretta*. Malcolm's dad is dying.

LORETTA. Oh no!

MALCOLM. Cancer's a bitch.

CANIHELPYOU?. My mom said he deserved cancer. Did you know that? She said he smoked when he was younger. She's so unforgiving.

THE SHOVELER. I'd say that's worse than unforgiving.

MALCOLM, *to CanIHelpYou?*. Your mom is a fucking asshole. No offense.

CANIHELPYOU?. None taken. Who would know this better than me?

LORETTA. My dad's gonna go to jail. When they find him. My mom's scared he'll find us first.

THE SHOVELER. Why's he going to jail?

MALCOLM. He tried to kill Aunt Missy.

LORETTA. His act was so boring! The audience hated him.

(*Silence.*)

CANIHELPYOU?, *to the shoveler*. Why'd you really carry that shovel around with you?

THE SHOVELER. I don't anymore.

CANIHELPYOU?. I mean when you did. And did you ever find the freak you were looking for?

THE SHOVELER. I don't know. I just carried it. And then she showed up one day and told me I should dig. Told me that the best things are underground or something. Sounds stupid.

MALCOLM. We *are* descended from potato farmers.

THE SHOVELER. True.

LORETTA. Potato farmers? That's no act. Where's the excitement?

CANIHELPYOU?, *to the shoveler*. Did she just vanish for you, too? Just *poof*!?

THE SHOVELER, *nods*. I thought she was a ghost.

MALCOLM. Wait. Brown hair, cut to here? (*He moves his hand to indicate neck length.*) Pale?

338

CANIHELPYOU?. Yeah. And tall.

MALCOLM. Looked like Uncle Matt.

THE SHOVELER. Who's Uncle Matt?

MALCOLM. No one talks about Matt.

CANIHELPYOU?. Even my mom doesn't talk about Matt and she talks shit about everybody.

THE SHOVELER. So, my mom has how many brothers and sisters? Three?

MALCOLM. Four. There are five of them all together. Jean (*points to CanIHelpYou?*), Harry (*points to himself*), Missy (*points to Loretta*), Matt (*shrugs and leaves his hands open and palms up*), and Amber (*points to the shoveler*).

THE SHOVELER. So, why doesn't anyone talk about Matt?

CANIHELPYOU?. Don't know. We should ask them.

MALCOLM. My dad used to talk about Matt. His only brother and all. The two of them didn't get along, and Gottfried and Marla liked Matt more. Popular jock type. Something like that. He moved away a long time ago. California.

THE SHOVELER. I didn't know any of you existed until now.

CANIHELPYOU?, *to the shoveler*. My mom called your mom the nomad of the family. I guess that's better than slut, but still—

MALCOLM, *to CanIHelpYou?*. Your mom. I remember the last time we came to Easter and she used the N-word and my dad argued with her.

CANIHELPYOU?. I remember that! I hid under the table. So embarrassing.

MALCOLM, *to CanIHelpYou?*. She still using the rap music excuse?

CANIHELPYOU?. Yep. So dumb.

(*Silence.*)

THE SHOVELER. So, do we all live near each other?

MALCOLM. Loretta lives here now. Katie lives east of town. I live south, near the turnpike, until I have to move back in here. You?

THE SHOVELER. I live in the city.

CANIHELPYOU?. So we all live in the same county.

LORETTA. And we never hang out together! That's a shame! We'd make a good troupe.

THE SHOVELER. So, what about Uncle Matt, then?

CANIHELPYOU?. Um.

MALCOLM. His daughter went missing. About two years ago.

CANIHELPYOU?. Out in California.

MALCOLM. No. In Pennsylvania.

CANIHELPYOU?. Different girl.

MALCOLM. Same girl. How do you not know this? Your mom is the biggest mouthpiece in the county.

CANIHELPYOU?. It was two different girls, Malcolm. The one here was the daughter of an artist or something. The one in California was the one my mom knew. Didn't know it was Matt's kid, though.

MALCOLM. The girl kidnapped from our mall was Matt's kid. Her mom left Uncle Matt for, like, four months. She had a job at the college here. Art teacher or something.

CANIHELPYOU?. I can't believe it.

THE SHOVELER. Wait. So Uncle Matt's daughter went missing?

MALCOLM. Right.

THE SHOVELER. And no one's found her?

MALCOLM. Not yet, no.

CANIHELPYOU?. My mom thinks she ran away. Probably with a boy.

MALCOLM. That's bullshit.

CANIHELPYOU?. You can pretty much bank on whatever my mom says being bullshit. Especially now that I know she was lying to me all this time.

MALCOLM. Sorry. I didn't mean to freak you out.

CANIHELPYOU?. She told me it was an epidemic. Girls disappearing from malls. Used it to scare me. I don't know.

MALCOLM, *to Loretta.* You okay?

LORETTA. It's sad. Just disappearing like that. And no one really knowing or caring.

THE SHOVELER. I'm sure her parents care.

LORETTA. I mean us. Our family. (*Points to CanIHelpYou?.*) Her mom didn't even tell her the truth about her own cousin. No one cares.

(*Silence.*)

CANIHELPYOU?. My mom doesn't tell the truth about anything.

(*Silence.*)

MALCOLM. Matt wasn't the nicest guy. Not to my dad, anyway. And not to his family in California, either.

CANIHELPYOU?. And my mom always says he's a great guy. So I guess that's what she's hiding. Jesus. Just when you think she can't stoop any lower.

(*Silence.*)

THE SHOVELER. I never even thought about having cousins. And now one of them is missing. I don't know. It's all weird.

CANIHELPYOU?. Says the guy who carries a shovel, who's friends with someone called "The Freak." (*Uses air quotes for that term.*)

MALCOLM. I saw the shovel in the back seat of your car when you were here painting. Just thought you liked being prepared or something.

THE SHOVELER. We can stop talking about the shovel any time you want.

(*Silence.*)

CANIHELPYOU?, *to the shoveler.* So this Freak girl. She's real?

THE SHOVELER, *nods*. She's some kind of magic or something.

CANIHELPYOU?, *to the shoveler*. Yeah. I don't know anyone else who can appear and disappear whenever they want.

THE SHOVELER. Yeah.

LORETTA, *to no one in particular*. It must be hard to have a missing kid. Poor Matt, wherever he is.

THE SHOVELER. She got me this job, I think. I mean, The Freak. Not Matt's kid. Left me a paper with the job circled in marker.

CANIHELPYOU?. What job?

THE SHOVELER. I just painted this whole house.

CANIHELPYOU?. You're the painter kid?

MALCOLM. I can't believe you painted this whole house and never knew anything about us.

THE SHOVELER. It's not like they have any family pictures. And my mom doesn't talk about it.

LORETTA. Seems like our parents don't talk about a lot of things. Dull show. But compared to my father's show, I guess it's okay.

CANIHELPYOU?. Hold on. Hold on. (*Holds her hands out in the stop position.*)

(*Silence.*)

CANIHELPYOU?. So the kidnapped girl from the mall is Matt's kid? And we've all been visited by this disappearing girl? (*Pauses. Shakes her head.*) Maybe I'm too stoned.

MALCOLM. What?

(*Silence.*)

The four teens look at one another.

(*Silence.*)

(*CanIHelpYou? looks at her phone. Types something in. Finds a picture. Shows it to the others.*)

THE SHOVELER. That's her.

MALCOLM. Holy shit.

LORETTA. She's been in my audience before!

(*Silence.*)

CANIHELPYOU?, *points to the picture on the phone screen.* This is our missing cousin.

LORETTA, *to Malcolm.* You're turning white.

THE SHOVELER. You okay?

MALCOLM. I know where she is.

CANIHELPYOU?. Dude. Don't bullshit. This is serious.

(*Silence.*)

MALCOLM. I know where she is.

CANIHELPYOU?. Seriously, Malcolm. Don't fuck around with this.

MALCOLM. I'm not fucking around. I know where she is.

(*Malcolm takes his phone out of his back pocket and shows the others a picture of a jerk-chicken-stained paper plate with GPS coordinates written on it.*)

(*Silence.*)

THE SHOVELER. I have a car. We should go.

LORETTA. This is exciting!

CANIHELPYOU?, *looking at her phone.* Dude. Did you search that on a map? It's in the middle of a forest . . . oh. Fuck. We should probably call the police.

MALCOLM. Maybe.

LORETTA. The police don't believe teenagers. Especially girls. Trust me. I've dropped into that net before. It never holds. We should make a plan.

Easter Conversation in
the Living Room

Harry and Amber are locked in a hug. Jean sits on Marla's floral couch and watches. Missy is in the bathroom. Marla and Gott-fried are in the kitchen, where Gottfried is telling Marla that Amber has come home.

HARRY. Oh my god!

AMBER, *through tears*. I can't believe you're here.

HARRY. Neither can I, believe me.

AMBER. Stop it. Some things aren't funny.

JEAN. Harry, are you going to hog her the whole day or do the rest of us get to say hello?

AMBER, *still hugging Harry*. Hello, Jean.

JEAN. Ha-ha-ha.

HARRY, *to Amber*. My god. You didn't age. (*To Jean.*) Unlike your ancient sister.

AMBER. Jean looks great. No more of that bullshit.

HARRY. This is my last Easter. I'm not going to make amends before I die. How else will Jean live if not feeding off the guilt she has for being such a bitch to us for so long?

JEAN. Jesus. If this how today's going to go, I'm not playing.

MISSY. Amber?

JEAN. It's her! In the flesh!

HARRY. Jean, don't they sell funny somewhere so you can buy it?

JEAN. Maybe the same place they sold you cancer.

HARRY. Clearly you have not found the humor store. Next you're going to tell Missy she's fat, right?

MISSY. I nearly died. Do you think I care if she says I'm fat again?

AMBER. You nearly died?

MISSY. You-know-who. You were right about him.

AMBER. Yeah. I know.

HARRY. Scumbag.

JEAN. Well, I—

HARRY. Don't say anything, Jean. Just don't say anything.

AMBER. Oh man. (*Hugs Missy.*) You okay? Loretta okay?

MISSY. That girl could walk through fire and still be happy, I swear.

HARRY. They all could. Look at them. Stronger than we ever were.

(*All four adults look out to the deck and spy their chattering kids; they smile and nod in agreement. Marla enters.*)

MARLA. Amber Marie! You came home!

AMBER. Hi, Mom. Nice to see you.

MARLA. Last time we heard from you, you were in Texas, I think.

AMBER. We were.

MARLA. Are you just visiting?

AMBER. We moved to town in January.

MARLA. Well, do I get to meet him?

HARRY. You can't hug your kid? After sixteen years? Seriously, Mom?

AMBER. It's fine.

MISSY. You know I was pregnant with Loretta before I got married. You didn't kick me out.

HARRY. So was Jean.

JEAN. What? No. I wasn't.

MISSY. Come on, Jean. Who cares? None of that shit even matters anymore.

JEAN. I got pregnant on our honeymoon.

HARRY. Sure you did.

AMBER.

MARLA.

JEAN. So where are you living?

AMBER. North city.

JEAN. Are you renting?

AMBER.

HARRY. Who cares, Jean?

JEAN. Just making conversation. Why are you all against me all of a sudden?

HARRY. I don't think it's sudden.

JEAN. If Matt was here, he'd stick up for me.

MARLA.

MISSY.

HARRY.

AMBER. What about Matt? Why do you all look like that all of a sudden?

HARRY. We should talk somewhere else. I have to catch you up.

JEAN. Matt's kid went missing.

AMBER. Why didn't any of you tell me this?

JEAN. Like we could find you?

AMBER. I sent my address to Dad. Every time I moved. He has my number.

HARRY.

JEAN.

MISSY.

MARLA. GOTTFRIED!

Gottfried isn't in the kitchen. He isn't in the garage. Marla looks everywhere and finally she sees him outside, talking to the kids. She weighs the possibility that her pineapple stuffing might burn if she goes outside to confront Gottfried. She decides it can wait. *Waited sixteen years already. Another few minutes won't hurt.* She goes back into the kitchen.

(*Amber sighs.*)

HARRY. Nothing changes.

JEAN. Amen.

MISSY. I can't believe I'm living here.

AMBER. So, why isn't anyone talking about Matt? Did he do something wrong? His girl is really missing? Like *missing* missing?

(*Silence.*)

AMBER. When did this happen?

MISSY. Like, two years ago, I think. Snatched from the mall.

AMBER. And no one's found her?

JEAN. Obviously not.

HARRY. No one knows anything.

AMBER. Shit.

JEAN. This family has been through the shit.

HARRY. Yeah.

AMBER. God, Harry. You especially.

HARRY. And you, Amber.

MISSY. And me.

JEAN. And Matt.

AMBER. It's so fucked up.

347

JEAN. Do you have to talk like that? It's Easter.

HARRY, *points at Jean.* That's exactly why our family is so fucked up.

JEAN. What? Me asking for civilized conversation?

MISSY. You've never had a civil conversation in your life, Jean.

HARRY. Maybe you can buy civility wherever they sell humor.

AMBER. I didn't come home for this.

JEAN. Well, tough luck. What you came home for is still what it always was. We're not going to miraculously change just because you popped in.

HARRY. It's my last Easter. If it doesn't suck, what pain will I have to bring to the Consciousness with me?

MISSY. Oh god, Harry.

GOTTFRIED, *enters through deck sliding door.* You guys have great kids! What a bunch of smarties! (*Shakes his head.*) But Marla worked a long time to hide those eggs and they're sharing the candy!

Marla calls for someone to fill water glasses, and Missy goes to the kitchen to get started. Harry sits down and closes his eyes as if he were meditating. Jean and Amber open the door to the deck to tell the kids to come in. The last thing Amber hears of their conversation is her son, David, saying, "We'll take my car."

THE FREAK LOVES PINEAPPLE STUFFING AND AWKWARD CONVERSATION!

The Freak is still in the trees. The Freak is still in the downstairs bathroom. The Freak is wherever she wants to be whenever she wants to be there. That's the beauty of being The Freak.

All this talk of her father is sad. Poor Matt. Wish he'd visit more often. Bullshit. This family is complete bullshit. Fact: Matt was a shitty father and a shitty husband and probably a shitty son and a shitty brother. Fact: If Marla and Gottfried would have loaned Matt a few thousand measly bucks, The Freak would not be wrapped in a dirt tortilla. There would be no dirt burrito. None of this would have happened.

The Freak is angry about this, but she's also not angry about this. It's not Marla and Gottfried's fault that she met that boy at the mall. It's not their fault that his brother was waiting in his car. It's not their fault that no one was listening when she yelled. It's not their fault that the people who did hear dismissed it as teenage drama.

But would they pay a few thousand bucks to have Matt there at Easter dinner? Would they pay a few thousand bucks to bring her back from the dirt? They say they would. Odds are, they'd call it a loan and collect interest. Odds are, they'd still treat her mom like shit even though it's not her fault that her dad is a giant asshole. Fact is, they can be bummed out about Matt all they want, but he's the biggest reason she's a dirt burrito. If he'd have grown up and known how to treat his wife and kid, then her mom would have never had to take the job in Pennsylvania, and The Freak would still be safe in her bed in California.

In case that's confusing, The Freak wants you to know the basic blame order: Blame the murderous brother-boys first, then her dad, then the half-wit high school bitches next, then her grandparents. And probably Aunt Jean. Because for all her talking about missing The Freak's dad, she's loaded and didn't loan him the few thousand measly bucks, either.

Greed trickles down in many forms. It made Harry a humanitarian who forgets the human he's personally responsible for from time to time. It made Amber and Missy happy with what they have, especially if their kids don't have any more. It made Jean a judgmental twat. But it just made The Freak disappear. No more pineapple stuffing for her.

CanIHelpYou?'s Easter Dinner

The one nice thing about having the whole family—what's left of it—at Easter dinner is that everyone here hates my lying, big-mouthed mother as much as I do. You don't think that's funny. You think I should grow up and move on. Right now her stupid bell is in a box under my bed. Maybe once I smash it with a hammer I'll feel better. Until then, keep your judgments to yourself.

Weird that the shoveler ended up my cousin. Weirder still that he's been working at my grandparents' house since January and none of them knew they were related.

My mother sticks her foot in her mouth the minute this is brought to light. "You let a teenager paint your house?"

Gottfried says, "He did better than any painter I had in."

"Mom, don't be rude," I say.

"I didn't think I was being rude." And she doesn't think she's a racist, either. None of us do. Ian is haunting my Easter dinner. He's making me see everything clearly. If I'm not careful, I'm going to feel fifty soon.

"So you three knew each other since January and didn't know David was your grandkid?" Uncle Harry says.

Marla can't stand the topic, so she eats faster. Not as fast as Loretta, though, who eats as if someone is about to take her food away. She's weird—always bowing and talking to an audience who's not there—but I like her.

"So, what kind of job are you working now?" Mom asks Aunt Amber.

"I do the books at a car lot."

"Which place?"

She says the name and no one has heard of it. Mom and Mom-Mom make a grunting noise as if they don't believe Aunt Amber has the job. And she notices.

"What? I'm thirty-four years old. Why would I lie?"

My mom says, "Don't be paranoid."

"I'm not paranoid."

Silence. More fast eating. More Ian haunting me. Because my grandmother is a racist, too. It's like I can see it. I can look at a person and see it. I'm afraid to look at everyone else at the table. I stare at my pineapple stuffing.

"Where are you working these days, Jean?" Aunt Amber asks.

"I don't have to work," my mom says in that way she says things. I want to stab her in the face with my fork.

Uncle Harry says, "Must be nice."

"I'm raising my daughter." Malcolm kicks me under the table. He must see me gripping my fork harder.

"And I'm raising my son," Harry replies.

The shoveler asks for more potatoes. Then he says, "Can I ask a question?"

Everyone nods.

"So, how come we sold the farm? Like—was it just a bad business or too hard or something?"

When the shoveler asks this, everyone at the table looks like they might stab one another with forks.

"Your grandfather is no farmer," Marla finally answers.

Gottfried finally swallows the lump of food he's been chewing. "I hated it. My brother and sister hated it. We didn't get along, either."

Marla chimes in. "And it's not like any of your parents got along enough to run a business. They all would have wanted to be in charge."

"Maybe that's because you raised us to be competitive," Uncle Harry says.

"Nothing wrong with that," my mom says.

"I mean, you could have at least taught these kids how to do an Easter egg hunt," Gottfried says.

The shoveler looks at the rest of us kids and raises his eyebrows. We have to eat. We have a plan. A mission. We need to hurry.

As I finish my plate of food, I try to imagine Ian at this Easter dinner. He'd be so funny and so great and he'd ignore the weird shit everyone is saying and he'd treat it like some kind of anthropology project. That's how he has to get through life here. Because every single person he meets is racist in some way and they have no fucking idea they are.

Loretta asks to be excused, and Marla says, "Are you feeling all right, dear?"

"Fine," Loretta says. "I just have an after-dinner act I have to rehearse one more time before I show it to you."

Gottfried looks uncomfortable and like he wants to say something, but he digs into his second helping of potato filling instead.

I stop thinking about Ian because I'm glad he isn't here and having to live through an anthropology project. I try to do that for myself. I put on my anthropologist's hat and look at my family.

It's a family-that-isn't-a-family. My mother hates all of them. Says so as often as she can. Uncle Harry is going to die and I barely know him. I essentially just met my two aunts and they seem cool—and maybe not nightmare racists like my mother, so that's good. But there's more than one missing part here. More than one missing cousin, or one missing uncle who lives on the West Coast. The hole in this family-not-a-family is big. It's bigger than a six-hundred-acre potato farm. It's bigger than this county that we all live in. I can't figure it out.

It's like some wall went up in 1970 when my grandparents got married.

It's like some wall went up when they had these children who are now grown.

It's as if those children are all trying to do better with us—their children—but they don't know how. You probably think I'm too stoned for Easter dinner. This Easter dinner, especially. But something tells me it's not the weed. You know damn well something's wrong with the roots of our family and I have a feeling we'll never know what it is.

Loretta, Act Three: Close the Show with a Bang

Loretta puts on her stage makeup in the upstairs bathroom. She can hear the audience chattering and laughing and she's as ready as she's ever been. Gerald and Dolly are in the lunch box arguing again about whose act is better and she's had it with arguments. She knows she can't go on like this forever. With her dad gone now, and her living in this pretty room, the troupe just doesn't fit into her life anymore.

She puts her hair up into a tight bun and fits her sequined hair clips into it. Does one final dusting of powder, grabs her balloons, and descends the stairs. The audience goes quiet.

Loretta feels it's wrong to introduce herself because she can't play two roles at the same time. She's Ringmistress, yes, but she's the talent now, too. So she starts blowing up balloons, and when she has four, she shapes them into two penis-and-testicle animals and gives them to David and Malcolm.

They laugh and start dueling with them, which makes the audience laugh, except for Aunt Jean, who doesn't laugh at anything. So Loretta blows up four balloons and ties them into perfect labia and leaves enough extra for the perfect clitoris. She hands it to Jean and points to the spot. She says, "This will come in very handy."

She bows. Then she makes one genitalia balloon for everyone at the table and then bows again and her smile is bigger than it ever was in the wagon.

"It's always a special day when my mom is in the audience," she says. "Everyone, a round of applause for my mom!"

The crowd goes wild, and Loretta feels as if she's distracted them enough. It was her part of the plan. They need dinner to move quickly, and nothing moves adults more quickly than teenagers acknowledging the existence of sex.

Marla Doesn't Really Like Dessert

Jean brought a Pavlova for dessert, and Marla is exasperated by it.

"What is it, even?"

Gottfried says, "Looks good to me."

"I think it's some sort of meringue. With fruit?" Marla says. "If you think kiwi is a fruit."

Gottfried walks to the garage and closes the door behind him. He takes a deep breath and stares at the two patches of painting on the walls. Thinks about the painter kid. *How about that? The painter kid is my grandson.* Part of him wishes he'd have known before he paid him all that money. The other part thinks of the robins again.

Such a waste. All he had to do was pay better attention. Slow down sooner. Anything to avoid this lifetime of being haunted by those damn birds.

"I'm not sure what to call you now," someone says. It's the painter kid—who's sitting over by the sink.

"You always called me Gottfried before. Still works."

"I guess I know more about my family now," he says.

"I guess you do. Sorry she kept it from you for so long," Gottfried says. "Our family has its problems, I guess."

"You kicked her out when she was pregnant," the kid says.

Gottfried thinks the kid's going to say more, but he doesn't. And Gottfried crashes into the robins a hundred times in his mind, watching them die over and over again. He says, "I think it's time for dessert!"

When they walk inside, everyone is sitting around digesting and marveling at Loretta's balloon genitalia. Gottfried announces dessert, and all the adults groan and say it's too soon.

Katie says, "Come on. Let's eat!"

Malcolm says, "I can't wait to try it."

Loretta says, "It looks so good!"

Marla says, "You know, I never really liked dessert. So, why not get it over with."

She watches Amber, her youngest child, move only once the others have moved. She watches her hands and the way she walks. She sees herself as a young woman. She regrets her whole life in an instant. That's dessert.

THE FREAK FEELS THE WIND IN HER HAIR!

The Freak has been waiting for this day for nearly two years.

The Freak is in your living room.

The Freak is in your TV show.

The Freak is frying you her great-grandmother's potato croquettes.

But really, The Freak is sitting cross-legged on top of a 2004 Nissan Sentra that's driving to New Jersey.

Inside the car are The Freak's four cousins. They're listening to loud music and are sharing the playlist. Everyone gets a turn. Her shoveler and Loretta, a master at balloon animals and the flea circus, are in the front seat. Malcolm and the girl from Arby's are in the back seat. They are on a mission. A mission that no one but them knows they're on.

The Freak feels nervous. This is rare. Impossible. Nervousness is reserved for the living, and yet she feels it all the same. Tonight will be a very important night for a lot of people. It will be the Easter they never forget.

The shoveler speaks. "So, you know I don't know who my dad is, right?"

"That's unfortunate," Loretta says.

Malcolm and Katie stay quiet in the back seat.

"Do any of you guys know who it was? Is there some family secret or something? Because my mom won't tell me."

"Isn't it on your birth certificate?" Katie asks.

"Just says *unknown*."

Malcolm says, "Huh. Why's it such a big deal to you?"

"Because he's my dad," the shoveler says. "You all know who your dads are."

"And outside of Malcolm, we all have shitty dads," Katie says.

"My dad can totally be shitty," Malcolm says.

"Maybe she'll tell you when you're, like, eighteen or something," the girl from Arby's says. "Moms do weird shit like that."

The Freak hears this conversation. She's in the stereo speaker. She's in the headrest. She's in the dashboard. She climbs into the back seat.

"A man who prides himself on his ancestry is like the potato plant, the best part of which is underground," she says. She leaves a bright green Easter egg on Malcolm's lap. It's a real egg. Malcolm holds it up, and the shoveler sees it in the rearview mirror.

"Holy shit," the shoveler says. "That's my egg from this morning. From the sinkhole."

No one in the car knows what he's talking about, but they nod anyway. Loretta is staring. The Freak feels weird about it. She wishes she could have saved Loretta from You-know-who, but sometimes there's nothing she can do. One time she visited Marla to tell Marla where she was. Marla only thought she might be going crazier. The Freak visited her parents a lot at first, but they never paid attention—which was surprising considering her mother is an artist and has paid numerous swindlers to read the lines on her palms.

The Freak knows the living have differing views about the dead—about what happens after you die. The Freak can't talk details. She just wishes the living paid more attention.

To make this point, before anyone in the car can ask her questions, she flickers.

360

The Shoveler: New Jersey

I feel like I'm in that dream with the ocean and the huge waves. Calm, dipping my body under the water while the storm moves overtop of me. The storm is Mr. _____ son. The waves are me.

The Freak was just in the back seat. She told me that the best part of me is underground. She may be right. I'm not sure how much I know the me that's aboveground. I just met my family at the age of sixteen. Before then, I didn't know they even existed.

"Okay," I say, and turn the stereo down. "Who here wants to buy a potato farm and just fulfill our destiny after we graduate high school?"

"Shut up," Malcolm says. "Turn the music back on!"

Loretta leans over and turns the stereo up again. "I'd do that," she says. "I love learning new things."

"But I'm serious," I say.

"Me too," she says.

Can I see myself starting a potato farm with Loretta? Yes. I can. It's very aboveground. Lots of variables, but none I can't handle.

She says, "So, this girl—this freak person. She was just here, but really she's dead, right?"

"Something like that," I answer.

When Loretta puts it that way, I'm sadder than I was before. *She's dead, right?* I thought she was the meaning of life. But she's dead. There's something in that, but I'm not sure what.

"So, the plan is to call the police once we get there?" Malcolm asks.

"I don't know," Katie says. "Loretta has a point. And I don't like cops, as a rule."

I say, "Let's see what we find when we get there. This could all be horseshit."

"Doesn't feel like horseshit," Katie says.

"I don't think it's horseshit," Loretta says.

I don't say it, but there's something about these three people in my car that feels familiar. As if my DNA had known all along what was going on. As if genes know more than we do as fully formed human beings.

Something about Malcolm and Katie and Loretta feels like I have a family now, and I guess I do. A crazy family who's going to New Jersey to find our missing cousin. Mom was right about it being a day I'd never forget.

Marla & Gottfried's Goodbye

Marla and Gottfried stand at the front door, waving.

Marla has her secret blood; Gottfried has his secret birds.

They watch four of their five grown children interact, and Gottfried can't help but grimace. *How did these four people come from the same household? My household?*

"We should really get together more often," Jean says to Harry.

"We should go out for a girls' night," Missy says to Amber.

The unspoken no has power here because all of them have it.

Jean gets in her car, and Marla can see her lips moving even though she's by herself. A lot of words that start with *F.*

Amber and Missy walk around the back of the house together. Marla doesn't want to know what they're talking about; she knows they're talking about her. She's as sure of it as she's sure Matt's daughter is never coming home. As sure of it as she's sure of how her body made defective children because of the blood.

The damn blood.

> I know it makes no sense. I know it's ridiculous. I know it's stupid and the longer I keep it, the worse it gets. I don't have anyone to tell. Thought I'd be able to tell Jean one day, but I gave her the same disease. Gottfried is useless. What would he say if I told him? I tried to tell the doctor once but that was after Matt was born. When I hit bottom.

Been drowning since. Thoughts
running so fast behind my eyes I
can't keep up with who I think
I am today. Who are you today,
Marla? You're a proud mother
and grandmother. You're a proud
maker of pineapple stuffing.

You are a fake, Marla.
You're no mother. You're
no grandmother. You're
only a maker of stuffing.
A hider of eggs. An inven-
tor of stories about why
you are the way you are.

It's not the blood,
Marla. It's the way
Jean and Harry
fight. It's the way
Matt doesn't come
home anymore.

It's not the blood. It's
you. It's the way you
are. Can't change.
Can't just be nice.
Tunnel never closes.

Loretta's Strainer

Loretta sits in the front seat of her cousin's car and the audience is fading. This is her last show. From now on, the audience will be her family. That'll take a while to get used to.

Malcolm, the one with the dying father, told her that she had real balls to make those balloon shapes after dinner. She still can't figure out why it's such a big deal.

She thinks about Gerald and Dolly and Cynthia. There's a dog that likes to wander the woods behind Marla and Gottfried's house. She reckons she'll put them on the dog and wave goodbye.

No place for a flea circus in that big house.

She's becoming someone else now.

The thought of this scares her.

She turns down the volume on her cousin's car stereo and says, "I'm scared to change schools." No one says anything, so she adds, "How do I fit in?"

"You'll do okay," Malcolm says. "The teachers are cool. It's just mostly entitled white kids as far as the eye can see. It's not like we have to go to a well to pump water for lunch, you know?"

Loretta says, "Well, that's always good."

There's silence in the car. The shoveler reaches for the volume dial on the stereo, and Loretta stops him.

"Can you guys just be my friends and that way I don't have to hang out with anyone else?"

"Sure," Katie says.

"Promise?" Loretta asks.

All three of her cousins agree. Loretta will be their friend.

The faint audience applauds and whistles. Loretta bows and smiles and picks up the roses thrown at her feet. She watches as people make their way into the aisles and out the tent openings until the center ring is dark and the smell of popcorn has faded. Now it's just Loretta in her sequins.

"Oh! Take the next exit. We're nearly there," she says.

Jake & Bill will never speak of it again

Bill Marks must have noticed he left Ashley at his parents' house about an hour after he left. Ashley was doing dishes with his mother when her phone, still on the dinner table, sounded an incoming text. She ignored it.

Suddenly, Bill Marks is in the kitchen with a pistol. Bill points it at his mother.

Ashley screams. "Fuck!"

Bill is wide-eyed. Sweating. *Meth?* Jake wonders. Bill looks like a mix of Bill and someone else. Something else. Something animal.

"Put the fucking gun down, Bill," Mr. Marks says. His cell phone is in his hand, and no one else in the room knows he's already dialed 911.

"Whatever he told you, it's not true!" Bill yells.

The four people not holding a pistol look at one another. Or more accurately, three of them look at Jake.

"I didn't tell them anything," he says.

"You said you were gonna tell them," Bill says.

"I didn't get to it yet."

Bill rushes forward and puts the pistol to Jake's head. "And you fucking won't!"

Mr. Marks lunges at his elder son and hits him in the middle. The gun flies into the air and lands with a thud. Bill starts punching his father, and Jake tries to pull him off.

Bill has something in him for sure. Has the strength of a horse.

Ashley's screams are the only normal thing in the house

aside from the décor. Everyone else is used to this violence. Everyone else is used to Bill's wake. Waves that ripple for weeks and months and years.

When the police arrive, they have no idea they're about to solve a missing-persons case that's nearly two years old.

Bill says, "I didn't do nothing! It was all Jake!"

Bill says, "I'm a quarter Mexican! This is police brutality!"

Marla & Gottfried's Beach House

Marla and Gottfried sit in their matching recliner chairs. Marla has the day's newspaper open in front of her, but she isn't reading. Gottfried is on his smartphone looking at his investment account.

He looks at Marla and wants to say something about how it was nice to have the family home, all in one place, for the first time in years. He says nothing.

Missy went to spend the night with Amber, and he can't say that doesn't make him happy. He can barely remember what things were like when the kids were growing up. He spent nearly all his time figuring out how to make the most amount of money from his hundred and fifty acres.

He puts his phone down and asks Marla, "Why didn't we do better by them?"

"By who?"

"The kids."

"They did fine on their own," she says.

"No. They didn't."

"You're not thinking about Matt, are you?"

Gottfried hadn't been thinking about Matt, but he was now. Poor Matt. "No."

"Stop thinking about the past," Marla says. "Nothing you can do about it."

"I can do something now, though."

Marla folds down the corner of the paper and looks at her husband.

"I want to buy a beach house," he says. Really, he wants to buy them each a house of their own. Except Jean—she's loaded.

"So do it. Buy a beach house."

"I want to give them all a key."

"Imagine the mess they'll make," Marla says.

"They're grown. They know how to clean up."

"That party Harry threw when we went to Atlantic City that one time," Marla says. "The V all over the porch."

Gottfried remembers what it was like for Marla to arrive home to vomit all over the porch. Beer bottles scattered in the backyard.

"That was 1994."

"Still," Marla says, from behind the newspaper.

"Jean turned out a lot like you," Gottfried says.

"She did."

Gottfried wants to say how much of a shame that is, but he knows Marla will never understand. He says nothing. Picks up his smartphone again and starts to look for beach houses.

Easter is over. All Marla did once the house was empty was complain about the mess. There was no mess. And that's the thing. Marla always saw a mess when there wasn't one. Always clung to her ideas as if something were holding her back from growing.

Gottfried can't blame her. He had his robins. They held him back, too.

Things were different. Nothing their generation can do about the next ones. That's what he says, anyway. Harry used to argue with him. Still does. Says Generation X got a raw deal. Now these younger generations are in the news all the time saying they got a raw deal, too.

Gottfried feels proud of what he did to survive. Never once

thinks about how it would feel if his own son would do the same to him as he did to his father. Just thinks he was smart to do it. Good father. Good husband. Good provider. He looked out for his family.

But the robins never fade. Every day he hears the unmistakable sound of impact. Sees the feathers flying. Cries in the car wash. They may have got a raw deal, but something about his kids and grandkids is different from his generation.

Until today, he'd never talked about the farm. Now, when he closes his eyes, he can see the logo from the family business. A potato plant. Leaves up top, potatoes down below. All those stems and roots joining the two—like veins and arteries. His father always said that families were the same. Everything was connected, everything worked in synchronicity.

Gottfried got to see the sun and he got to flower. His kids were harvested from shallow soil. His grandkids, accidental plants for the most part, would eventually mature and one day they, too, would rise up from the dirt, their brittle roots still connected.

It's the best anyone can hope for.

The Shoveler's Strainer

I take the exit onto the New Jersey Turnpike. Malcolm says there's about twenty minutes to go. I see a sign for Rancocas State Park and point at it. Loretta acts excited. Malcolm and Katie whisper in the back seat. I need a cigarette, but it feels rude to smoke with all these people in the car.

Katie says, "It's not like we can dig her up, right?"

"Jesus, no," I say.

"Aren't we going to look suspicious considering you have a shovel in the car?" she asks.

"I told you. I don't carry that anymore."

"Right," Katie says.

Loretta starts to cry. From excitement to tears in one second flat. I've never met anyone like her.

"What's wrong?" I ask.

"If this is all true. All of this? Then we're about to find a dead person. Our dead cousin. That's sad is all. Really sad."

"I wish I would have known her," Malcolm says. "I never really met her, I don't think."

"None of us did," Katie says. "Matt didn't want any of us to know her."

It's all too much for me. I wanted a family, not another mystery. But maybe all families are mysteries. Maybe all families have secrets. Maybe none of us is perfect, ever.

Suddenly not knowing who my dad is seems small. Realistically, I am someone's son and I always have been. Mom has always been here. Always.

"Exit five to Mount Holly—that's us," Loretta says. "Maybe Katie's mom was right and the girl ran away."

"Maybe there's no body to find," I say. "That would be a relief."

I put on my turn signal and get off on Exit 5.

"She left me the plate," Malcolm says. "It was her. I'm telling you. I'm getting messages from the Consciousness. We're going to find her."

"The Consciousness?" Loretta asks.

"Long story," Malcolm says. "Just trust me."

Every car I pass on the small road into Rancocas State Park is Mr. _____son's. He's there to camp. To fish. To hike. He's there to bury a body. To dig one up. To hide Easter eggs. To watch the stars. He's there to relax after a hard week at the office. He's running from the law. Variables.

My last set of variables. Because this has to stop now. Life's too short to live the whole thing underground. *Hey, Mr. _____son! I don't give a shit anymore.*

"Almost there," Loretta says, staring at the phone map.

"Park and we'll have to walk in," Malcolm says.

"Duh," someone says. "It's a forest."

We park. Get out of the car. Stand facing the coordinates.

"I'm scared," Loretta says.

"Me too," everyone else says.

It's dark as hell in here. None of us brought a real flashlight.

THE FREAK LOVES SCARING THE SHIT OUT OF PEOPLE IN THE FOREST!

The Freak's been doing this for what feels like eternity, but it's only been about two years. Flickering. Haunting. Jumping out from behind trees to scare lovers who thought this was a good place to make out.

Four people are approaching. Two girls. Two boys. She knows them all. She was just in their back seat quoting a Spanish proverb. Fact is, she doesn't want to leave them. She wants to be like Loretta—a new friend. She wants to be alive.

Alive. Almost every one of the living takes this for granted.

Taking things for granted is the privilege of existence. The living don't even think about it, same as boys aren't scared to go missing at the mall. Same as her white cousins can drive over the speed limit across state lines to New Jersey. Same as her grandfather didn't think twice about selling the family farm.

She flickers so she can get her fill of the world. First to a place with kangaroos. She waves to the kangaroos. Then to a large city filled with people on bicycles. She waves to the people. Then to what feels like the coldest place on Earth. She waves to the snow. She flickers to so many places so she doesn't have to meet her cousins. Not looking like this. Not as a dirt burrito. Not naked.

Sheep, eagles, penguins, whales, water, trees, mountains, stars, fresh air she can't breathe. Flickers. Flickers.

CanIHelpYou?'s Freakish Cousin

As we walk closer to the coordinates, the air gets colder. None of us talk. I want to stop and take a breath, but they're all walking so fast I don't want to lose them.

We're using our phone flashlights, and it's weird having three beams of light shining toward the same nothing. Just forest. More trees. Loretta's sequins throw light around the trunks and scare the shit out of me.

I need a Xanax. I need a joint. I need something to make this okay.

Finding a body. Solving a mystery. Being with my cousins and actually feeling like I have a family. Like—these are my family members. They have potential, which is more than I can say about the rest of the guests at Easter dinner.

Somebody's phone rings.

"It's my dad," Malcolm says.

"Please tell me you turned off your phone finder," I say.

"I did."

"Don't answer it," I say.

"I have to. He could be dying."

We all stop. Fifteen yards from the coordinates, we stop. Malcolm answers his phone. Tells his dad he's just hanging out with us at Dairy Queen.

You can't figure out why we're doing this. And frankly, neither can we. Look at our faces. None of us has any idea why we're doing this. You'll blame our underdeveloped prefrontal cortexes.

You'll blame our lack of responsibility. You'll blame anything so long as you don't have to blame yourselves.

There's a dead girl in the forest.

We'll find her.

You didn't.

"So what do we do now?" David asks. He says he wants me to call him the shoveler, but I can't. I can't call Loretta the Ringmistress, either. I want to be called Katie from now on, too. We have names. We're just so used to being labeled, we took to it.

We all point our flashlights at the spot. The forest floor looks normal. Nothing out of place.

"Maybe we're not in the right spot," I say.

"Look," Loretta says, pointing to something five feet away.

It's a lighter.

"Look," she says again, pointing the other direction.

It's a pink plastic egg with a wrapper from a mini Hershey bar next to it.

"Look," she says again. She's pointing at me.

I'm your weed dealer. I'm your fast-food dealer. I'm your advice dealer. Never in a million years did you think I was smart enough to solve a crime. And maybe I wasn't. But I bet you don't have the balls to do something like this. The food made you slow. The drugs made you tired. The advice made you lazy.

"What?" I say.

But behind me, there's a voice.

"You should call the police now," The Freak says. "You don't want to see what's under there."

David looks at me and then back at The Freak. He has tears in his eyes.

We all back away from the coordinates. The Freak comes with us.

Malcolm calls the police. He says, "We think we found the body of a missing girl . . . it's doesn't really matter how . . . we can tell you when you get here . . . we're her cousins." He gives them the coordinates and says we'll wait. When he hangs up, he says, "I don't know who said that. It was like my voice was controlled by something else."

"That was me. Sorry," The Freak says.

We all stare at her. Frankly, and this is probably bad timing, but I think about how cool it would be to be able to control other people's mouths. Like force-fed healthy bacteria.

"I'm suddenly realizing how stupid our story's going to sound," David says.

"It's not stupid," Loretta says.

"A ghost came to us and told us where to find her?" David says. "That's crazy."

"I'm not a ghost," The Freak says.

"You look like a ghost to me," Loretta says. "I'm scared."

"That's only because we haven't met," The Freak says.

"True. She's really nice," David says. "But our story's still going to sound unbelievable."

The Freak says, "We don't have much time. I have things to tell you."

She looks at me. "If you don't stop selling drugs, you're going to end up in prison," she says. "And you're right about your family."

"Okay."

She turns to Malcolm. "You know what's about to happen. Keep loving him. We'll take good care of him."

"Okay," Malcolm says.

The Freak gets serious on her face and looks at Loretta. "Your dad is at a Super 8 motel outside of Morgantown, West Virginia. I'll make sure the right people know about that, okay?"

"Okay," Loretta says.

She turns to David. She walks to him and hugs him, and his arms grip real flesh—not some Scooby-Doo apparition. She pushes the hair away from his eyes and says, "You're not missing half of you. You're whole. A whole person. You're better off than a lot of people who know who their dads are."

"Will she ever tell me?" he says.

"She can't tell you. She doesn't know. Do you understand?"

He nods into her shoulder, and she releases him.

The Freak looks at me and David. "Some stuff runs in our family. In our genes. Like depression and anxiety. Marla has it. Gottfried, too. You all have it in your own ways. It's a real thing, but people don't really talk about it. It's why you have your tunnels. Talk about it with one another. Look it up on the Internet. Don't go through life like this just because your parents don't believe there's anything wrong with them. How do you think you got it?"

All this time you thought the tunnel was a lie. You thought I was running from my bad decisions. From racist parents. You thought I was being dramatic. Turns out you were wrong. Did you ever think of that? That maybe you were wrong?

The Freak looks at us. "The best part of all of you is underground if you keep thinking those people define you.

"Our grandparents were rotten seed. Kept secrets. Worshipped money. Pitted their kids against one another. But we aren't them. We can break free." She shakes her head. "Or you can, at least."

"And you're just . . . dead," Loretta says.

"Yes."

"Do you know who killed you?" I ask.

"Yes."

"Will they go to jail?"

"I'm taking care of that," The Freak says. I shiver.

"Jesus, what's taking them so long?" Malcolm says.

The Freak says, "I'm an old case."

We all hold hands and stay quiet. We eventually hear a car coming. No red-and-blue lights or any of that. We keep holding hands.

Five cousins.

Five accidental cousins. Volunteers.

Descended from potato farmers.

Underground.

Now emerging.

You think this is crazy. You think this is too cosmic to be real. You think what you want. This is the best buzz I've ever had, and I've tried it all.

The Shoveler: See You Later

We hear the car doors close and see their flashlights in the distance.

It's time for me to say goodbye to my perfect Freak. The meaning of life.

"That's potatoes," The Freak says.

"What's potatoes?" Katie asks.

"The meaning of life," I say.

"Depends on how you cook them," Loretta says. "Mom-Mom makes this thing called Au Gratin and it's disgusting."

"Shhh," I say. "Let's say goodbye."

The Freak says, "I prefer see you later."

"Okay," I say. "Let's say see you later."

We can hear the police coming. We hold hands, five cousins. I no longer care who Mr. _____son is or what he's doing. I duck my head under raging waves of variables and remain calm. *Control the brain and the rest is easy.*

Malcolm is crying, so I hug him into my side. Loretta catches the other half of him. Katie squeezes into my other side.

The Freak says, "Thank you."

Before we can say thank you back, she's gone.

High-powered light lands on us, and two state troopers stop in their tracks when they see four teenagers holding one another, one of them sobbing himself dry.

"What's going on here?" one of them asks.

Loretta says, "It's a very long story but the facts you need to know right now are, our cousin has been missing for two years. Her body is buried here. Her killer is in Pennsylvania and already in custody. Sorry. *Killers*. Brothers. I have their names when you need them."

"How'd you find the body?" he asks.

Loretta answers, "We looked hard enough."

Loretta seems as surprised by what's coming out of her mouth as we are, but Malcolm keeps crying and Katie keeps a hold of my right side while I hold him up with my left.

"You need to vacate the crime scene," the trooper says. "Mark here will take your statements over at the police department."

The Freak whispers in my ear.

Don't worry. I'll tell them everything.

Malcolm Knows Where He Belongs

I can't wait to tell Dad about this. All of it, including how he's going to die soon. He already knows he's going to die soon. He'll die a lot happier knowing that the Consciousness is real. Or whatever you want to call it. Belief systems are all pretty much the same if you peel back the layers.

I've decided I'll live with Marla and Gottfried when Dad dies. Moving to Jamaica would be nice, but people there already know the truth about poverty. They don't think it's a coincidence that they're descendants of slaves and also poor in a country that was ruled by Colonialists for so long.

I'm needed here because this is where the ignorance is. Even my own.

I'm needed here because I now have three cousins to hold me up when I cry.

I'm needed here because somebody has to help this family face their shit.

I'll still see Eleanor. She will become prime minister, maybe. I'll take over Dad's business, maybe.

Dad and I have a lot to talk about.

I look around the township police department, listen to the state cops and the local cops discuss how to deal with our case. Ours is a special situation. David keeps asking if we can go—if they can drive us back to his car. Loretta is eating every last piece of candy in the place—lucky it's Easter. Katie is taking a nap on the couch.

The Freak is entertaining me. She appears outside the window and pretends she's swimming. She appears by the coffee-maker in the tiny kitchenette and mixes a cup of coffee, and delivers it to the chief's desk. He says thank you. He looks up to see who delivered the coffee, and she's already gone. Outside the window, miming. Hilarious.

She stares at the chief. He says, "You guys can go now."

She stares at the state cop who drove me and Loretta here. "Come on, I'll get all of you back to your car."

Some of us take a minute to use the bathroom before we leave. I go last and I flush the toilet twice, just to marvel.

THE FREAK HAS
BEEN STRAINED!

The Freak has something to say. She says it to the men exhuming her from her dirt burrito. She says it to the coroner. She says it to the funeral director. She says it to you.

DON'T LIVE UNDERGROUND FOREVER!

NOT EVEN IF YOUR DAD WAS AN ASSHOLE! NOT EVEN IF YOU GET PUNCHED IN THE FACE BY A HALF-WIT BITCH! NOT EVEN IF YOU HAD TO DOUCHE WITH TURPENTINE! NOT EVEN IF YOUR MOTHER OWNS A DISGUSTING BELL! NOT EVEN IF YOU MAKE COLOSSAL MISTAKES!

MAKE SMARTER MISTAKES!

STOP BEATING YOURSELF UP!

CONTROL YOUR VARIABLES!

BLEND AND STRAIN!

CHANGE YOUR MIND!

The Freak knows this sounds corny because you're so used to looking at hateful shit, right? News shows and conspiracy theories. Rape jokes and dank memes. You're so used to the humor of the put-down that you didn't see that you slid down a hole and into a tunnel.

DIG YOUR WAY OUT!

The Freak knows you want to know what happened next. You want to know if her cousins went home and met up for movie nights or badminton. But all that really matters is if you do that, not them.

DIG YOUR WAY OUT!

The Freak is tired of the Easter egg hunts, the race—the competition. She wins, okay? She's dead, okay?

NOBODY WINS!

CHANGE YOUR MIND!

The Freak knows everything now. She knows some days you try to make sense of your life and you fail. She knows you are not taken seriously. She knows you're only as smart as the textbooks and the textbooks lie.

DIG YOUR WAY OUT!

The Freak knows you are not a potato.

DON'T LET ANYONE PUT BUTTER ON YOU!

The Freak knows you are not a set of car keys.

DON'T LET ANYONE DRIVE YOU AROUND!

The Freak knows you are not a door.

DON'T LET ANYONE WALK THROUGH YOU!

The Freak knows you can't control all of these things. Look at the power she has. She can go anywhere and do anything. The one thing she can't do is change the minds of the living.

THAT'S YOUR FUCKING JOB!

Easter Conversation in a Nissan Sentra

Four cousins drive home from New Jersey. None of them are talking. The shoveler drives. Loretta, next to him, stares out her window. In the back seat, Malcolm and Katie have their eyes closed and their heads back.

Until today, they were strangers, pretty much. Now, they are bonded for life.

Katie is thinking about her racist family and trying to figure out what to do about it.

Malcolm is thinking about having to live with Marla and Gottfried for the next two years and what to do about it.

Loretta is thinking about how she and her mom are going to have a nice life now, without You-know-who, and what to do about it.

And David, our shoveler, is thinking about how the four of them are underground. Like potatoes. He thinks: *Underground is where everything starts. It's not so bad.*

No one puts on music.

The conversation in the Nissan Sentra is internal.

KATIE. I need a new job. And I have to get a new number on my phone so no clients can find me. Then the car. Then move out of that house. But first, I smash the bell.

DAVID. I don't get why I think I should live with my mom forever. And I never thought about life after this. Always too busy moving. I have no idea what I'm doing.

MALCOLM. I thought maybe I didn't love Eleanor, but I do. It's

386

not just her ankles or anything empty like that. I really love her. I know I'm white and I know she's Jamaican. And I know that it all seems like I'm chasing a culture and not a person, but I love her. I really do.

KATIE. I can't stop thinking about Ian and how I used him all those years. I really did. I didn't mean to. I can't figure out when he went from being my best friend to the worst best friend my mother could imagine. I miss him.

LORETTA. Why do I miss my father? That makes no sense.

KATIE. I always thought I was so much better than other white people. Since my ninth birthday party, I was part of *us*. The tunnel would protect me from *them*. But I think I might be *them*. Shit. I think we're all part of *them*. I guess that means I'm finally out of the tunnel, then.

DAVID. I will never know who my dad is. I'm not sure how to tell Mom I don't care about it anymore. I only care that she's my mom.

MALCOLM. I don't know what to do about my dad dying.

LORETTA. This family is like the train act. But not with Holloway. More like Gerald. Nothing will move the train.

KATIE. I don't think I'm as bad as my mother, though. I mean, I can still be the healthy bacteria. Maybe we can have an intervention or something.

LORETTA. I miss my father because I'm not used to people being nice to me.

DAVID. I have to talk to Mike about his tattoo. I have to tell him how sad I am that he turned out to be such a loser. Control the brain and the rest is easy, my ass.

Four cousins make plans in their minds.

They are coming for their parents. They are coming for their grandparents. They are coming for you.

KATIE. An intervention could work. We should have it at Marla's house. Maybe I can smash the bell there. In front of everyone.

DAVID. Mike is wasting his existence on the wrong words. I don't understand how he doesn't see it. I guess no one sees it. I guess that's how things got this way.

LORETTA. I think they're only being nice to me because they feel bad for me.

MALCOLM. Loretta and I have to hold some kind of intervention with Marla and Gottfried now that we both live there. No more lamb. No more bullshit judgments. I bet they can't help it. I bet they're going to be like this until they die. It's in their genes.

Malcolm is the first to speak. "It's in our genes," he says. "We have to attack it on a cellular level."

Katie says, "Totally. Cellular."

Loretta says, "Maybe we have their genes, but we can still be fine. I'll never be anything like You-know-who."

David says, ". . ."

"What's that smell?" Loretta asks.

Malcolm sniffs the air and answers, "That's the stench of human history!" When none of his cousins seem to understand, he says, "Landfill."

Katie says, "You want to know the truth about people, always look at their trash."

David nods at this and pictures his mother in the neighbors' trash bags, finding the truth. Never finding his father.

Four cousins drive up the cul-de-sac and park next to Marla and Gottfried's garage doors. They sit in the car for a while and say nothing. This is the beginning of something. Something good. Something new. Something you can't paint over.

Jake & Bill in a strainer

Jake Marks writes letters to his brother, Bill, but never sends them. He's been doing it since the online therapy. That kooky woman said it might help him work out his feelings. Jake doesn't know how he feels. He feels like he's in a blender most days—surrounded by so many ingredients and trying not touch any of them while they all swirl around. It's dangerous. Never know what you're going to find in a blender. Never know what you're getting mixed with.

Bill hasn't called—not even for bail. Ashley has spent the night at her mother's house. The wedding is off. The snake escaped from their car and could slither into anywhere, now.

Jake is happy for the snake, happy for Ashley, and happy for himself. Living a lie is more dangerous than any blender/any snake/any brother.

Sometimes at night, he sees the girl in his room. She's got a lighter. He's afraid she's going to burn him alive, but all she does is burn his therapy letters to his brother. It means something. It means he has to stop thinking of Bill as family.

Marla & Gottfried's Curtain Call

Gottfried watches his grandkids pile out of the painter kid's car from an upstairs window. They stand around and talk—even Loretta. He's happy for her. He wondered if she was well adjusted enough to talk to people her own age.

He shakes his head and decides to tell Marla that the kids are too old for egg hunts. Next year they may as well just put a bowl full of candy on the table so everyone can share.

Marla is in bed. She said something to Gottfried before she closed the door to the bedroom. She said, ". . ."

Doesn't matter what she said. Gottfried realizes that it never mattered what she said. He wasn't listening. Too old to learn now.

He makes his way to the garage to eavesdrop on the kids. They're trading phone numbers. One of them tells Loretta that she should get a cell phone now that she's free. One of them says they'll make a group text. One of them says they should have a picture from tonight because it was such an important night. Gottfried is touched to think they found the day special after all Marla put into it. He imagines them on the other side of the garage door, taking pictures.

But then he hears them talk about their dead cousin.

Dead. That's what they say.

Dead and buried. Solved a crime. One of them says, "I can't believe she made me say things!" Another explains how the dead cousin would appear and disappear with no warning. Another says she used to light snowflakes on fire and read minds. Loretta says that's how she got the red-sequined dress. Gottfried feels a pull in his gut like the time his mother made him eat green potatoes to teach him a lesson. He looks around the garage for something to vomit into.

Dead. Dead and buried. Solved a crime.

He knows who they're talking about.

The Freak—Gottfried had seen her.

She was talking to him all along.

The robins told him a thousand times that he was on the wrong path, but people on the wrong path don't often listen to reason.

Usually, they only listen to themselves.

Gottfried can't stop the tears that arrive. He makes a promise to himself.

Inside the garage, four white walls are all he has to talk to.

Pay attention to the robins, he says.

Mate with purpose, he says.

Pay attention to love, he says.

Tunnel closes.

ACKNOWLEDGMENTS

When my mother first told me about how they used to separate blood in Arkansas, it fit the narrative of what I knew already about the South in the early 1960s. I was disgusted but I wasn't surprised. She and my dad had a lot of stories from their time when my dad was drafted and served. I don't remember a time in my life when I wasn't thinking about race and racism and asking why our world is like this. I owe thanks to my mom for every time she pointed out the racist and sexist system in which we live. There's no one out there like you, Mom. I'm glad I'm your daughter.

~~~

This book is supposed to be uncomfortable. I'd apologize, but I'm not sorry.

The man with the tattoo is real. He really did loan me a shovel. I really did have to wait until spring to see his arm. I don't know what to say except: You can't strip-search your potential friends, so pay attention.

If you read this book and want to know more about the move forward to an equitable society, find the real history of America. Find the truth about slavery, the Civil War. Then have a look in your social studies textbooks and find the missing pieces. (Hint: the systematic robbery from, and slaughter of Native Americans was not a "Clash of Cultures on the Prairie.")

Pam—our time in Wichita changed my life. You probably don't know that. But I know that. Thank you.

I owe enormous thanks to the team at Dutton—all of you—thank you. Andrew Karre, thank you for everything. Like, everything. Michael Bourret, I have the design for the M.B. action figure ready. It's rad! Drew, Kirstin, Z.O.B., e., Carrie, Lizzy K., Kephart, good friends make life. G & L, thank you for understanding that your mom has a weird job and for being awesome daughters. Topher, you are so radical. 32 years, FTW.

Teachers, librarians, I think you're the most important people alive. Booksellers, thank you for your support. Indies, I love you. Student readers: a few years ago, in the back of a book, I said that I'd flip off the adults in your lives who don't think your opinions count. My fingers are tired. How do you put up with this crap?